THE VIVALDI CIPHER

VATICAN SECRET ARCHIVE THRILLERS
BOOK ONE

GARY MCAVOY

LITERATI
EDITIONS.

Printed in the United States of America
Hardcover ISBN: 978-1-954123-06-9
Paperback ISBN: 978-1-954123-07-6
eBook ISBN: 978-1-954123-05-2
Large Print Edition ISBN: 978-1-954123-17-5

Library of Congress Control Number: 2021913720

Published by:
Literati Editions
PO Box 5987
Bremerton, WA 98312-5987
Email: info@LiteratiEditions.com
Visit the author's website: www.GaryMcAvoy.com

0323

This is an original work of fiction. Names, characters, businesses, places, long-standing institutions, agencies, public offices, events, locales, and incidents are either the products of the author's imagination or have been used in a fictitious manner. Apart from historical references, any resemblance to actual persons, living or dead, or actual events is purely coincidental.

BOOKS BY GARY MCAVOY

FICTION

The Jerusalem Scrolls

The Avignon Affair

The Petrus Prophecy

The Opus Dictum

The Vivaldi Cipher

The Magdalene Veil

The Magdalene Reliquary

The Magdalene Deception

NONFICTION

And Every Word Is True

The *Sestieri* (Districts) of Venice

PROLOGUE

T he first symptom of the poisoning began as a fever.

Sitting at one of two long white-silk-draped tables in the Sistine Chapel, along with sixty-seven of his fellow cardinal-electors, Pietro Ottoboni cast his vote for Pope on the eighth day of the conclave to replace the late Pope Clement XII.

Enfeebled by fever, the 73-year-old Ottoboni made his way toward the front of the chapel to a small altar below Michelangelo's majestic fresco *The Last Judgment*, dropped his ballot onto a brass saucer, then tipped the saucer, letting the ballot fall into the large brass urn beneath it.

A few moments later, having returned to his seat, the cardinal collapsed onto the table, the high temperature having sapped his energy. Shocked, the other cardinals stood to better see what was happening to their colleague. The master of papal liturgical celebrations suspended the conclave while they moved Ottoboni to his apartment under the care of a Vatican physician.

LONG CONSIDERED favorite among the *papabili* to succeed Pope Clement, Pietro Ottoboni was born in the Most Serene Republic of Venice to a rich and noble family, whose most distinguished member was his grand-uncle, Pope Alexander VIII. Ottoboni had held every important post in the Vatican during an illustrious career, and as cardinal-bishop to several churches in Italy, his annual salary exceeded fifty thousand gold *scudi*—the present-day equivalent of six million dollars per year.

Cardinal Ottoboni had been a prolific paramour with a countless number of lovers, many of whom were married to the great patricians of Venice. In fact, the famous masks unique to Venetians were introduced not to ward off the plague, as many later believed, but to officially disguise the wearer's identity— thus permitting anyone, noble or peasant, to do or say whatever one pleased. With this ingenious permissiveness, *affari di cuore*— affairs of the heart—were as common as the fleet of gondolas plying the canals of the celebrated city, without legal recourse. Having taken full advantage of this liberal device, Cardinal Ottoboni was known to have produced up to seventy children in his lifetime among his various mistresses.

Though he lived well in Rome's grand Palazzo della Cancelleria, Ottoboni's greatest passions were music and art, and he was a generous patron to some of the most renowned masters in both fields: Arcangelo Corelli, Alessandro Scarlatti, Giuseppe Crespi, Tintoretto, Veronese—and most of all, to his close friend and protégé, the prodigious *maestro di violino* of Venice, Antonio Vivaldi.

As he lay on his deathbed, Ottoboni summoned Vivaldi to his side. In a low, rasping voice, the cardinal confided to his friend a tale of great importance, a scandalous operation run by the notoriously corrupt Cardinal Niccolò Coscia in league with the feared secret Mafia organization known as the Camorra.

In fact, he added with struggling breath, he was convinced it was Coscia, acting on orders from the Camorra, who had poisoned him to keep him from acting on what he knew. With information gleaned from one of his many spies, Ottoboni had discovered the ongoing scandal days earlier and approached

Cardinal Coscia with a warning that he and his Camorra would soon be out of business, at least as the Vatican was concerned. Were it not for his required attendance in the papal conclave, he would have put a stop to it sooner, especially if he was elected Pope, an elevation to supreme power that was expected by everyone.

The following day, however, Cardinal Ottoboni succumbed to the poison, killed for a secret now known only by Antonio Vivaldi.

LIKE MOST ITALIANS, Vivaldi survived cautiously within the Camorra's Venetian sphere of influence. The secret society's tentacles reached into everyone's life, and their strict enforcement of the seal of *omertà*—the sacred code of silence— ensured clan activities remained discreet and wholly within *la familia*. The family.

Since the late 17th century, the Camorra had carved out its territories, starting in Naples and moving northward, into the Lombardy and Veneto regions of Italy encompassing its most lucrative prizes, Milan and Venice. Competing with La Cosa Nostra in Sicily and the 'Ndrangheta of Calabria, the Camorra's criminal enterprises included prostitution, gambling, smuggling, kidnapping, and art theft—but also the unusual niche of producing and selling fine art forgeries of the highest order.

During the earlier reign of Pope Benedict XIII, who cared little for managing his vast realm of Papal States, Cardinal Niccolò Coscia oversaw all Vatican government operations, taking advantage of his authority to carry out substantial financial abuses, virtually draining the Papal treasury. But his ongoing misdeeds eventually caught up with him. In 1731 he was charged with corruption, tried and convicted to ten years' imprisonment, and excommunicated from the Church.

However, still not without influence, he managed to get his heavy sentence commuted to a mere fine. He was also mysteriously reinstated as a cardinal, allowing him to take part in the papal conclave of 1740—the one during which Cardinal Ottoboni had died.

~

WITH OTTOBONI out of the way, Cardinal Niccolò Coscia could now carry out his master plan without hindrance. In his not-so-secret role as *capo* of the Roman Camorra, Coscia led development of the Veneto branch of the Mafia clan, based in Venice and headquartered in his own newly acquired Palazzo Feudatario on the Grand Canal. Purchased with funds he had discreetly absconded from the Vatican treasury, Feudatario would be a most fitting place to carry out his planned forgery operation of the Vatican's most profound works of art.

Niccolò Coscia was a meticulous diarist and, owing to all the business he conducted outside the Church, he had created the first book to record the activities of his new organization, naming it *Il Giornale Coscia della Camorra Veneta*—The Coscia Journal of the Veneto Camorra. In it he would secretly record careful notations of all paintings by artist and title, including each work's provenance and to whom the forgeries or originals were sold, depending on which he chose to return to the Vatican—for many were prominently displayed in public, while most were simply returned to the Vatican's vast art storage vaults, unseen by anyone.

The Coscia Journal would be passed down to each *capintesta*, head of the Veneto Camorra, for generations.

Unfortunately for Coscia, Cardinal Ottoboni's spies had discovered not only the Camorra's abhorrent plan for art forgeries, but the very existence of the Coscia Journal for recording such transactions. At that point Ottoboni's death was preordained, for no one could ever know such proof existed.

~

ANTONIO VIVALDI, who at age 25 was ordained a Roman Catholic priest, was now at a crossroads. He feared possessing knowledge of the treacherous secret passed on to him by his esteemed patron in his dying moments. Putting himself at odds with the Camorra was not just an unappealing prospect, it could end up costing him his life, depending on what he did with what he knew.

But Cardinal Ottoboni had one last request of his protégé.

Intent on stopping the sinful and unlawful activities of Cardinal Coscia, Ottoboni had pleaded with Vivaldi to see that Coscia was brought to justice, to pay for his felonious actions. Distressed by letting his friend and mentor die without the satisfaction of such a promise, Vivaldi agreed to do what he could. He would ensure that the authorities were informed, the Coscia Journal would be found, and the matter would be settled.

AFTER THE CARDINAL'S stately funeral, Vivaldi waited for the right moment to fulfill his promise. But as he waited, he became more apprehensive. He was just a lowly priest, after all, and not a very good one at that. The violin was his life, and teaching it was his life's work. Besides, who would believe him? Where was the proof? And what would the Camorra do to him if he were to expose its business? He had seen the results of their retribution —those who crossed the Mafia were dealt with harshly. Beheadings were not uncommon, and those who weren't beheaded were drawn and quartered—alive. No, he must find a way to honor his pledge without exposing himself to such horrible consequences.

An idea came to him. He would hide the messages in plain sight, in his musical compositions.

Picking up a sheet of staff lined manuscript paper, Vivaldi began to assemble the first of many, his *Scherzo Tiaseno in Sol*.

~

VENICE, ITALY—PRESENT DAY

AN ENORMOUS FLIGHT OF PIGEONS, hundreds of them, flocked overhead, diving for potato chips and bits of bread sticks tourists had enthusiastically tossed out for them, as Father Michael Dominic and Hana Sinclair made their way across the Piazza San Marco.

Despite the ban on pigeon-feeding in St. Mark's Square, little children were oblivious to the law and more amused by the flapping gray-and-white spectacle than frightened by the few *gendarmerie* patrolling the square, whose policing efforts to stop the feeding were futile. Venetian health experts estimate over 130,000 pigeons had roosted in the historic center—well over optimal concentrations for such a small public space—and efforts to rid the city of the determined birds had failed miserably. The damage to the marble buildings and statuary was considerable, not to mention possible pathogenic health hazards.

Locals knew it was often prudent to cover one's head with a newspaper or magazine when crossing the vast piazza, lest strollers subject themselves to the inevitable bombardment of bird droppings from above.

An old hand at the practice, Father Dominic had kept pages of the newspaper he had read at breakfast for that very purpose, knowing he and Hana had to cross the piazza in order to get to Venice's Biblioteca Marciana, the Library of Saint Mark.

The director of the library had requested the Vatican's help with a planned exhibition of manuscripts held in its stacks, and as Prefect of the Vatican Secret Archives, Michael Dominic had accepted the invitation, while also taking a week's vacation time in the fabled city. At only 31 years old, his access to the Vatican's vast number of historical manuscripts still humbled him. The Biblioteca Marciana was yet one more repository of ancient wonders that fascinated him.

Lovingly named La Serenissima by Italians devoted to its "most serene" natural and historical wonders, Venice was also Michael Dominic's favorite city in the world. He loved its vibrancy, its rich history as a major world trading port up to and through the Renaissance period, and of course the inherent romantic nature of the people and their ancient ways.

"I'm so glad you could join me, Hana," Dominic said as they walked through the piazza. "Have you ever experienced Carnivale before?"

Holding the newspaper awkwardly over her stylish wide brim straw hat, Hana replied with a contented sigh. "I was here once, years ago, but Carnivale had just ended. I've been meaning to be here for the real festivities for some time now, and since my editors wanted a piece on the celebration for *Le Monde's* Weekend Section, I volunteered for the assignment."

She looked up at the priest and smiled. "Thanks for letting me tag along with you, Michael. I don't mind that you have a little business to attend to. I need some time off myself and can always float around in a gondola and take notes while you're occupied."

Dominic laughed as he removed the newspaper from over his head, having passed the worst pigeon zone. He took Hana's paper and tossed them both in a trash receptacle alongside the library façade. "I can just see you now, laid out on a shiny black gondola, that fetching hat drawing everyone's eye as you cruise the canals. A fashion photographer's dream. But let's have some fun together while we're here as well."

"Agreed. I can get some writing done after dinner each

night," she said with a sly grin. "So, what's in this library that you've been asked to weigh in on?"

"I'm meeting with Paulo Manetti, the curator of the Marciana's Cardinal Bessarion Library, a special wing containing the original founder's collection of books and precious manuscripts from 1468. The Vatican has an original translation of Homer's *Iliad*, a companion version to his *Odyssey*, but the Marciana has the oldest actual texts of the *Iliad*. Manetti has asked me to consider lending ours to the Marciana for a temporary exhibition on Homer. They also have the only autograph copy of commentary on the *Odyssey* from the 12th century, so it should be a fine showcase."

Fascinated as she was by Dominic's explanation, Hana's eyes glazed as the warm sun took hold of her, her white cotton midi skirt fluttering in the light breeze. They had passed the tall brick Campanile and were now walking through the piazzetta between the Marciana Library and the Doge's Palace, heading toward the entrance to the Grand Canal. It wasn't quite noon yet, the appointed time for Dominic's meeting, so they settled onto a stone bench near the *traghetto*, the gondola landing overlooking the Church of San Giorgio Maggiore on the island across the lagoon. *Vaporetti*, gondolas, and sleek mahogany water taxis plied the calm waters as they sat there, each in their own dreamy state of mind, an effect Venice has on every visitor.

As the tower bells of the Campanile struck twelve, Dominic leaned back for a deep stretch to rouse himself, then stood and reached out for Hana's hand to help her up. With one last glance over the lagoon, they headed toward the library.

CHAPTER
ONE

T he entrance to the Marciana Library Palace—heavy wooden doors flanked by two larger-than-life Greek marble statues—opened into the opulent vestibule, where a two-flight staircase took visitors to the upper loggias.

Looking up as they walked the marble halls, Hana fixated on the ceiling, which featured twenty-one roundels, circular oil paintings by seven notable Renaissance artists commissioned in 1556. They looked as fresh today as at the time they were painted, Hana mused, overwhelmed by their unusual spherical beauty. Reaching one of the reading rooms, sunlight streamed in from the high glass ceiling, bathing the three-story room in a diffused natural light. Surrounding the reading tables on all sides were a series of Doric arches with a handsome frieze on one wall featuring rosy-faced cherubs and garlands of fruit and flowers.

A slim, well-dressed man with long black hair who looked to be in his fifties was walking toward them, a welcoming smile on his face. Dominic smiled in response as the man approached.

"Padre Michael, welcome back to the Marciana!" he beamed as he extended his hand.

"Paulo! What a great pleasure to see you again. This is my

friend and colleague, Hana Sinclair. Hana, this is Paulo Manetti, curator of the Bessarion Library here."

The three exchanged handshakes and pleasantries. Then Manetti turned, gesturing for them to follow him.

"We'll be using my private office to view the *Iliad*. Better to keep tourists from flocking around us. I already have it set up."

He led them through the upper loggia and down a corridor leading to various offices, entering a corner room that overlooked the piazzetta and the lagoon.

"Not only do you have a stunning library here, Signor Manetti," Hana remarked, "but you probably have the best office in the building!"

Manetti grinned shyly. "Please, call me Paulo, Miss Sinclair. And yes, I am very fortunate to have such a wondrous place to work. What you see around you is my life. Like our friend Michael here, my love for antiquities of the Old World has no bounds."

Dominic nodded his head in agreement, then turned to his companion. "Hana, if you'd like to better explore the library while Paulo and I are working, please feel free. We should only be a half hour or so. Take it all in, it truly is a marvelous old building filled with treasures you won't find anywhere else."

"I'll do that, thanks. Just come find me when you're ready." Hana turned and left the office, making her way back to the reading rooms and their glorious artworks and statuary.

A LARGE TABLE in the center of Manetti's office held several reference books, various implements for examining documents —a digital microscope, magnifying glass, blacklight, leather sand bag weights—and several large parchment manuscripts which had been laid out on it. One in particular was the chief item of interest: the only copy of of the commentary on Homer's *Odyssey* written entirely by the hand of the author.

Putting on a pair of white gloves, Dominic handled the

manuscript guardedly, gazing at the beautiful script by the hand of Eustathius of Thessalonica, the Byzantine scholar and rhetorician of the twelfth century.

"This is our finest treasure, Michael, and one of the oldest in the library," Manetti said. "It will be one of the principal features of our exhibition. But now, look at this."

With a gentle flourish, Manetti reached across the table and pulled over two comparable manuscripts.

"These are *Venetus A* and *Venetus B*, the oldest texts of Homer's *Iliad*, with centuries of Greek scholia written in the margins."

As Dominic recalled, since the first century ancient commentators, known as scholiasts, would insert grammatical or explanatory notations, even critical commentary, in the margins of the manuscripts of early authors. Over time, centuries in fact, successive copyists or those who owned a particular manuscript altered the scholia, and sometimes the practice expanded so much that there was no longer room for scholia in the margins, so it became necessary to produce them as separate works. No copy machines, just dedicated scribes working with Egyptian reed pens and feather quills to patiently reproduce one-of-a-kind originals.

"These are truly extraordinary, Paulo," Dominic declared, his hands shaking slightly as he held the ancient parchments. "I can certainly see why you'd want to share these in your exhibition. I can confidently say the Vatican will cooperate in any way we can. I'll make arrangements for the original translation of Homer's *Iliad* to be couriered to you when I return to Rome. I assume you'll have appropriate security arrangements in place?"

"Of course, Michael, apart from our own security detail, the federal Carabinieri has offered to provide full protection for us. We are simply the custodians of these masterpieces, but they are part of Italy's proud heritage and the government takes that responsibility quite seriously.

"And thank you for your generous contribution, Michael," he

continued. "Your *Iliad* will be in excellent hands, I can assure you."

"When we spoke last week," Dominic said, "you mentioned another piece you wanted to discuss?"

Manetti turned somber. "Yes, there is something else I need to show you, and I'd like to get your opinion on it. This came to us recently from a local donor who wishes to remain publicly anonymous, and while its value is undeniable and a welcomed donation to our collection, I am not quite sure what to make of its meaning."

The curator rummaged about the other manuscripts on the table, his gloved hands repositioning each document carefully, until he found what appeared to be an autograph musical manuscript, with staff lines and bars of musical notations, placed inside a small Mylar protective sleeve. While it was in relatively good condition, given its apparent antiquity, its corners had been chipped and there were many creases across the paper, as if someone had folded it many times at some point. Its size was quite small, a half sheet of standard paper at most.

"Well, this looks interesting, though I must admit I know little about musical manuscripts. Who is it by?" Dominic asked.

As Dominic peered closely at the manuscript, Hana returned from her brief tour of the library, and walked up to stand silently next to the two men. She glanced at the object of their attention while Manetti continued.

"This, my friend, was penned by the hand of Venice's own *maestro di violino* Antonio Vivaldi. He gave it the title 'Scherzo Tiaseno in Sol,' and it appears to be a scherzo in the truest, most literal meaning of that word—a joke! It is a fair enough piece of music, but nowhere near the level one would expect from a Baroque master like Vivaldi. If it is a joke, then the question is, why? And for whom? There must be more than meets the ear.

"This is marked as page two, so there may still exist a page one somewhere. The donor was rather circumspect on the matter, but as Vivaldi was her sixth great-grand-uncle, the provenance is well established." Manetti looked up at Dominic questioningly and shrugged his shoulders.

As Hana read the notes, she weighed in. "You're right, Paulo. This isn't anything close to what Vivaldi was known to have composed. And scherzos are normally in three, like a waltz, but this has the bar lines in the wrong place. There must be some other meaning to it."

"You read music?!" Dominic asked her, somewhat taken aback.

"Of course, I studied music for years at St. Stevens School, and I play both the piano and cello," she replied, a shy smile playing across her face.

"Will wonders never cease with you?" Dominic asked, grinning mischievously.

"Oh, please," she said modestly. "We all have our secret talents. And I can hardly travel around with a cello."

Turning to the curator, she asked, "Paulo, may I have a closer look at this?"

"Of course, signorina," he said encouragingly.

Hana accepted the Mylar sleeve from Dominic and took a seat by one of the windows. Reading the music, she hummed the notes, emitting a series of high, low, and mid-range sounds which produced no tune whatsoever.

"Okay, this is really strange. There is nothing here that might even imply that an artist with Vivaldi's genius was creating anything good, much less great. But why would he do that? From what I know, he wrote beautiful music feverishly, wasting not a precious second on something like this. But there *must* be a reason."

"I completely agree, signorina," Manetti said, nodding his head. "But what are we to do with this? We must have some kind of explanation for such an artifact if we are to display it."

Hana had a thought. "Paulo, can you make a copy of this for me? I have an old friend, Dr. Livia Gallo, my former music teacher at St. Stevens, who is an expert in Vivaldi and other Baroque masters. Maybe she has some idea of what this might represent?"

Manetti was delighted. "Yes! I would be happy to provide you with a copy if it helps to better understand this. You must assure me that you will not share it with anyone else except your colleague, yes? Until we understand it better, I wouldn't want speculations to be awkward for our donor."

"Yes, of course, only Dr. Gallo will see it. For that matter, it's small enough that I can just take a photo of it with my iPhone. Would that be acceptable?"

"Better yet," Manetti replied. "That way there are no loose copies to get lost. Oh, and please do not use flash."

Hana returned the manuscript to the table, removed her

phone from her bag, then took a full frame shot of the piece under natural light.

"Paulo," Dominic asked, "might we get an introduction to your donor, this Vivaldi descendant? Hana and I may be able to get more relevant information from her that can assist Dr. Gallo. Where does she live?"

"Here in Venice, in one of the great palazzos on the Grand Canal. I don't think the contessa would mind at all, actually. She's quite the conversationalist."

"A contessa?!" Hana asked, surprised.

"Oh yes, she comes from a very old noble line herself and married well, besides. Contessa Donatella Vivaldi Durazzo. She must be in her eighties now, a delightful woman, very generous in her philanthropy. She is one of the jewels of Venice, a wonderful patron of the arts, adored by everyone. She lives in Palazzo Grimaldi in the Dorsoduro, not far from the Guggenheim Museum. I would be pleased to make an introduction."

"Excellent! We'll be here all week, Paulo, and it would be a treat to see one of the famed palazzos on the Grand Canal," Dominic said excitedly. "Not to mention meeting Italian nobility." Manetti smiled assuringly at his old friend.

"We're staying at the Ca' Sagredo, Paulo," Hana said. "You can reach us there, but here's my mobile number if you need us at any time." She wrote down her number on a slip of paper and handed it to Manetti.

"Grazie, signorina. I will make the call this evening and let you know when she is available."

"Where to now?" Hana asked Dominic as they left the building, having said their goodbyes to Manetti.

"I thought we'd have a bite of lunch at Quadri then saunter over to St. Mark's Basilica and say hello to a friend of mine from my seminary days. We've come all this way, and I'd hate to miss seeing him."

"Lead the way," Hana said breezily, placing her wide-brimmed straw hat back on her head. "I'm ready for some fresh seafood, aren't you?"

"You bet. Just watch out for pigeons, though, as I've tossed the newspapers."

CHAPTER

TWO

Among the many fine palazzos lining the Grand Canal is an understated three-story ochre palace, somewhat more slender than its neighbors but nonetheless impressive. Its more observable features include a grand entrance off the gondola traghetto, with a black scalloped awning over the brick staircase leading up from the water's edge; several full-width balconies with ornamental balustrades at each end; heavily draped arched picture windows overlooking the canal—and a cadre of armed security guards posted around the grounds of Palazzo Feudatario.

As a glossy mahogany water taxi approached the dock, two beefy men appeared from the palazzo's entrance to greet the sole visitor on board, a priest called to administer last rites to the dying master of the house—a man known to all of Venice as Don Lucio Gambarini, the *capintesta,* or head-in-chief of the Veneto Camorra.

A stout man in his sixties, Don Gambarini had suffered a paralyzing stroke some weeks prior, and as his health had further declined, his death was not unexpected. In the meantime the *capintriti,* heads of the twelve districts under Don Gambarini's leadership, had assembled in the grand house, set

17

to squabbling as to who would take over as leader of the clan when the great *capintesta* met his end.

But that was hardly on Gambarini's mind when Father Carlo Rinaldo entered the formal master bedroom to hear the Don's confession and administer extreme unction, the final anointing with last rites before death. Rinaldo had never met Gambarini before, though he was aware of the Don's reputation, one deserving of a robust confession if he were truly repentant.

The large, well-appointed bedroom had many people standing around, vying for the boss's attention should he wish to suddenly name one of them as his successor. But Gambarini would have none of it yet, demanding the bedroom be cleared except for the priest, who would hear his confession privately.

As everyone ambled out of the room, giving each other dark glances, the door was closed as Rinaldo placed a violet stole around his neck, then reached into his black leather bag and withdrew a small bottle of holy water, a crucifix, and his Bible.

"Don Gambarini, my name is Father Rinaldo, from St. Mark's. Do you wish to make a confession?"

"Where is my regular priest, Father Viani?"

"I'm afraid he is on sabbatical, signore, and will not return for some time. He entrusted his duties to me in his absence."

Gambarini looked wide-eyed at the priest for a long while, trembling, gauging his predicament. Rinaldo found terror in the man's eyes. Not an uncommon occurrence for one so close to death, but there was something more. Some heavy burden the man was struggling with. All the priest could do was wait for his penitent to make the first move.

"Father, I do wish to make a confession," Gambarini began, "but it is not one you are going to like."

"I make no judgments at all, signore. I am but the Lord's servant in this matter. He alone passes judgment. But that depends on how you wish to leave this life, carrying with you the dark burden of your transgressions, or absolved of sin in His light." Rinaldo gestured upward as he said this.

Gambarini paused, glanced around the room, then looked deep into the priest's eyes. "Before we begin, Father, I must ask of you an important favor, for my sins are so great, my penance must include some action on your part—but only after I am dead.

"What I am about to tell you involves a serious crime against the Vatican itself, an offense which has been ongoing for centuries, and still takes place to this very day. I fear I will not have God's full absolution unless this matter is revealed once and for all. And you must be the one to tell it to others, so that it will stop. Is that agreeable?"

Such an unusual request completely mystified Rinaldo. Never had he been asked to play a part in a confessor's penance. And to do so he would have to break the sacred seal of the confessional; he was uncertain if having permission to do so by the penitent absolved him of that restraint. He would have to speak with someone about that later.

He walked across the room and picked up a chair. Placing it next to Gambarini's bed, he took a seat. He paused a moment to consider the situation.

"Let me hear your confession, my son. If it is within my power, I will do my part as you ask."

CHAPTER

THREE

Once the private chapel of the Doge of Venice—whose 15th-century palace sits next to the spectacular church—Saint Mark's Basilica is the main focal point of Piazza San Marco, a 9th-century ecclesiastical Byzantine wonder.

Entering the basilica, one's gaze is naturally drawn upward, to the domed cupolas featuring thousands of golden mosaic tiles artfully depicting early saints and other religious figures. Not one bit of space had been untouched by the talented hands of many famed artisans of the day, even underfoot, with its inlaid marble floor. Byzantine archways abound, with murals portraying biblical scenes and divine imagery, nearly all leafed in gold, hence its ancient nickname *Chiesa d'oro*, Church of Gold.

As she and Dominic entered the atrium, overwhelmed by the splendor of it all, Hana marveled at what each panel might have represented in the mind of its creator, since there seemed to be no common theme throughout apart from the universal adoration of religious iconography, some 8,000 square meters of it in the basilica proper alone.

While tourists meandered through the church, Dominic led Hana through the crowd and directly toward the back of the basilica, to a door marked *Privato* off the east sacristy, leading to a suite of administrative offices. The receptionist there greeted him warmly as he announced his business as visiting his old friend Father Carlo Rinaldo.

"He is on the telephone now, Padre, but I will inform him you are waiting," the receptionist said. She wrote something on a piece of notepaper, then stood and walked back to one of the offices, disappearing through its door. A moment later, she returned.

"Don Rinaldo will be with you in a moment," she said, using the Italian colloquial term for *Father.*

A few minutes later, a good-looking priest in his early thirties came out of the same office, approaching Dominic with a wide smile.

"Michael Dominic, as I live and breathe! What brings you to Venice?!"

"Carlo!" Dominic exclaimed with joy.

As the two men embraced, Hana watched with amusement. *Another devilishly gorgeous priest?!* she thought. *What's wrong with this picture?!*

"Carlo, I want you to meet my good friend, Hana Sinclair. Hana, this is Carlo, my best friend from seminary at Fordham."

"Pleased to meet you, Carlo," Hana said, meeting his own light blue eyes with admiration. "What is it with all you handsome priests? A girl doesn't stand a chance these days."

Both Carlo and Dominic laughed as they held each other by the shoulders, clearly happy to be together again.

"Please, come into my office," Rinaldo offered, leading the way. "Would either of you like tea or water?"

Both declined the gesture, each taking a seat on old brown leather wingback chairs in the priest's office.

"To answer your question, Carlo, we're mostly here for a bit of vacation. Hana is a journalist for Paris's *Le Monde* newspaper and we go way back, so we'll enjoy Carnivale while we're here, something she has yet to experience.

"But I did have a little business to attend to, a meeting with your neighbor across the piazzetta, Paulo Manetti at the Marciana Library. The Vatican will contribute one of its manuscripts for the library's upcoming exhibition, so I wanted to look at how they'll be presenting it. And hopefully we'll be meeting with Contessa Vivaldi this week as well."

"Ah, yes, the lovely Donatella," the priest remarked. "A most gracious patron of St. Mark's too. You will find her pleasant company, I'm sure, with a stunning palazzo on the Grand Canal. This will be quite the Venetian experience for you, Hana. Everything worthwhile in one visit! Few visitors get the chance to see inside one of the great palazzos of our city. Where are you staying?"

"At the Ca' Sagredo," Hana said matter-of-factly.

"Well, you're already enjoying the best Venice has to offer then." His glance turned to Dominic. "And you, Michael?"

"I have a room there as well."

Rinaldo's eyebrows shot up. "They must pay very well at the Vatican nowadays!"

Dominic blushed as he looked over at Hana. "This is Hana's treat. The style to which she is accustomed... As she would be the last to tell you, coming from a wealthy family has its benefits."

"So, Carlo," Hana said, modestly changing the subject, "how long have you been at St. Mark's?"

"Going on two years now. It is a great honor to work here. I fell in love with Venice on my first visit, when I was just nineteen and serving in the US Air Force at Aviano Air Base, so it's great I could one day make a home here. Though I was born in New York, I have dual citizenship since my parents are both Italian."

The telephone rang. Rinaldo held up a pausing hand to his guests as he answered the call. He listened attentively as his demeanor changed from glad to serious, then said a respectful goodbye and hung up the phone. For a moment he was lost in thought, the room quiet. Then he looked up at Dominic, holding his gaze as he considered something.

"Hana, I hesitate to ask this, but would you be so kind as to give Michael and me a few minutes to discuss an important spiritual matter? I don't mean to be rude, but—"

"Not at all, Carlo," she said. "I'll take in your gorgeous basilica and be back in a while, if that's okay." Rising, she left the office and made her way back to the church interior.

"What is it, Carlo?" Dominic asked. "Something I can help with?"

"Michael, that was Cardinal Abruzzo, the Patriarch of Venice, on the phone, or what you would know as our archbishop. I turned to him earlier today with a thorny problem, since it involves breaking the seal of confession. But he did not have an answer, leaving the decision to me."

"Wait, I'm lost," Dominic said, his eyelids fluttering in confusion. "Breaking the seal of confession? You mean as in, something that can never be allowed? And what would the archbishop be afraid of?"

"Well, under pain of potential excommunication, let me start from the beginning…" Rinaldo said, as he recounted the deathbed confession of Mafia boss Lucio Gambarini.

"Since the 18th century, the Camorra has administered a long string of Vatican art thefts and forgeries, involving a continuous line of corrupt insiders. The very idea is inconceivable to me, that something of this vile nature hasn't been exposed long before now. Or maybe it has, and those potential informants either gave in to participating in the illicit operation or met with certain dark fates if they proved unwilling.

"The Camorra is like a monstrous octopus, Michael. Its criminal enterprises are vast and varied, and they 'own' many political and religious leaders throughout Italy, much like the Sicilian Mafia and the 'Ndrangheta do in their own regions. That fact is widely known, but most people simply turn their heads thinking, '*Ah, just business as usual with the Vatican.*'

"Don Gambarini's confession is unique, though, in that he feared God's eternal wrath unless he did what he could to expose the practice before he died. And he wanted *me* to be his executor in this matter!

"As I said, I turned to the Patriarch seeking his advice, and he just now flatly turned down my plea. Perhaps it was because he wanted none of the details, nor the name of the penitent, a quandary in itself." Rinaldo glared at the telephone, recalling the conversation as he wrung his hands in distress.

After his friend finished, Dominic sat there, stunned at the enormity of the situation. And he now understood that, given permission by the penitent, perhaps the rules of confessional sanctity had been slackened a bit, though he was still dubious.

Rinaldo continued. "I share this with you for a couple of reasons, Michael. First, you're the one friend I can turn to for unvarnished ecclesiastical advice. Second, you're a Vatican insider, and must have some kind of influence on any prolonged and ongoing crimes that may take place there. That the Vatican Museum even today has an undercurrent of criminality to it must shake you to your core. It certainly does me. And the man is dying, so I know very soon my promise to help him must be fulfilled and these secrets revealed. So, what do we do now?"

After the word *"we"* surprised him, Dominic took a moment to reflect on the situation, steepling his hands beneath his chin as he resettled himself in the leather chair. He knew about the Camorra's reputation and didn't want to put anyone in their menacing path, least of all himself. If all this was true—and he had real trouble believing the practice had been ongoing for *centuries*—then yes, it needed to cease.

"You mentioned art forgeries, Carlo. Was Gambarini more specific about that? As in, what had been outright stolen, or which artworks had been replaced by forged replicas?"

"No, he spoke in broad terms, nothing specific. But can you imagine how much damage this will have to the credibility of the Vatican as having one of the world's foremost museums?

We're talking about thousands of works of art from the greatest masters in history. Michelangelo, da Vinci, Raphael, Caravaggio... the list goes on. No doubt these would have all ended up in the most private collections worldwide, for they could never be put on the market."

"Yes, I imagine someone could also store them in freeports, where many wealthy collectors keep their finest treasures for tax and security purposes." He thought back to an earlier adventure, the Zharkov affair involving a veil from Mary Magdalene, reinforcing the likelihood that what Gambarini confessed could be true.

"I need to give this some thought myself, Carlo. Gambarini said take no action until he's dead, correct? So I see no reason to rush into a decision right now, anyway. Time is on our side, regardless. I still cannot believe this has been going on for a couple hundred years. Maybe that's just a legend the Camorra cooked up to build mystique around its reputation. It is the oldest Mafia organization in Italy, after all."

"Perhaps you're right. But that doesn't mean we should just stand aside and let it continue unabated. The question is, how to stop it?"

FOUR

With its splendid panoramic terrace on the Grand Canal, the L'Alcova Restaurant at Ca' Sagredo Hotel was the perfect way to end their day. Across the water was the famed Rialto Market, busy with locals searching for the day's freshest ingredients to prepare their own homemade suppers for the evening.

Hana and Dominic had each ordered Punzoné vodka martinis, which they sipped while looking over menus.

"I'm famished, but there are so many fabulous choices here," Hana enthused. "What looks good to you?"

"That Yellowfin Ahi Tuna seems to have my name on it," Dominic said. "'*Caught fresh this morning off the waters of Sicily.*' No wonder it's so expensive."

"This is the Ca' Sagredo, Michael. Everything here is pricey. But it's worth it," she said assuringly, "and don't forget, this is on my expense account."

Dominic felt a twinge of discomfort with Hana's generosity, but accepted that if this was her comfort zone, he shouldn't carry any burdens about it.

"I think I'll have the Ahi as well," she decided.

After the server took their orders, they both sighed

contentedly and looked out over the canal. Gondoliers in their striking red and white striped shirts and beribboned straw hats dug their oars into the placid waters, their sleek, sinuous black gondolas escorting tourists to no place in particular, simply taking in the magnificent palazzos bordering the Grand Canal. The larger *vaporetti* water busses ferried hordes of tourists from one stop to another, creating large foamy wakes in their path which the expert gondoliers handled with ease.

Before long, the server returned with their meals. Each plate was an artistic masterpiece: thick slices of fresh seared Ahi Tuna, garnished with colorful dabs of garlic-lime aioli and soy ginger lemon dipping sauces, topped with a single red pear tomato and razor thin slices of mandarin orange, and a side of steamed asparagus with butter and garlic.

Both of them gazed at the displays before them, then looked up at each other with satisfied smiles.

"Isn't this Venice at its best?" Hana asked. Dominic nodded as they dug into their meals.

They ate in silence, savoring each delicious bite, interspersed with sips of a fruity New World Pinot Noir the sommelier had recommended for the spicy, seared tuna.

Glancing at Dominic from time to time, Hana noticed a distant look in his eyes, as if his mind seemed to be elsewhere.

"Everything okay, Michael?"

Dominic lifted his head abruptly, interrupted in his thoughts. He considered her question for a moment, then relented. Looking around to see if others were close by, he leaned forward, speaking in a near whisper.

"Remember Carlo wanting to speak with me privately at St. Mark's?"

"Of course," she whispered, nodding. "I've become used to having to wander off like a tourist when your business calls." She smiled impishly, as if it were a private joke.

"Yeah, sorry about that. Normally this wouldn't be

27

something I'd be permitted to discuss, but this situation tosses out some of the rules.

"Carlo told me he had just heard the confession of a dying man as he administered last rites. But not just any man. This guy was a Mafia *padrino*, or godfather, head of the Veneto Camorra clan. And in the confession—which I tell you in the strictest confidence, Hana, only because the confessor permitted Carlo to relay certain information to others—he revealed an astonishing operation involving the theft of Vatican artworks, occurring over *centuries!* It seems inconceivable, I know, and yet this guy was in mortal fear for his soul, which understandably persuaded him to reveal everything before he dies."

Setting her knife and fork down, Hana folded her arms on the table and leaned forward.

"Do you mean to tell me that for some hundreds of years the Vatican has been the victim of art theft? That can only mean it's been an inside job for generations! How is that even possible? I agree with you. It seems inconceivable."

"I can hardly believe it myself, to be honest," Dominic said, shaking his head. "You would think someone, at some point in time, would have tried to put a stop to it. *Somebody* would have noticed the disappearance of such major pieces—though the Don did say it also involved art forgeries taking the place of the originals. That might be possible. There are some very talented forgers out there, fooling even the brightest experts for centuries.

"I'm not sure what to do in this situation, Hana. Where to even begin. Carlo also stressed the dangers of interrupting the Camorra's business operations, and if we do get involved, that's not something to take lightly."

"*We?!*" Hana blurted.

Michael realized he'd done the same thing to Hana that Carlo had to him, involving him just by revealing the situation. However, he also knew her reaction would be the same as his had been. "Well, you asked what was on my mind, so now that you know, how can you walk away from something so intriguing?" Dominic offered an engaging smile.

"You do know me well, don't you?"

"But think of it. If what he says is true—and I still have my doubts about his claim of this spanning centuries—there must be a well-tuned mechanism by certain forces within the Vatican who are aware of, if not enabling, what's going on there! How do we go about finding them and stopping the practice? And if we do, how will the Camorra respond? This could be a pretty dangerous gamble."

"So this godfather character is based here in Venice, meaning this is likely the center of their operations. And since he's either dying or dead by now, someone else will take his place. We should do a little snooping first, see what the score is."

"Listen to you, talking like some goombah in a gangster movie."

"I just calls 'em as I sees 'em," Hana said, continuing the impression.

"By the way, did you contact your friend who might know something about that Vivaldi manuscript?"

Hana brightened. "Oh, yes, I emailed Livia that photo I took and she replied saying she'd get back to me tonight." She checked her watch, then opened the Mail app on her phone. Sitting there was an email from Dr. Gallo. Hana tapped on it.

After opening the message, Hana read it aloud. "*Quite the mystery you have here, Hana, and I'm thrilled you shared this with me. I think I know what this is, but I'd rather explain it in person. May I join you in Venice tomorrow? I can take the train from Rome and be there by 1:00. Know of a good place I can stay?*"

"I think we have her interest," Hana said, smiling at Dominic. "I'll get her a room here at the hotel." She tapped out a reply message confirming she'd be welcome to join them, and that her accommodations will be taken care of at Ca' Sagredo.

"I wonder why she's making the trip rather than simply talking about it on the phone?" Dominic asked.

"If I know her, she'll want to get her hands on the original, to see it for herself, and such opportunities don't come by very often for most people, wouldn't you say? Especially one we're asking a favor of."

"No, you're right. I understand the attraction of in-person experiences with ancient artifacts like that. I don't think Paulo would mind at all, especially if she has some sensible solution for us. And for her to make the trip, I expect she does.

"But back to the Camorra and this art heist operation. I think I'll call Cardinal Petrini and explain the situation to him. He's likely to have some opinions on the matter."

"That would be an understatement. If I were him, I'd go ballistic. I am a little concerned about messing with the Camorra though, Michael. Why don't you ask him if he can send Karl and Lukas to join us here, just in case?"

Dominic considered this wise, and given the possible consequences if they started asking too many questions, hoped Petrini would agree. The guys would enjoy some time in Venice, too. He'd relied on them in past situations, trusting their guidance and assistance implicitly.

"Good idea. I'll ask."

Just then Dominic's phone vibrated, signaling an incoming text message. He opened it.

"It's from Paulo. Contessa Vivaldi has invited us to her palazzo tomorrow evening! This has been quite the day, hasn't it?"

"No kidding! And tomorrow looks just as exciting.

"So, meanwhile, what's for dessert?"

CHAPTER
FIVE

At the end of its four-hour journey from Rome, the glossy apple red Frecciarossa bullet train had just left the Venice Mestre station before crossing the long causeway across the lagoon and on into Venice, with its terminus at the Santa Lucia station on the Grand Canal.

Dr. Livia Gallo collected her suitcase and laptop bag and waited patiently for the low snout of the train's locomotive to reach its buffer stop so travelers could disembark.

As she descended the steps, she heard her name being called from among the crowd of people on the platform. Looking up, she saw her former student Hana Sinclair and a priest walking toward her.

"My goodness," she said as they reached her. "Do you always greet old friends with a priest at hand?"

They all laughed as Hana made introductions, and they exchanged hugs and handshakes.

"Michael is at the center of our Baroque mystery here, Livia, since his expertise is in ancient manuscripts. He's Prefect of the Vatican Secret Archives and a good friend to have." She glanced at him admiringly, pleased to introduce the two of them.

"I think I should get settled in at the hotel first, then let's meet up and talk about your manuscript," Livia said.

"I think you're going to enjoy this evening, Livia," said Hana. "We're meeting with one of Vivaldi's descendants, Contessa Donatella Vivaldi Durazzo, at her palazzo on the Grand Canal."

"Oh, my! How on earth did you manage that?"

"The curator at the Marciana Library, Paulo Manetti, arranged the meeting for us. The contessa donated the manuscript to the library, and Paulo said she would be happy to give us more background on it. Michael thought it would be a good idea to get as much information as we can, if we're to understand why Vivaldi wrote such an odd piece of music."

"Well," Livia added, "I think I may have an idea about that, which is why I brought my laptop with me. We can discuss more after I'm settled in."

WITH LIVIA ENSCONCED in the suite Hana had arranged for her, she laid out her laptop on the meeting table, prepared it for what she intended to display, then texted Hana and Dominic to join her.

A few minutes later, there was a knock on the door. Opening it, she welcomed them inside.

"First, dear Hana, I must thank you for arranging such a delightful room, and at the Ca' Sagredo, no less. You do know how to live well!"

"Oh, Livia, it's the least I could do for your generous time and travel to help us out," Hana replied. She noticed her friend's MacBook Pro had a wood panel cover. "What a gorgeous laptop. I didn't know they came in wood!"

"I had that custom made. It's African Padauk. I love the warmth wood gives to cold machines. It's kind of a quirk of mine.

"Now, as to our little mystery," Livia went on. "I'm certain I've come up with the solution. Vivaldi's Scherzo appears to be a relatively normal piece of music, but has subtle eccentricities that are clues to something more for the right audience. I believe he composed his manuscript with what's known as musical cryptography—the embedding of certain note styles that are covertly intended to convey secret messages.

"As a little background, the practice of musical cryptography dates back to the 9th century, but it wasn't until the Baroque period when it gained wider acceptance, and the Baroque was very much Vivaldi's era. Many composers—among them Bach, Brahms, Haydn, Schumann, and perhaps others—are known to have integrated cryptographic motives into certain of their compositions, mainly for fun or as an intimate secretive jest for friends or lovers.

"Looking at your manuscript, it appears as any other piece of standard music might. But, what piqued my interest," Livia continued, "was the use of the word *Tiaseno* in the title."

"I'd wondered about that myself," Dominic said. "I've never seen the word before. Is it a special musical term?"

"No, it isn't a word. Those are seven frequently used letters in most European languages. Vivaldi was probably counting on a trained *cifristo*, or cryptologist, being able to recognize it."

"Ah, so 'Scherzo' was to trick most people into thinking it was a joke, while *Tiaseno* was to signal to those in the know that there was a hidden message?"

"But you're not a *cifristo* yourself, Livia," Hana said. "So how did you figure it out?"

"Well," Livia replied, "I recognized *Tiaseno* because the same word appears in the musical code called Solfa Cipher, something I happened upon many years ago inspecting another manuscript. Solfa Cipher maps letters of the alphabet to the steps of a major scale: T-I-A-S-E-N and O is the order of the first seven notes. Vivaldi *must* have been using an early version of the system."

"Are you saying there is actually a secret message in this manuscript?" Dominic asked excitedly.

"You'll see," Livia said coyly, "but first, to translate the notes back into Italian, we need to know which major scale Vivaldi was using. Fortunately, I think he gave us another clue as part of his 'joke.' The manuscript looks like it is in F major, but that didn't make sense to me because the title is 'Scherzo Tiaseno *in Sol.*' In music, 'Sol' means '*in the key of G*'."

"Wow," Dominic marveled. "So the key was in the title and is the key to mapping this out. Ingenious!"

Livia reached for a blank sheet of composition paper from her bag. "Exactly. Let me illustrate it for you." She began laying out the notes.

"You see, if we swap the clef and key signature at the beginning of each line to G major, with one sharp, we should be able to read the correct letters. Look at the message that starts to emerge when I map these onto Vivaldi's manuscript."

"What about the rest of the alphabet?" Hana asked. "There are only seven notes in a major scale."

"Yes, in Solfa Cipher, T-I-A-S-E-N-O always appear on the downbeats; the other letters of the alphabet use the same seven notes, but fall in between the beats."

"That would explain why the bar lines don't match with a normal ¾ scherzo meter," Hana said. "Vivaldi was showing where to place the beats to extract the message."

"Right," Livia confirmed. "The third clue of his musical joke! For example, these notes match the letters R-C-H and U."

"I can almost make out actual words now," exclaimed Dominic. "That looks like it could be *chiunque trovi*...'whoever finds.' Can you decode the rest of the manuscript?"

Using musical composition software on her laptop, Livia had overlaid Vivaldi's staffs, clefs, and notes from the image Hana had sent her, which then assigned each note its appropriate scale degree. The result on the laptop display produced a four-line stanza in what appeared to be a continuous string of Italian words:

"Extracting the Italian took a bit of careful parsing," she noted, "but after determining the proper word endings, when it was finished a coherent message emerged."

chiunque trovi questo messaggio

deve causare questa pratica
cessare con tutta la dovuta fretta ma
essere cauti nello sforzo

"Then it was just a matter of converting the Italian into English." She read aloud the translated version:

whoever finds this message
must cause this practice to
cease with all due haste but
be cautious in the endeavor

"Brilliant!" said Hana, ever the puzzle fan. "This is amazing work, Livia."

"As I said, I've had a little experience with it. And since the music itself represented nothing of what we would normally expect to be from the hand of Vivaldi, that's what led me to thoughts of steganographic cryptography—information hidden inside other information.

"No one knows the origin of the Solfa Cipher," she added, "but I am wondering if Maestro Vivaldi may have actually been the inventor. This is the earliest use of it I have ever seen. And I believe he left us one more clue in the manuscript. The key of G in Italian is *Sol*, but the other key, F major is..."

"...It's *Fa!*" Hana said jubilantly. "Of course: Sol and Fa!"

Astonished by the outcome, Dominic shook his head in admiration. He had one last question.

"So, this accounts for being page two of Vivaldi's original score, but where is page one? This secondary translation relies completely on whatever came before it."

"Hopefully your contessa might shed some light on that," Livia said. "I'm so looking forward to meeting her. This is the most fun I've had in ages."

CHAPTER

SIX

As the water taxi navigated between the *pali da casada*, the colorful striped gondola poles at the entrance to Palazzo Grimaldi, Dominic shouldered Livia Gallo's laptop bag and stood firmly to steady both her and Hana as the boatman attached the mooring lines to the cleats on the narrow dock.

Dominic disembarked first, then held out a hand to both women as they stepped onto the dock. He paid the driver, then they walked up to the grand doors of the palazzo to announce their arrival.

A few moments later the door was opened by a small and very old butler who introduced himself as Francesco. He led them into the magnificent foyer of the mansion.

"Welcome to Palazzo Grimaldi. The contessa is engaged at the moment but will be down presently. She has asked me to entertain you in the meantime and offer you whatever you might like to drink. Please, follow me into the parlour."

Despite being several hundred years old, the palazzo was well-maintained and tastefully decorated, with a remarkable abundance of fine oil paintings and tapestries lining the walls, lavish Persian and Oriental rugs on the old wooden floors, exquisite Murano glass chandeliers in all rooms with antique lighting sconces in the hallways, and tall arched windows draped in white sheers giving each room copious yet soft natural light.

The parlour was spacious, with two separate plush seating areas divided by a polished white Fazioli grand piano, the dominant object in the room. Against one side wall was an elaborately carved mahogany bar with a large antique mirror behind it.

"What cocktails may I prepare for you?" Francesco asked. "I am confident we can accommodate every taste."

After the three guests each gave him their request, Francesco slipped behind the bar to prepare the drinks. As he did so he gave them what sounded like a long-rehearsed, or at least oft-repeated, history of the palace.

"It may please you to know that Charles II, Lord of Monaco, originally built Palazzo Grimaldi in 1578 as a retreat from his principal residence in Monte Carlo. It has been passed down through the Grimaldi family for generations until the contessa's family acquired it in 1872. The signora was born in this very house and has lived here ever since.

"There are many styles of *palazzi* on the Grand Canal: Byzantine, Gothic, Renaissance, Baroque, and Neoclassical, the earliest built starting in the 5th century, if you can imagine that. Many are still standing from the earliest periods, though they have been meticulously restored. Palazzo Grimaldi is of the Renaissance period, modeled after classical ancient Roman and Greek forms."

It was clear the butler had given this talk often, implying the contessa likely had many guests from time to time, and Francesco served as not only bartender but tour guide while the lady of the house was preparing herself for her visitors.

As Francesco distributed each drink from his bar tray, the contessa entered the room, wearing a resplendent Armani light mauve gabardine crew-neck jacket with darted palazzo trousers and chic Ferragamo ballet flats.

"Oh, good evening, everyone. I had a small business matter to attend to, which took longer than I had hoped. I am sorry for having made you wait, an unforgivable breach of courtesy."

"Not at all, Contessa," Dominic offered with a smile as they all stood. "Francesco has been keeping us quite entertained by the history of your beautiful palazzo. It is a breathtaking home."

"You're too kind, Father..."

"Dominic. Michael Dominic," he said, reaching out his hand. "And this is my friend and colleague Hana Sinclair, and Dr. Livia Gallo, who just came in from Rome to help us with your Vivaldi manuscript."

The contessa shook each of their hands, graciously placing her left hand atop each exchange. Francesco stood next to her, a ruby red Negroni resting on his bar tray, which she then reached for. With his duties for the moment complete, he left the parlour.

"A great pleasure meeting you all. Before we begin, would you like to see some of the artwork in my collection? I am very fond of paintings and delight at sharing them."

"Yes, please," Livia said enthusiastically. "I, too, am a fan of great art."

A keen observer, Hana estimated the contessa to be in her eighties, though she maintained herself superbly. Fit, with a lively step, a sharp mind, and exquisite taste in clothing and how to wear it.

She also noticed a sizable ruby ring on the contessa's left hand when she first embraced them all.

"That is a stunning ruby, Contessa. Is there a story behind it?"

The old woman held up her hand to look at the stone. A look of loving reminiscence crossed her face.

"My husband, Count Durazzo, gave this to me for our engagement. I treasure it every day, and except for cleaning, it has never left my hand. Now, follow me, please."

As she led them through various rooms on the ground floor of the palazzo, she stopped at various notable paintings she favored in particular, giving a brief background on each one. Raphael, Caravaggio, Tintoretto, Titian... many of Italy's finest artists were represented in the various rooms of the palazzo.

Finally, she directed their attention to one impressive oil painting over an enormous fireplace in the library: a depiction of the Crucifixion, with bold strokes of the composition having rough edges that swiped back and forth between the agonized Christ figure and terrified observers at the base of the cross. The whole of it depicted the artist's chiaroscuro contrasts cast in a cold light.

"This piece, *Crucifixion with Apostles*, has quite a history to it," she said admiringly. "Originally attributed in 1740 to the eccentric Giovanni Battista Piazzetta, it turns out to have actually been painted by a female Venetian artist named Giulia Lama, a most intelligent, educated woman who was also an accomplished poet with a comprehensive understanding of mathematics and philosophy.

"As a woman in the male-dominated 18th century, her work was sophisticated and highly desirable, but over time had been falsely attributed to her male adversaries—men who simply could not allow a woman, especially one of such unappealing physical appearance, to receive higher commissions than they were getting for their own work.

"As if *looks* should even have mattered," she concluded, rolling her eyes with a disparaging wave of her hand.

"Many of Lama's paintings had been assigned under Piazzetta's name, and scholars later determined that no less than 26 of her paintings and some 200 drawings had been previously attributed to other well-known artists. A sad reflection of the times, I'm afraid.

"As a matter of fact," she continued, "Giulia Lama was a very close friend of my ancestor, Antonio Vivaldi. He tutored her in the violin at the orphanage where he taught, and she was an apt pupil, from what I understand. Such a talented woman, treated shamefully by her male counterparts. This painting is among my favorites now for that reason. I only just recently acquired it from a local gallery, and it thrilled me to have discovered her."

"You have quite the admirable collection here, Contessa," Hana said appraisingly. "And thank you for enlightening us on Giulia Lama's background. What terrible challenges she faced. Thank goodness times have changed."

"They have not changed enough, my dear," the contessa grumbled, exasperated. "There is still a long way to go.

"But now, let's discuss Signor Vivaldi's manuscript, shall we?"

While the others followed the contessa down the hall and into the parlour, Hana hung back, taking in Giulia Lama's painting for a few moments longer. Inspired by it, she reached for her phone, taking a photo of it to admire later.

CHAPTER
SEVEN

The contessa led them back to the parlour, where Francesco was again behind the bar, ready to refresh everyone's cocktail. As he did so, Dominic began the discussion.

"As you know, Contessa, I met with Paulo Manetti at the Marciana Library, where he presented me with what appears to be a secondary page of your Vivaldi manuscript. By any chance, might you know where the first page is?"

"Why, yes, it's in my safe, along with other music and letters from the maestro. Would you like to see those, Father?"

Dominic was suddenly exhilarated, not just at potentially finding page one of the manuscript, but having the chance to see other letters of Vivaldi's.

"*Gentile Signora*, I would love nothing better! Thank you for so generously offering."

"Of course, it is my pleasure. I shall return in a moment," she said, turning to leave the room.

Livia's eyes shone brightly as well. "I can't believe my good fortune taking part in this! I am indebted to you both for inviting me, and cannot wait to transcribe Vivaldi's first page, much less hold his original letters in my own hands."

"To be on the safe side," Dominic said, "it's best if I handle them with conservation gloves and share them with you that way. Our hands accrue natural oils which can damage old papers." He reached into his pocket and withdrew his pair of white gloves, sliding his hands into each one.

A few minutes later the contessa returned carrying a large black portfolio box. Setting it on the expansive inlaid-leather sofa table in front of Dominic, she took a seat next to him and opened the case.

"These manuscripts have been in my family since around 1780, initially acquired by my great-great-great-great-grandfather-in-law, Count Giacomo Durazzo, from a Venetian senator, who bought them from Vivaldi's brother after the maestro died."

Dominic noted that each document had been wisely inserted into its own acid-free Mylar sleeve, consistent with exacting archival methods, making handling of the manuscripts that much safer. No gloves were needed.

The first one he picked up was a one-page letter in Vivaldi's hand dated 1735 and addressed to Alvise Pisani, the ruling Doge of Venice. Dominic read it aloud to the others, translating from the Italian. It seemed to be a heated correspondence concerning the city's Sumptuary law.

Dominic explained. "During the Renaissance, Venice was such a commercial powerhouse that the more well-heeled merchants and nobles spent a great deal of their wealth on excessive vanity luxuries: food, drink, conspicuous styles of dress, adornments to their palazzos and even their gondolas. Patrician women in particular were singled out for their ostentatious fashions, and the law came down especially hard on them. It restricted even courtesans from wearing pearls, as just one example.

"That's where Carnivale came in handy, a time during which sumptuary laws were suspended and people could dress as they pleased. The custom of wearing masks, in fact, hid a person's

station in life, so nobles could mix with commoners and no one
was the wiser.

"In this letter, it seems Signor Vivaldi was venting his
opposition to the law for various reasons. An interesting but
unremarkable specimen." He held it up for Livia to take,
fulfilling her desire to hold one of the maestro's letters.

Dominic flipped through the rest of the material in the
portfolio until he came to several musical scores. Peering closely
at each one—thrilled at the privilege of being able to do so—he
sought out that singular page one that would match the other
manuscript they had already seen.

And then he saw it. He took in a sharp breath.

"Here it is! Found it."

Signed by Vivaldi himself, and bearing the same folded and
crumpled appearance as the second page but flattened in its
sleeve, he handed it to Livia to examine. Her eyes shone as she
held it.

"Contessa, may I play this on your piano?" she pleaded.

"Of course, Dr. Gallo, be my guest."

Livia walked over to the Fazioli, sat down on the bench, and
placed the sheet on the music rack. With trembling fingers, she
began to play.

What emerged was what she expected. A jumble of tonal notes, unlike Vivaldi's typical style. She smiled.

The contessa, however, was bewildered.

"Is that really something Vivaldi wrote? I do not play the piano myself, nor do I read music. But I do have a good ear, and that sounds... off!"

Dominic explained the similar surprising reaction they had when reading the first manuscript they had copied from her original donation to the Marciana Library, and Hana's humming of it, showing something about it was indeed 'off.'

"We then sent it to Dr. Gallo, who is versed in a specialty area known as musical cryptography, and she discovered a secret message Vivaldi had encoded into the notes.

The contessa was not only visibly surprised, she was thrilled at the prospect of a mystery given rise to by her ancestor.

"Oh, and you've already translated it? What did it say?!"

Livia reached into her bag and withdrew the earlier output from her laptop, along with the translated message.

"This is simply extraordinary!" the contessa exclaimed after reading it. "But what is he talking about? What 'practice' must cease? And to what 'caution' does he refer?"

"That's what we're hoping to find out on this first page of his manuscript," Dominic said, hoping she would take the bait.

"Well, can we do the same thing for that page?"

Dominic barely contained himself, unobtrusively pumping his fist in the air at his side.

"I was hoping you would ask!" Livia said with delight. "And the answer is *yes!*" She took out her phone, took a photograph of the document, then transferred it to her laptop, which she had placed on the sofa table. Working with the composition software, she repeated the steps as before, decoding the Solfa Cipher, then arriving at the transcribed four stanzas on her laptop display:

In un vergognoso atto di arroganza.
il Vaticano viene derubato.
cieco dalla Camorra in campionato.
con Cardinale Niccolo Coscia.

Which, when she translated it into English, read:

In a shameful act of hubris
the Vatican is being robbed
blind by the Camorra in league
with Cardinal Niccolo Coscia

Everyone in the room fell silent, each pondering the meaning of the document as they heard it.

Dominic and Hana were stunned. *Here was proof of what Father Rinaldo heard in the Camorra Don's confession! It* had *been centuries old!* Looking at each other, they said nothing.

It all baffled the contessa.

"Well, that is quite the indictment, wouldn't you say, Father Dominic?" she faltered. "That the Vatican was being 'robbed blind'?! What do you suppose that was all about? I know who the Camorra is, of course; they are still quite active here in Venice even today. Is it not fascinating what one can learn from historical documents such as this? What should we make of it?"

Dominic was circumspect, preferring to reveal as little as possible.

"Oh, I'm sure that era entertained all sorts of skullduggery between the Church and the aristocracy. The Camorra is a curious addition, though. It does raise one's interest, doesn't it?" He smiled, as if to pass it off lightly. Glancing at Hana, he imperceptibly shook his head, implying, *Leave it alone for now.*

"May I see what else you have here, Contessa?" Dominic asked, striving to change the subject. He sat back down on the sofa and rifled through the remaining manuscripts, remarking on one or another, passing some around for all to see and hold.

"This is simply the finest collection of Vivaldi's work I have ever seen," Dominic commended her. "And I've seen some pretty remarkable things.

"Thank you so much for sharing these," he concluded.

"It was my pleasure, Father," she said as she returned all the documents to the portfolio.

"Now, as a last request, you must join me and my guests for our annual Carnivale celebration here in two days' time, on Saturday. Please come, you are all such lovely people, and you would be most welcome back to my home. There will be many prominent Venetians here: the Mayor, most of the city council, celebrities, various bishops and cardinals— you'll feel right at home, Father Dominic. And please bring your own guests, the house is open to all for this celebration.

"Until then, I bid you *buona sera*," she said as she stood and led them to the entrance foyer. "Francesco has already called your taxi, and it is waiting."

As she opened the door, sure enough, a canopied water taxi was already docked in front of the palazzo, waiting for its passengers.

"Thank you so much, Contessa, for your time and generosity," Hana said on their behalf as she kissed each of the older woman's cheeks in the familiar *il bacio* embrace. "It was a wonderful visit, and of course we'd love to attend your Carnivale celebration!"

WHILE THEY WERE on their way back to the Ca' Sagredo, the harmonious bells high atop Piazza San Marco's Campanile struck at the unusual time of 7:48, which could only mean one thing: the death of some notable figure in Venice had been announced.

Though neither Dominic, Hana, nor Livia understood the bells' significance yet, word soon spread quietly throughout the city that it was indeed the passing of Don Lucio Gambarini that caused the tower's bells to strike their mournful tune. Despite the Camorra leader's line of business, he had been accepted as a prominent personage in the city, and respect was accorded to all such high-profile Venetians.

While many breathed sighs of relief, others were troubled by who might replace Gambarini. Would the new capintesta be a kind soul, one who looked out for his fellow citizens in the course of the Camorra's business affairs? Or would it be someone with more barbaric inclinations, suffering intolerance for anything or anyone standing in his way?

BACK IN HIS HOTEL ROOM, Dominic called Cardinal Enrico Petrini, the Vatican Secretary of State, to update him on matters and request a favor. Although Dominic had only recently learned the cardinal was his biological father, he still held to the appropriate conventions of address, an accord to which they had agreed.

"Eminence, there is something here you should know, something very important."

He explained the entire situation: his meeting with Paulo Manetti at the Marciana, Father Rinaldo's surprise revelation of

Don Gambarini's shocking confession, the discovery of Antonio Vivaldi's manuscripts, and the Contessa's generous involvement. And that the Camorra is still in the picture and will probably not look well upon Dominic's involvement in bringing their operation into the light of day.

Michael acknowledged that they had no proof other that Vivaldi's accusation hidden in a coded sheet of music a couple hundred years earlier and a present-day man's dying confession. How did Vivaldi know this as fact back then? Even if it were true in Vivaldi's time, could this crime possibly still be taking place centuries later? Yet the coincidence of the confession coming to light at the same time as Vivaldi's accusation ... Michael left his thoughts unspoken. But the sigh by Cardinal Petrini hinted that the same thought had passed his mind: was divine providence at play? At the least, a coincidence so intense that they couldn't ignore it. And surely a deathbed confession would not include such a heinous lie, so there must be, in fact, truth to this matter. Yet, still, where was the proof?

"Is that your intention, Michael? To prove and stop this aberrant behavior?"

"I am only thinking of the Vatican's historical and priceless treasures, Eminence. This kind of theft cannot continue. Plus, if true, you have one or more moles in your bureaucracy there, and the Veneto Camorra must have some sort of efficient operatives here in Venice, and Rome as well. We must do what we can to uncover and stop this. And it looks like I'll need to take more time here in Venice, if you can arrange that with my assistant in the Archives."

The cardinal was silent for a moment, evaluating the situation.

"Difficult as it is to believe, we need to pursue this. But I will only allow it if you'll permit me to send two Swiss Guards to be at your side at all times, Michael. You will no doubt need protection while you're there. And yes, take the time you need."

Dominic laughed. "That was the favor I was going to ask. I'm hoping you can send Sergeant Karl Dengler and Corporal Lukas Bischoff at the earliest opportunity. They know how I work from past experience."

"Consider it done. They'll be on the first train in the morning."

"Oh, and please have them bring a change of street and dress clothes. It seems we're all going to Contessa Vivaldi's Carnivale soirée at her palazzo. The guys should love it—of course, they'll be on duty at all times," he added quickly, reinforcing the seriousness of their mission.

"Do be careful, Michael," Petrini cautioned. "I don't want harm to come to anyone over whatever may be going on with the Vatican's artworks."

"Of course, Eminence. And thanks," he said, then ended the call.

A few moments later, a text message came in on Dominic's phone from Carlo Rinaldo: **Don Gambarini just passed away.**

CHAPTER
EIGHT

J ust off the Rialto Bridge, at the center of the Grand Canal, rests the posh Studio Canal Grande. Venice's San Polo sestiere, or district, enjoyed many palazzos including this one that doubled as a commercial studio and gallery featuring many of Italy's finest artists, both Old Masters and contemporaries in the Venetian School of fine oil paintings.

Its dignified proprietor, Signor Renzo Farelli, always struck an imposing presence, the epitome of the Italians' prized appearance standard known colloquially as *la bella figura*—the handsome figure. He was never seen without *la sciarpa* around his neck draping the fine Italian suits he wore. In cold weather, the scarf protected him from chills; in sweltering summers, it helped to catch sweat or wipe it from his brow. Farelli selected his clothing carefully each morning, attiring himself for the wealthy clients he was sure to meet that day.

Admiring himself in front of a full-length mirror, he glanced at his Patek Philippe watch. His personal tailor would arrive soon, preparing for him a bespoke costume for Contessa Vivaldi's Carnivale party, *the* event to see and be seen at for every season. He never missed a one, for her friends were always the choicest potential clients for his thriving art business.

BEFORE HE DIED, Don Lucio Gambarini had named his successor, one Angelo Gallucci, as the new *capintesta*. Gallucci had been a capable underboss for Don Gambarini, and despite their personality differences, it was only fitting he be promoted to the top rank.

But Don Gallucci was more feared than loved by those who knew him, and he made it clear from his earliest hours of command that his leadership style would differ from that of his predecessor. Over his twenty-year reign, Gambarini had grown old and too easily persuaded, resulting in suboptimal revenues across the whole Veneto organization. His closest aides acknowledged he seemed more worried about his spiritual legacy than his corporeal standing in the centuries-long Mafia clan. There were even rumors he might have confessed things he shouldn't have to Father Rinaldo when the Don was given last rites in private.

But Angelo Gallucci had no such feeble inclinations. Taking possession of Palazzo Feudatario, the Camorra's Venetian headquarters for centuries, the new Don gathered his *consigliere* and newly promoted underbosses for a radical strategy and reorganization session. First on the agenda: find out what the confessor priest knows, and how to deal with him.

It was a new day in the Venetian's beloved La Serenissima.

KARL DENGLER and Lukas Bischoff had just arrived at the Santa Lucia train station on the late afternoon's Frecciarossa *Red Arrow*'s Rome-to-Venice run. Knowing Hana had reserved a room for them at Ca' Sagredo, they grabbed their gear and boarded the *vaporetto*, making their way up the Grand Canal to the chic hotel.

"Don't we have the best job in the world?" Karl asked Lukas, taking a deep breath of the fresh salty air.

His partner looked at him warmly and grinned as they both leaned on the deck rail, watching the activity on the canal. "I'll say. This is my first time in Venice, and we're already invited to a contessa's swank palazzo party! Life is good, Karl."

"Of course, we have a job to do, too." Karl said soberly. "Is it just me, or does my cousin Hana and our Father Michael always seem to get into trouble on these missions?"

"He *is* an inquisitive man," Lukas replied thoughtfully. "I admire him for his courage and sense of adventure. But yeah, his curiosity often comes at a price, and Hana's too. I feel privileged that Cardinal Petrini entrusts us with their safety. Now," he looked at his fellow Swiss Guard with a grin, "all we need to do is keep them safe. And enjoy ourselves at the same time!"

CHAPTER
NINE

T he stalwart leather and wood-paneled interior of the famed Harry's Bar, just west of Piazza San Marco, was the perfect spot for dinner as Dominic, Hana, Karl and Lukas sat at a window table overlooking the Grand Canal. The sun was just setting, casting radiant glows off the orange and pale brownish yellow-colored buildings across the lagoon.

Once the familiar haunt of Ernest Hemingway, Truman Capote, Alfred Hitchcock and other notables—whose photographs lined the walls of the narrow restaurant—the 1930s decor and white-jacketed waiters created a literary ambience that made the spot so beloved by Venetians that it was designated a national landmark by the Italian Ministry for Cultural Affairs.

Though Karl and Lukas had just arrived, the others were wearied after a long afternoon of taking in various Carnivale activities, but everyone was hungry. Sipping Harry's distinctive Bellini cocktails—Prosecco with peach—while studying the generous menu, they variously ordered Scampi with Finferli Mushrooms on Risotto, Green Tagliatelle with Pesto Sauce, John Dory with curry sauce and rice pilaf, and Chilean Sea Bass. Until their meals came, they sampled a beautifully plated appetizer of firm ripe cantaloupe wedges wrapped in razor-thin aged *prosciutto di Parma.*

"I've tasted nothing so incredible before," Hana gushed. "For such simple ingredients, there must be some secret recipe Harry's has."

"You could just be starving, too," Karl smirked. "Anything tastes good when you're famished. But the menu said this prosciutto has been aged a full three years. That's probably the secret. Just time."

"So, Michael," Lukas asked keenly, "we haven't yet discussed why we're here. Cardinal Petrini said you might need protection —but from whom?"

"Oh, it may be nothing, Lukas," Dominic said. "But it's good to have you here. There is much to do."

He then gave them the background of the past couple days: their meeting with Paulo at the Marciana Library, the time spent with Contessa Vivaldi at her palazzo and the additional documents she shared, Dr. Gallo's brilliant discovery of Vivaldi's secret musical manuscripts—and the strange confession of the Camorra *capintesta*, since it was relevant to their being in Venice.

"His Eminence thinks the Camorra may respond disagreeably to our raising questions about Don Gambarini's last words. And if it *is* true—which Vivaldi's own manuscript would seem to confirm—we need to find out if it's still going on and do what we can to put a stop to it."

Karl was astounded. "You can't really believe such an ongoing theft has been occurring, can you, Michael? I mean, the safeguards for moving art outside of the Vatican alone are nearly impenetrable. It wouldn't make our security look very effective, if it is true."

"We'll be working on the assumption that it *is* true, Karl, but hope it isn't. Wherever the blame lies, we'll deal with that at the appropriate time. Meanwhile, I've asked Cardinal Petrini to discuss the issue with Marcello Sabatini, curator of the Vatican Museum, to get his reaction."

"I can't imagine Signor Sabatini would be involved in such disgraceful activity," said Karl. "I've worked with him before, frequently. He's a good man, committed to his work."

"Well, someone on his staff may be complicit," Dominic replied. "That's what we need to find out. How to go about it is the problem."

Two waiters appeared, each holding two plates of steaming food, which they set down in front of each patron. Karl leaned over to take in the fresh scent of the day's catch, John Dory, poached and laid out on a bed of seaweed and hay topped with seared brined capers.

Lukas sneered at the dish. "That has to be the ugliest fish I've ever seen."

"Ugly, yes," Karl beamed, "but it is also the tastiest. Looks can deceive, my friend."

The others absorbed the delectable aromas of their own meals before digging in. As Hana savored her scampi and creamy risotto, she posed a suggestion.

"After dinner, why don't we take in the Guggenheim Museum. They're sure to have some Carnivale celebration going on."

"Great idea," Dominic said. "We'll just take a gondola ride across the Canal."

CHAPTER
TEN

The setting sun over Rome cast long dark shadows across the Vatican grounds as Cardinal Enrico Petrini and Museum curator Marcello Sabatini walked through the papal gardens.

The red-faced Sabatini held his chin up, his face tight as he retorted. "It simply isn't possible, Eminence."

"I'm not accusing you of any wrongdoing, Marcello," Petrini explained to the disturbed man.

"But Eminence, there is no evidence, no clue you've provided to substantiate something so unthinkable."

Petrini nodded. "But if what Father Dominic told me is true, you have a profoundly important task ahead. One that needs to be handled delicately, but promptly."

Sabatini now pleaded, "But I would not know where to even begin! Nothing shows as missing from our inventory. I have dependable mechanisms in place for such things. We display some 20,000 pieces securely mounted throughout all our galleries, leaving the Vatican's remaining 50,000 pieces in safe storage. Each item is bar-coded, and any transfer is diligently tracked. The only time they move is when we rotate exhibitions, send them out for restoration, or loan them out to reciprocal institutions. It is a mystery to me how someone might even go about managing such a corrupt scheme. I contend it is unthinkable that it happened at all!"

Petrini allowed a moment's pause as the curator calmed. Then he asked softly, "And you have been curator for how long?"

Sabatini took a long breath, realizing he would need to abide by whatever the Cardinal requested of him, no matter how difficult to achieve. "I have only been at this job for ten years now. So, yes, Eminence, there's no telling what happened before I stepped in as curator."

Just then Petrini's mobile phone pinged, signaling an incoming text message. He read it, a thoughtful expression creasing his face.

"Let's go to my office, Marcello. Miss Sinclair, a colleague of Father Dominic's in Venice, sent me images of the Vivaldi manuscripts they discovered. We'll look at them on my computer."

PETRINI TOOK a seat at his desk as Sabatini stood behind him, both watching the computer display as it lit up. The cardinal opened the email from Hana and found several attachments. He opened one at a time as he and Sabatini peered at the screen, reading the Vivaldi musical transcriptions prepared by Livia Gallo.

"Amazing," Petrini said. "These, combined with Lucio Gambarini's purported confession to Father Rinaldo, would seem to confirm the case for some kind of ongoing scheme. Are you familiar with this Contessa Vivaldi Durazzo?"

"Yes, Eminence, I well know who Contessa Durazzo is, though she prefers to use the Vivaldi surname, for obvious reasons. She is one of the preeminent art collectors in Venice. Her family's collection is legendary. We have met on several occasions, and she would surely remember me."

Petrini clicked on the third attachment. A moment later, a large religious painting filled the screen.

Sabatini gasped, turned white, and began trembling. "Eminence! *This is one of the Vatican's own works!* It is called *Crucifixion with Apostles*, painted by an obscure Venetian artist named Giulia Lama. I happen to know this because she is one of the very few female painters in our collections, and certainly cannot be counted as among the Old Masters. I am truly shocked seeing this!"

As he looked at the Lama painting, Petrini's interest piqued. "This is extraordinary. But how is it possible? We must ask Hana about this."

Looking up her number on his phone, he made the call. A few moments later, Hana answered. Petrini put her on speakerphone.

"Hana, this is Enrico Petrini. I have you on speaker here with the Vatican's Museum curator, Marcello Sabatini."

"Good to hear from you, Eminence," Hana said cheerfully. "Is there something I can do for you?"

"First, thank you for sending these Vivaldi images. They are certainly compelling in support of Michael's claim. But I must ask: why did you send this photo of the painting?"

"A painting?" Hana questioned. "Oh, I'm sorry, Eminence, I must have tagged that as an unintended attachment. It was a photo I took yesterday at the contessa's palazzo. Just ignore it."

"But that's the thing, Hana—we *can't* ignore it! Signor Sabatini here recognized it as an art work belonging to the Vatican! It *is* by a female artist named Giulia Lama, correct?"

"Why, yes, it is a Lama," said Hana, surprised. "Are you certain it's the same painting? Is it possible the artist could have painted more than one?"

Sabatini demurred, shaking his head. "Signorina, this is Marcello. Yes, it is absolutely the same piece. And no, it is unlikely an artist would do such a thing in that era. I cannot understand this at all."

"Well," Petrini said, looking up at the man, "the question is, Marcello, how can one painting be in two places at the same time? I suggest you look into this as soon as possible. Track down that painting in our collections, and if you do find it, it may reveal part of the solution to this mystery."

"Of course, Eminence. I shall do so at once." Sabatini bid farewell to Hana, then left the room.

"Hana, do you think it would be possible for Marcello to come to Venice tomorrow, and perhaps have a look at the contessa's painting? Assuming he finds the one supposedly in our collection, he can make a more visually informed analysis of the two."

"As a matter of fact, Eminence, the contessa has invited us to her annual Carnivale gala tomorrow evening at her home, Palazzo Grimaldi, and has encouraged us to bring our own guests. So yes, Signor Sabatini would be most welcome, I'm sure."

"Excellent," Petrini said. "That is most gracious of her, and should help us better understand things. Sabatini and the contessa have met before, he tells me, which might make the situation... well, seem less intrusive."

"Oh, that's helpful, yes. And be sure to tell him to bring a costume for the Carnivale theme, or at least a mask. Or to purchase one when he arrives; mask shops are everywhere here."

"I will pass that on to him, Hana, and thank you for everything. How are Michael and the boys holding up?"

"Everyone's fine here. We're filled with curiosity about this so-called Vatican art operation and intend to follow leads wherever they take us."

Recalling an earlier conversation he'd had with his old friend Baron Armand de Saint-Clair, Petrini added, "Oh, I spoke with your grandfather this morning and filled him in on your developments. As always, he is concerned about your own safety. So you take good care, Hana. We'll speak again soon."

"Thank you, Eminence. We'll keep in touch."

MARCELLO SABATINI HAD RETURNED to his desk in the Museum's administrative offices and conducted a search on Giulia Lama's art piece. Noting its location ID in the repository, he left his office and took the elevator down to the underground warehouse beneath the Belvedere Courtyard.

Thousands of undisplayed paintings were stored in the vast climate-controlled space, each hung on tall, modern, sliding stainless steel racks as far as the eye could see in any direction, works of art that had been kept here for hundreds of years, catalogued by artist.

Sabatini checked the ID code he had written on a slip of paper and proceeded to that location. Finding the proper rack, he slid it open out into the aisle, revealing several glorious artworks by various Old Masters and relatively unknown artists alike.

Expecting not to find the Lama, it stunned Sabatini when he looked up and saw the very same painting he had seen in Hana's photo. *Impossible!* he thought desperately. *There cannot be two of them!*

And yet, hanging before him was *Crucifixion with Apostles*, nestled inside a meticulously gilded wooden frame, the contrasting chiaroscuro treatment of light and dark visible even in the low-lit LED conditions of the dim warehouse.

The artwork was stunning. The mystery of it shocking.

Removing his phone from his pocket, he took a photo of it to share with Cardinal Petrini.

Clearly, he had a problem.

CHAPTER

ELEVEN

ana was in her element, surrounded as she was by exquisitely custom-tailored Venetian Carnivale costumes at Antonia Sautter's famed atelier in the San Marco *sestiere*.

Both Hana's and Livia's eyes shone as they swept the room, seeking the perfect bespoke ball gowns for the contessa's soirée. Sautter's signature couture fabrics—rich velvets, damasks, brocades and Venetian silks, paired with period shoes, wigs, hats, gloves, fans, jewels, and of course, masks—were the most sought after in all of Venice.

There was one costume Hana could see herself in—a stunning bright scarlet silk gown with matching cascading cape, and a brocaded décolletage with shoulder-to-elbow half-sleeves.

Livia chose a more demure ivory gown with a gold brocaded bustier, and a huge auburn curled wig topped with pure white overlapping ostrich feathers.

Both of them chose handheld Venetian stick masks matching the colors of their gowns.

· · ·

ACROSS TOWN, AT THE FAMED CA' Macana mask workshop in the heart of the Dorsoduro, Dominic, Karl and Lukas were only seeking the shop's signature hand-produced masks. The two soldiers had brought their colorful Swiss Guard Gala Renaissance uniforms as their own costumes—something probably not sanctioned by the rules but, as they reasoned, they *were* on duty at the instruction of Cardinal Petrini—so they only lacked appropriate masks. Both of them had chosen traditional black Bauta masks which covered the entire face with a flat, stubborn chin line. They left their chest armor back at the Vatican, of course, and rather than bring their feathered armor helmets, they brought the more informal black berets—which packed far more easily, anyway.

At first Dominic himself decided he would forgo a costume and come as—surprise!—a priest. But the boys cajoled him enough to surrender to wearing the traditional Venetian shoulder capelet with a tricorn hat known as the Zendale, made from black satin and macrame lace, including the floor-length Venetian cloak, cape, and white Bauta mask. Begrudgingly, he rented the costume.

AFTER THE TRAIN came to a stop, Marcello Sabatini nervously descended the steps of the Frecciarossa, landing unsteadily onto the platform at Santa Lucia. The two martinis he'd had on board had taken effect, but his hotel, the Boscolo Bellini, wasn't far from the station. With his rolling suitcase trailing behind him, he headed northeast two hundred meters or so to the Bellini's entrance, then checked in for his two-night stay. After unpacking in his room, he headed back downstairs to the bar.

Though a capable curator of the Vatican Museum, Sabatini was a short, highly strung man in his forties, obsessed with details but often brittle when his competence was questioned. And though Cardinal Petrini had dealt with him kindly—given the unusual situation they'd found themselves in—Sabatini was apprehensive about his role here in Venice. *What am I to do if I find an identical Lama painting? Accuse the contessa's family of forgery? Or maybe we have a forgery!* Such worrying thoughts overcame him such that he couldn't enjoy the unique pleasures of La Serenissima, which was more the pity since he could use a vacation to rid his mind of this particular burden.

"*Un gin martini, per favore*," he mumbled to the bartender, reaching for the bowl of pretzels on the counter.

CHAPTER

TWELVE

The procession of waiting black gondolas lined up in front of the entrance to Palazzo Grimaldi, their elegant brass lanterns casting shimmering reflections over the waters of the dark canal as the sound of live classical music drifted out from inside the palace.

Sure-footed gondola tenders—servants wearing powdered wigs and black waistcoats with golden breeches and white leggings—stood on the dock, helping guests out of each arriving gondola, taking special care with ladies and their voluminous gowns.

Standing at the door to the Reception Hall, Contessa Donatella Vivaldi welcomed each arriving guest. Her own costume, designed by the renowned Nicolao Atelier, was a dazzling lampasso brocade gold-white gown with a close-fitting bodice and square neckline, decorated with white pearl trimmings in a gold base tableau, embroidered with precious stones and white paillettes. In her left hand she held an eye-catching Charleston fan with silky black Marabou feathers.

All manner of guests filled the Grand Salon wearing spectacular period costumes, most harkening to the Renaissance, others of the more common variety one might expect at a

Venetian ball celebrating Carnivale. The varied face coverings were of particular note: the long-beaked Volto mask, originally used to hold herbs and flowers that would filter the air and cover up the smells of 14th-century plague victims; dramatic Commedia dell'arte masks based on familiar characters in stage performances—the crooked and crippled Pulcinella, and figures such as Pantalone and il Dottore and Scaramouche. All of them hid the faces of rich and famous and commoners alike as everyone roamed the room, seeking attention for their fashionable efforts.

Dominic, Hana, and Livia Gallo had already arrived, along with Karl and Lukas, two imposing young men who were drawing much attention wearing their gala Swiss Guard uniforms behind mysterious black Bauta masks. All five were gathered together at one of several massive round tables of food, featuring ice sculptures and cascading rivers of fruit, figs, nuts, cheeses, and other finger edibles.

"Have I mentioned how stunning you look this evening, Signorina Sinclair?" Dominic said in a gentlemanly manner.

"Why, thank you, Padre. You cut quite the dashing figure yourself tonight. That black cape and white mask add a beguiling air of inscrutability to your already mystical nature," she purred, embodying the faux persona as she shamelessly heaved her cleavage in the flirt.

As she spoke, another tall, dark, handsome stranger approached Hana from behind Dominic, his eyes holding hers in a sensual stare as he joined them.

"Mademoiselle Sinclair, I presume?" the man with a suave French accent inquired. Dominic turned to see the new arrival, a military type with ramrod stature wearing short black satin knickers with white leggings below a long brocade style coat with fancy cuffs.

Somewhat dazed that she had been recognized but did not recognize her charming opposite, she blushed.

"And to whom do I owe the pleasure, sir?" she asked, taken aback.

The man theatrically removed his mask and smiled.

"*Marco!*" she gasped.

"Monsieur Picard, at your service." He bent over in a formal bow, his taut costume outlining a fit, muscular frame.

"Marco!" Karl and Lukas blurted, reaching their arms out to exchange handshakes.

"How on earth did you get invited?!" Hana inquired, blushing. "How did you even *know* about this party?"

"I am here at your grandfather's insistence," the bodyguard admitted. "Somehow he'd heard you might need discreet help while in Venice. The baron and the contessa go back a long way, I'm told. I will keep my distance, of course. You won't even know I'm here." He smiled mischievously while instinctively eyeing others near his charge.

Hana murmured in a clipped tone, "Yes, I expect that would be Cardinal Petrini's doing. He did speak to Grand-père about my presence here."

"It's great to see you again, Marco!" Karl said cheerfully. "Looks like we've got a proper party going now. How long are you in Venice for?"

"For as long as it takes," he said circumspectly, glancing at Dominic as the two shook hands.

"Good to have you here, Marco," Dominic said. "We have no idea what we're going up against yet, but another capable body is certainly welcome."

As the men spoke, Hana couldn't take her eyes off the handsome Frenchman. *Capable body, indeed.* His wavy long black hair slightly unkempt beneath that dashing tricorn hat, his deep blue eyes as penetrating as she last remembered them. And that captivating smile. Like a schoolgirl with a crush, she stared dreamily at him, her imagination taking flight.

Just then, she felt a gentle elbow nudge.

"Earth to Hana," Dominic said teasingly, with a sideways glance. "Here comes our hostess."

Hmm… is that resentment I hear? she wondered as she turned to face the priest, smiling primly.

The contessa was making her way through the crowd toward their little group with a man in tow, one dressed in flashy Carnivale costume attire. Once she had reached them, she introduced the two.

"Father Dominic, I would like you to meet Signor Renzo Farelli, a prominent art dealer here in La Serenissima. He has asked to meet you," she said with a knowing smile as she turned to mingle with other guests.

"A pleasure to meet you, signore," Dominic said, extending his hand.

"And you, Padre. So, I understand you to be the Prefect of the Apostolic Archive, is that right?" Farelli asked. "And the contessa tells me you're here on some interesting business?"

Though somewhat troubled that his 'business' was becoming common knowledge, Dominic acceded to the man's question.

"Actually, it's just a little mystery involving the contessa's ancestor, Antonio Vivaldi. Something to do with a musical manuscript and works of art, that's all.

"Oh, I'm sorry," he added, more to change the subject. "May I introduce my colleagues Hana Sinclair and Dr. Livia Gallo?"

Introductions, handshakes, and costume compliments went around the group. Karl, Lukas and Marco had casually stepped aside, moving away from the others, preferring to be inconspicuous associates for now.

"I heard you mention works of art earlier," Farelli said. "That is *my* line of work, and if there is anything I can do to help with your 'little mystery,' as you call it, you have but to ask. I own the Studio Canal Grande gallery in the San Polo *sestiere*, and you are most welcome to visit."

An older bespectacled gentleman approached them. Dominic

had noticed him earlier, closely admiring the various paintings on the walls of the palazzo.

"This is one of my colleagues, Father," Farelli said. "May I introduce Giuseppe Franco, the lead restorer at Palazzo Feudatario? Giuseppe has an exquisite eye for fine art."

The older man held out his hand to the priest. Dominic took it in his own.

"It is a pleasure meeting you, Giuseppe. You must be the one who does all that careful restoration on the Vatican's pieces, I take it?"

Giuseppe blushed as he smiled self-consciously. "Si, Father Dominic. It is among my greatest honors to work on the Vatican's incredible art works. I take great pride in it." He looked around nervously, as if he didn't belong there and his presence would be discovered at any moment.

As the men continued to talk, Hana and Livia wandered off to see more of the palazzo and take in the pageantry. A live string ensemble in a corner of the ballroom was performing classical works, foremost among them many of Antonio Vivaldi's own masterpieces, including *The Four Seasons* and *L'Estro Armonico*.

Walking up the grand staircase to the upper levels, Livia noticed many beautifully framed pieces on the walls as they ascended, a cluster of original musical compositions signed by various famed composers: Bach, Beethoven, Liszt, Pachelbel and several other maestros. Stopping to inspect one in particular, she gasped.

"*Hana!* There's more handwritten music signed by Vivaldi here!" Peering at it, she hummed a few bars, then recognized that it, too, seemed to be constructed using the Solfa Cipher, for its notes were like the previous works she had seen.

Removing her phone from a small pocket in her outfit, she took a photograph of it, thrilled to have discovered yet another page, and curious why the contessa hadn't mentioned it. She couldn't wait to decode it.

From across the room, Karl looked around to see where Hana and Livia were, just to keep track of them. Seeing them on the grand staircase, his mind was eased. He continued watching as they were approached by another guest.

Descending the stairs above the two women was an older gentleman dressed in a *Medico della peste* outfit, that of a Renaissance doctor with a long, ugly bird's beak nose, a black ankle-length overcoat and black tricorn hat. He had an air about him Hana instinctively took a dislike to; perhaps it was in his prideful swagger, or the way he blatantly stared at her décolletage. Apart from his masked eyes, she could see a snarl of a smile showing rotten teeth on a face wrinkled with age. Probably from too much smoking, she figured.

"*Buona sera, le belle Donne,*" he said as he stopped just above the wide step they were standing on, making him all the more intimidating. He continued in Italian. "My name is Don Angelo Gallucci. And you are...?"

"Leaving, I'm afraid," Hana said in English, then, "*Non parliamo italiano... scusaci.*" As she and Livia kept moving up the stairs, Hana hoped he didn't speak English, for she had just excused herself quite capably, telling him they did not speak Italian.

He turned in silence to watch both women ascend the staircase.

Though Don Gallucci did, in fact, speak perfect English, he chose not to pursue the conversation. Besides, his informants had already told him who the two women were. He wondered what their purpose was for being in Venice, if not just for Carnivale.

No, no need to engage them now. He was certain their paths would cross again.

Observing the encounter, Karl made a mental note to keep an eye on the man.

THIRTEEN

"Why did you put him off so harshly?" Livia asked.

"I'm not sure," she smirked. "There was just something creepy about him. And isn't '*Don*' the formal title for a Mafia capo?"

"Well, yes, but it could also be used for addressing a priest."

"I can assure you, that man was no priest. I couldn't seem to stop my breasts from staring at his eyes."

Livia giggled, then the two of them burst out laughing, breaking the tension of the encounter.

BACK IN THE GRAND SALON, Dominic had run into his old friend, Father Carlo Rinaldo, who had been speaking with other party guests until they wandered off.

"Hey, Carlo, shall we go find a beer and catch up?"

"Great idea, Michael. I see a bar in the corner over there." He nodded in that direction, and they set off through the crowd. Having gotten served two bottles of Birra Moretti, they stepped outside onto the portico, leaning up against the concrete balustrade overlooking the Grand Canal to watch the festivities on the water.

"Quite the soirée, isn't it?" Rinaldo asked.

"I'll say. Hana and Livia are having the time of their lives. I imagine it's rarely they get to dress up in such fantastical outfits and hobnob with Italian aristocrats. Me too, for that matter, though I'd just as well stay home and read." He smiled at his friend, then took a swig of beer.

Looking back inside the great arched windows, Rinaldo pointed out one of the guests.

"See that man dressed as a cardinal? That's not a costume, he is one. Cardinal Salvatore Abruzzo, the Patriarch of Venice. A very powerful man here. You may want to introduce yourself at some point, he could be useful in your work here.

"By the way," Rinaldo continued, "I'm celebrating Mass at St. Mark's tomorrow at 11:00. I'd love it if you and your friends can come, provided you're awake by then." He grinned.

"Of course, we'll be there. I'd even join you if you needed the help."

"That's a great idea. You can be my concelebrant. And perhaps we can have lunch afterward?"

"You bet," Dominic replied. "I'm sure everyone would love that."

"By the way, Michael, have you given more thought to that dilemma I'm dealing with? With Don Gambarini dead, I feel we have to do something, but I must confess, I do fear repercussions by the Camorra. Don Angelo Gallucci took over as the new *capintesta*, and he has a nasty reputation which can only grow worse given his promotion. I saw him inside just a short while ago, talking to Hana and Livia on the staircase. You must tell them to avoid the man."

"Hana is pretty capable of taking care of herself, but as it happens, we're not without protection. Those two guys dressed as Swiss Guards in their colorful striped pantaloons you saw among the guests? They're real Swiss Guards, both friends of mine. And Hana's grandfather sent his personal bodyguard here to make sure Hana comes to no harm. Not that the situation should demand it, I hope.

"There's something else I should tell you, though," Dominic said, going into detail about the encoded Vivaldi manuscript and its confirmation of what Don Gambarini had confessed.

"So, it does go back for centuries!" Rinaldo said, astonished by the revelation. "Then I have to ask again—how can this possibly be?!"

"That, my friend, is what I intend to find out."

As he said this, Dominic looked back through the window into the ballroom, recognizing someone he knew. The man was dressed in a simple business suit, wearing only a standard black eye mask as his only accommodation to the festivities.

He invited Rinaldo to join him as they went inside to greet the man.

"Marcello! What are you doing here?"

Startled at being recognized, Sabatini looked at the masked man who approached him, with not a clue who it might be. Dominic lifted his mask, a welcoming smile on his face.

"Father Dominic! Finally, someone I know... I'm here at the request of Cardinal Petrini to learn more about the Giulia Lama painting you and your colleagues found in the contessa's library." He looked around him, his voice dropping to a near whisper.

"May I see it?"

"Of course. Yes, Cardinal Petrini told us you were coming. But first, let me introduce Father Carlo Rinaldo, an old friend of mine from seminary who is, well, somewhat involved in this matter."

The two men shook hands.

"Now," Dominic continued, "let's find my friends, then we'll all go see the painting together."

Taking his phone out of a pocket, he texted Hana, asking where she was. A moment later she replied: *We're just chatting here in the library, where it's quiet.*

Perfect. "Just follow me."

The three set off for the library on the ground floor at the other end of the palazzo. Once there, Dominic made introductions. Then Sabatini stood gazing up at Giulia Lama's painting, a mixture of fear and bewilderment on his face.

"Astonishing. It appears to be identical."

"Identical to what, Marcello?" Hana asked, confused.

"To the same painting we have in the Vatican Museum."

CHAPTER
FOURTEEN

"But, how is that possible?!" Hana asked, incredulous.

"How is what possible?" an older female voice inquired.

Everyone's head turned from the painting to the door, where Contessa Vivaldi was standing next to Renzo Farelli.

"Why, Signor Sabatini!" she exclaimed, recognizing Marcello. "I am delighted to see you again, and all the way from Rome! Are you a guest of Father Dominic's?"

Quickly appraising the situation, Dominic replied for him. "Sì, Contessa. Marcello came at my invitation to view your lovely art collection. As curator of the Vatican Museum, he jumped at the opportunity. We were just admiring your Giulia Lama piece. I was about to tell him about her background, which you so kindly shared with us."

"Lovely," she responded with a warm smile. "I'm afraid I don't have the time to tell the story myself just now…" she said, glancing out into the hall at other guests vying for her attention, "… but I am sure Signor Farelli here would be happy to fill you in on any details. It is from his gallery I purchased the painting." The contessa placed a comforting hand on Farelli's shoulder, smiled, then turned and walked out the door to speak to other guests.

Taken by surprise, Farelli paled for a moment. A careful, prepared man under optimal conditions, he did not care for being ambushed.

"Please, excuse me," he mumbled hurriedly, turning toward the door. "I do not mean to be rude, but there is an important potential client I absolutely must speak with before he leaves. Might we continue this discussion a bit later?"

Without waiting for an answer, he left the room.

Everyone stood there, blinking in silence.

"Did anyone else find that rather strange?" Hana asked.

"I certainly did," Livia huffed. "For all he knew, *we* could be *important potential clients.*"

Sabatini fixed his gaze on the empty doorway. "I know of this Signor Farelli. He owns the Studio Canal Grande in the San Polo district. He is a prominent art dealer, yes, but one also known amongst a very few for, shall we say, somewhat shadier practices.

"I wonder if our collective focus on this particular painting was cause for his agitated departure. Perhaps... issues of provenance he couldn't explain?"

"Marcello," Hana said, "before they came into the room, you were about to explain the duplicate paintings."

An exasperated Sabatini tossed his hands into the air.

"That's just the thing. I *can't* explain it! They do 'seem' to be identical. I saw its twin in the Vatican just yesterday. But one of them *must* be a forgery. I would stake my reputation on that. Only which is the question." He drew his face closer to the canvas.

Peering closely at one small section in a corner of the painting, the curator pointed to a series of small cracks in the pigment.

"In paintings of the Italian Renaissance, typical patterns called craquelure resemble a series of tiny disordered bricks, much like we see here. Look closely at Leonardo da Vinci's *Mona Lisa*, for example, and you will find similar craquelure as this. By comparison, such rifts in French paintings tend to look like spider webs, branching outward from a central nexus. Different locations and their periods, such as Dutch and Flemish artists, often had distinctive aging signatures like this in the oils and canvases they used; even the air of the environment in which they worked had a contributing effect. The natural faults in this painting seem to exhibit what one would expect. But I will, of course, compare what I see here to our counterpart in Rome, but first I need a sample...."

Hana, Livia, Dominic and Rinaldo all peered from behind the curator for a glance at the craquelure, intrigued by the mystery. As Sabatini reached into his pocket, he looked at the door, then at Dominic. He pulled out a small leather case. Opening it, he withdrew a set of stainless steel Dumont conservation tweezers, selecting the one he needed for this task, one that had a small magnifying glass attached to it.

Understanding what the curator was about to do, Dominic stood at the door, keeping guard. He nodded at Sabatini, who then got to work extracting an infinitesimal speck of green pigment; something that, without damaging the canvas, would go unnoticed by the casual observer. He removed a white handkerchief from his suit pocket, then dropped the particle onto it, carefully folding and re-pocketing the cloth.

DRESSED in his sinister bird-beaked costume, Don Angelo Gallucci stood on the lower steps of the ballroom staircase, looking out over the crowd for someone he wished to speak with. Seeing his quarry, when their eyes met, Don Gallucci motioned for the man to join him.

As Renzo Farelli made his way through the crowd to the stairs, the Don stepped down, walking toward a remote corner of the Grand Salon. Farelli followed him.

"So, Renzo," he began as he continued scanning the crowd, "one of my men tells me that Don Gambarini may have *jittari i virmiceddi* with Father Rinaldo on his deathbed. Do you know anything about this?"

Farelli scowled. His refined sense of culture never much cared for the old Sicilian Mafia slang phrase—roughly translated as 'vomit the pasta,' meaning to 'cough it up,' or divulge innermost secrets—but he took Gallucci's meaning.

"I have heard this too, Don Gallucci. Word gets around."

"So what are we to do with this Rinaldo priest? Is the seal of the confessional good enough to protect Operation Scambio?"

"I do not know yet, signore. I must make further inquiries," Farelli whispered. "There is a small group of people in the library, including Father Rinaldo. They were inspecting the Lama painting I recently sold to Contessa Vivaldi. They had questions about it, but I avoided answering them for the moment.

"There was another man there, too, someone from the Vatican Museum, whose presence gives me pause. I'd rather not have anyone looking too closely at our work like that."

Though a respected art dealer in his own right, Renzo Farelli possessed another prominent title few people were aware of: Camorra capo of the San Polo district, or *capo di sestiere*. His forte, appropriately, dealt in the sale and acquisition of fine art pieces, whether legal or illicit. And business was brisk on both counts.

"This is all making me quite uncomfortable, Renzo," the Don muttered, an edge of anger to his low voice. "This is your area. I expect you to take control of it. I want a progress report. Soon."

CHAPTER

FIFTEEN

A t the prompting of Palazzo Grimaldi servants who circulated the room, all guests were encouraged to step outside onto the balcony overlooking the water for an immense fireworks display the contessa had arranged as the fitting denouement to a magnificent evening.

Hana and Livia stood alongside Dominic, with Karl, Lukas and Marco next to them, leaning on the balustrade. Marcello Sabatini had already left the party, eager to get back to Rome and analyze the speck of pigment he'd taken from the Lama painting. Looking around, Dominic couldn't find Carlo Rinaldo, but figured he too may have left.

Oohs and aahs erupted from the assembled guests as each spectacular display flew high into the sky and exploded over Venice, launched from a barge in the center of the Grand Canal.

EARLIER, as the guests had filed outside, two burly white-masked men dressed in black Bauta capes had approached Farther Rinaldo, asking him to accompany them for a 'religious emergency.' Confused by their meaning, but being an accommodating sort, Rinaldo walked with the men to an alley out behind the palazzo, stepping into a waiting private motorboat at their insistence.

"Where are we going, *signori*?" he asked as he settled himself on the aft seating area. "What is the nature of this trouble, may I ask?"

Both men were silent as the motorboat started up the dark canal, bright glints of color from the fireworks reflecting off the quiet buildings lining the narrow waterway.

The priest grew anxious as the craft made its way along the canal, passing under low bridges and moving farther away from peopled areas, without a word being spoken by anyone. Rinaldo's mind whirled with fear, the impulse for 'fight or flight' demanding an action. He leaned slightly to peer into the inky black water passing the craft. Instantly the one man sitting next to him pressed the barrel of a gun against his right side. Escape was not an option.

Too late, Father Carlo Rinaldo feared he was in God's hands now, praying for mercy.

WITH THE FIREWORKS ENDING, everyone on the palazzo's balcony began applauding, thanking the contessa for a splendid evening as they gradually made their way to the entrance dock and a fleet of waiting gondolas and water taxis.

"Did everyone have a good time?" Dominic asked, looking around at his now unmasked friends.

"It was *fantastic*, Father Michael!" Lukas gushed. "What a great introduction to Venice. Such a romantic city." He glanced at Karl, who took his hand.

"I agree," Karl said. "It will be hard to compete with this kind of experience when we do return someday."

"Oh," Dominic said. "Carlo has invited us to tomorrow's late morning Mass at St. Mark's, then we'll all go for lunch afterward. Sound good?"

Hana looked at him and smiled. "What would a trip to Venice be without taking in a Mass at St. Mark's? Count me in."

"Me too," Livia added. "I like Father Rinaldo. He reminds me of you a little, Michael. Suave, handsome, and unavailable."

They all laughed, then took their place in the line forming for gondolas and taxis.

A few minutes later, Dominic's cell phone hummed. He answered it.

"Michael, it's Carlo," the voice said tersely. "I need a favor."

"Carlo! You missed the fireworks. Where are you, my friend?"

There was a long pause, then Rinaldo spoke again. "Michael, I need you to take my place celebrating Mass tomorrow. I know it's a big favor, but would you do this for me?"

Dominic noticed Rinaldo's strained voice, as if he was in pain.

"Are you alright, Carlo?"

"Ye... yes. I'm... I'm fine," he stammered, clearly struggling. "You know the standard Mass already, but because it's Lent, have the choir sing *Gloria in excelsis Deo*. You know, from Vivaldi's RF-590 setting." He emphasized 'R-F' as he spoke each letter.

Dominic's breath caught as he grasped the undercurrent of fear hidden in his friend's words. Carefully, he measured his response. "Of course, Carlo, I'll be happy to take your place at Mass. Will we see you afterward, as planned?" He tried hard to listen to any other sounds on Carlo's end, but those around him in line were talking too loud.

"I have to go now, Michael. Take c—"

The connection went dead.

Dominic looked at his phone, overcome with a sense of doom. He leaned over to Hana and anxiously whispered in her ear.

"Carlo is in trouble, I'm certain of it."

"What makes you think so?"

He explained the brief conversation.

"Maybe he's just ill from something he ate," she offered.

"Hana, we do *not* sing Gloria during Lent! It would be inappropriate, in fact. It's mainly sung at Christmas, and Carlo knows that." Michael's mind spun as he sorted the facts that made no sense. "And his mention of Vivaldi's 590 setting was wrong for two reasons: first, it's titled RV-590, not RF-590. Second, the RV-590 is presumed lost! Nobody knows the music, since mention of it only exists in a brief entry in the old Kreuzherren catalogue.

"And he emphasized the letters R-*F*, not R-*V*. Why would he change those? The identifier comes from a standard catalog for Vivaldi's music, called the Ryom-Verzeichnis. Hence, RV."

"Sounds to me like he was passing on some kind of code, then," Hana reasoned, ever the puzzler. "But what does RF represent? Are you sure you heard it right? And why mention music at all if he's in danger?"

At that moment, they were next to board a waiting water taxi. Dominic helped Hana and Livia on board, then Lukas, Karl, and Marco jumped on after them. They all gathered inside the covered cabin, out of earshot of the driver, as the craft headed toward the Ca' Sagredo hotel. Dominic filled the others in on what was happening.

"As I was just about to tell Hana before we boarded, Carlo's focus on the *Gloria* music reference was the only logical way for him to tell us something else—that whatever is happening to him now is seriously wrong! I fear he's in grave danger. The Camorra must have found out about Don Gambarini's confession."

"We have to assume that they might believe *we* know," Marco said. "Our security protocols have just escalated."

CHAPTER
SIXTEEN

S unday morning offered a brilliant sunrise as Dominic pulled himself out of bed and flung open the drapes of the huge arched window in his room.

He hadn't slept well, fearing for Carlo's well-being. After showering and dressing, he called Hana's room.

"Up for some coffee?"

"I am, yes. Meet downstairs in ten minutes?"

"Sure, see you then." He hung up the phone.

Leaving the room and making his way down the old elegant elevator, Dominic again tried calling Carlo's cell phone. Each time, the call went straight to voicemail. Each time, he grew more worried.

Entering the princely frescoed ballroom where breakfast was served, Dominic took a seat by the window, watching the activity on the Canal while he waited for Hana. A server brought him a thermal carafe of Italian Roast coffee, pouring a cup for Dominic. Looking up, he saw Hana approaching.

"Any word yet from Carlo?" Hana asked as she took her seat.

"Nothing. Not a word. I also called the church and nobody there has heard from him either. I'm worried sick about this,

Hana. I hate not having control of situations I'm involved in. Somehow this feels as if it's all my fault."

"You can't take this on your shoulders, Michael. Father Rinaldo is the one who heard that Camorra Don's confession, not you. Perhaps he shouldn't have mentioned it to anyone else."

"Yes, well, he mentioned it to *me*. And I confess a certain guilt about having told others, given the seal of confession. I understand these are unusual circumstances, but still, I have certain responsibilities..."

"Is it possible someone may have overheard the confession?"

"I wasn't there, of course, but I suppose anything is possible where corrupt gangsters are concerned. Maybe they bugged the boss's bedroom, who knows? And besides, the Don *asked* Carlo to bring the practice to a halt. It was his dying wish, to absolve his soul from a life of dirty deeds. The man was terrified of the spiritual consequences."

"Well, despite being raised Catholic, you know how I feel about heaven and hell..." said the agnatheistic journalist.

Dominic smiled at her while taking a sip of coffee. "Don't get too cozy there. We'll bring you into the light soon enough...."

Looking up, they saw Karl and Lukas approaching.

"Good morning, boys," Hana said breezily. "Sleep well?"

The Guards looked at each other and just smiled. "We need coffee." They took a table next to their friends, waving for the server to come over.

"Have you seen Marco this morning?" Hana asked.

"He left the hotel earlier, saying he had a few things to check on," Karl said. "That guy's pretty impressive. I wouldn't be surprised if he's already cleared up Father Rinaldo's disappearance and that whole art heist scheme thing. Has Carlo still not checked in, Michael?"

"No. Not as yet." The look on Dominic's face told Karl all he needed to know.

"So, what time is Mass?" Lukas asked.

"Eleven," Dominic replied, deep in thought. "I'm still trying to figure out what 'RF' means. I'm sure he intended for me to grasp its meaning. Might be something unique to the church. I'll ask someone when I get there, maybe they'll know."

As TWO YOUNG altar boys helped Father Dominic don his vestments in the Sacristy, the sacristan prepared the red wine and water in separate crystal cruets, ensuring the chalice, ciborium, paten, and other sacred utensils were clean and ready for the Liturgy.

At the appointed time, Dominic and his two altar servers began the procession out into the basilica and up the chancel to the altar. As the choir sang *Attende Domine* in glorious plainchant, Mass began.

Dominic loved the ancient rituals of the Mass, and he usually performed them in a state of near transcendence. But even though he had been handed the great privilege of celebrating the Liturgy in the fabled ancient Basilica of St. Mark, his mind was elsewhere.

Though he respectfully observed the rote ceremonies, he did so this day without the usual joyfulness that accompanied his celebration of the Blessed Sacrament, for the fate of Carlo Rinaldo was foremost in his thoughts.

After the Rite of Consecration, Dominic invited the assembly to partake in Holy Communion. People stood from their seats and, walking forward, began kneeling at the Communion rail while others waited their turn in line.

As the choir began singing another hymn, Dominic and his altar servers slowly walked up the line presenting each communicant with the sacred Eucharist, as he uttered '*Il Corpo di Cristo*'—'the Body of Christ'—to each one, many of whom he recalled seeing at the contessa's party the night before.

The next person kneeling before him he recognized as that

thickset art dealer who had rushed out of the library... *what was his name? Ah, yes. Renzo Farelli.*

As if electrified, the wafer fell out of Dominic's hand with a jolt, then dropped onto the golden paten held by the altar boy, who looked up at the priest questioningly.

Renzo Farelli.

R.F.

Regaining his composure, Dominic softly apologized, then picked out a fresh host from the ciborium and placed it on Farelli's tongue, his hand shaking.

That's got to be it. Carlo was telling him Renzo Farelli is involved in his disappearance!

Farelli's coldly assessing eyes held Dominic's own as his tongue—nearly black from poor hygiene and years of smoking cigars—accepted the pure white Host. The eyes relayed an unambiguous message: *Stay away.*

Dominic almost wanted to call him out, right then and there, and have him account for Carlo's disappearance. But he had sacred obligations remaining. Without thinking, he sped up serving Communion, wanting nothing more than the Mass to be over so he could take up this fresh development with the others.

There was work to be done.

CHAPTER

SEVENTEEN

Back in Rome, Marcello Sabatini had just left Mass at St. Peter's himself, then headed to his lab next to the Vatican Museum's administrative offices.

It being a Sunday, few others were in the building, giving him open access to all the equipment he would need to analyze the tiny green speck he'd taken from the contessa's Giulia Lama painting.

He took a chair at the table where the lab's optical microscope sat, then retrieved the handkerchief containing the sample from his pocket. Using tweezers to place the speck on a glass slide, he inserted it into the microscope, then peered through the lens. After a few moments, he removed the slide, surprised with the results and festering a growing concern.

Next, he inserted the sample into the lab's X-ray Fluorescence analyzer to check for lead, a common element used by early painters until the risks of using it were later discovered in modern times. If lead was missing from a painting of this age, it would certainly raise questions about the work's authenticity.

The XRF analyzer completed its testing—revealing the presence of lead.

No… This can't be!

Sabatini anxiously got up and went into the art repository beneath the Belvedere Courtyard. Returning to the location where *Crucifixion with Apostles* hung, he pulled out the steel wall rack, took out a small LED flashlight and his tweezers from his pockets, then inspected a similar part of the painting where he had extracted the speck from the contessa's painting. Carefully positioning the tweezers, he scraped off an infinitesimal sliver of paint, dropping it inside a small circular glass vial.

Returning to the lab, he put this sample through the same processes.

This time the XRF revealed *no* presence of lead. Sweat began forming on Sabatini's forehead.

He needed one more test for a more definitive analysis. Moving over to the Raman spectrometer, he inserted the sample into the unit's analysis chamber to measure spectroscopic reflectance in the ultraviolet, visible, and near infrared ranges. A few minutes later, the analysis discovered the presence of Phthalocyanine Green G, a synthetic green pigment from the group of phthalocyanine dyes which, as Sabatini well knew, were not available to Renaissance painters, being a modern discovery.

Sabatini sat there, devastated, his hands shaking.

The Vatican's painting was a forgery. Contessa Vivaldi had the original.

HIS BACK SET against a stucco wall, his feet planted firmly on the cobblestones, Marco Picard held the thug's neck in a firm chokehold, waiting for him to tap out and give the former Green Beret the answer he'd demanded.

The victim's body flopped around, trying to free himself from the stronger man's ironclad grip, to no avail. Wrestling in a fetid back alley on Venice's more industrial Giudecca island, there was little chance of anyone happening upon them.

Finally, the squat but burly man repeatedly slapped Marco's arm, struggling for breath as Marco let him fall to the ground.

"One last time, Enzo," Marco threatened, pulling on the man's hair as he shook his head around. "*Where* is Father Rinaldo?"

"Don Gallucci will have me killed if I say anything!"

"*I'll* kill you if you don't," Marco snapped, grabbing and pulling the man's arm hard as the soldier's foot pressed against his neck.

"*Okay! Okay!*" the man gasped, wincing in pain. "We dropped the padre off at a small warehouse on the Rio del Vin canal, just east of St. Mark's. Two other guys came out to take him inside; I do not know who else was in the building. After dropping him off, our job was done."

"And who is this Don Gallucci?"

Enzo looked at Marco in abject fear. "I... I should not have even m... mentioned his name," he sputtered, glancing around nervously to see if anyone else had heard.

"Who... is... *Gallucci!*" Marco forcefully growled as his leg pushed harder on Enzo's neck.

Enzo screamed in pain as his arm nearly popped out of its shoulder.

"*Don Gallucci is head of the Camorra!* That is all I know. *I swear to you!*"

"It's not polite to swear," Marco said, releasing the arm and kicking the man viciously as he lay on the cobblestone alley. "Now get out of here. If any harm comes to my other friends, I'll be looking for just one man to get answers from. And you won't like the questions."

Enzo got up unsteadily, then did his best to hobble off as far from his attacker as possible, nursing the injured arm.

Straightening his light jacket and brushing his long hair back with his hands, Marco headed for the mahogany motorboat he had rented and parked on a nearby canal dock. Starting the ignition, he aimed the boat for the Grand Canal, then sped across the lagoon heading for the Ca' Sagredo hotel.

As he approached the entrance to the Grand Canal, he saw several police boats grouped east of St. Mark's Square, their blue-lighted masts flashing. Taking out a map of Venice from his pocket, he confirmed they were clustered at the opening to Rio del Vin canal.

He had a bad feeling about this.

Steering his craft in that direction, he also noticed the *Medico Legale*'s boat pull up—the coroner had arrived. Slowly motoring to the scene to monitor events, as other rubberneckers around him were, Marco put the engine in idle as he watched a man's dead body being fished out of the water and placed on a low gurney on the coroner's vessel. He was wearing black clothing, with a white collar encircling his neck clearly visible in the bright lights of the Carabinieri's boats shining on the water.

Father Carlo Rinaldo.

Marco took out his phone and snapped a photo of the scene. Turning the boat around, he headed up the Grand Canal and back to the hotel.

CHAPTER
EIGHTEEN

The six Camorra capos, one from each of their designated *sestieri* in Venice proper—San Marco, Cannaregio, San Polo, Dorsoduro, Santa Croce, and Castello—had gathered in Palazzo Feudatario at the request of Don Angelo Gallucci along with another guest.

"My friends," he said in a low brooding voice, "we have dealt with the meddlesome priest who heard Don Gambarini's confession, which broke our sacred seal of *omertà*. Unfortunately, this cannot be undone.

"I speak of the confession, of course." The six men laughed quietly, uncomfortably, as the Don looked around the table with a steely gaze.

One of the capos spoke up. "My men are the ones who took Rinaldo from the contessa's party, but they were reluctant to take the life of a priest. They said he told them he would confess everything he knew if he were allowed one call, which they gave him. He then called the priest named Dominic, asking him to take his place at Mass the next day. But he was of no use to them after that, so he was expendable."

"We do not know if Rinaldo spoke to anyone else about these things," Gallucci continued, "but I did meet, more or less, two of his associates at the contessa's party. Two women—one quite rude, as women can be—but there are others, I am told."

"Yes," said Renzo Farelli, "one of them is a fumbling priest who couldn't manage holding a Communion wafer if his life depended on it."

Another round of subdued laughter.

"Salvatore," Gallucci asked, turning to a large man in a black cassock with red piping and a scarlet cap, "what do you know of this priest?"

Cardinal Salvatore Abruzzo, the Patriarch of Venice, took his time responding. He took a deep sigh before speaking.

"Father Michael Dominic is the Prefect of the Vatican Apostolic Archive—which you may know as the Secret Archives —and is here on a brief vacation, I am informed. He is a harmless sort, very bookish, but he has significant connections in the Church. His godfather is Cardinal Petrini, the Vatican Secretary of State, and the two men are very close. I would exercise caution in dealing with him.

"He is also here with a companion, apparently an old friend who is a reporter for the French newspaper *Le Monde*. And I noticed at the contessa's party that he has two Swiss Guards with him, whose presence here is very unusual, but which could only have been approved by Petrini. Their purpose here is unknown."

Gallucci thought for a few moments.

"I don't like it. But, until they do something that warrants our attention, leave them be for now. Keep a watch on them, though." He glanced around the table to make sure everyone understood his meaning.

"Now, as for our next shipment from Rome. Salvatore, are your men bringing us the Raphael on Monday?"

"Yes, Angelo, all is in order for the shipment. Our man in the Vatican Pinacoteca has made the arrangements, as usual. We do not expect any problems."

"Good. That is what I like to hear. We prepared our artists

and restorers upstairs with the materials they need for it, and they are eager to work on their next masterpiece."

"Which they shall have tomorrow," the cardinal confirmed.

∾

AFTER BERTHING HIS BOAT, Marco made his way up the dock to the entrance of the Ca' Sagredo. As he was entering the foyer, he ran into Karl, who was heading out for a quick run.

"Hold up, Karl," he said, raising a hand. "We all need to meet. Now. Are Michael and Hana here?"

"Yeah, they're having lunch with Lukas upstairs on the Terrace. We can take the elevator." Karl saw the hard set of Marco's eyes, the tight bands in his neck; the news was serious.

After the slow lift to the Terrace restaurant, the two men exited the car and made their way to their friends' table.

"This is a pleasant surprise," Dominic said, setting down his fork and wiping his mouth with the napkin. "Are you joining us?"

Marco and Karl took chairs from adjacent tables and pulled them up.

Looking around the room before he spoke, Marco leaned in close. The others followed suit.

"I'm afraid Father Rinaldo is dead. I watched as the police lifted his body out of the lagoon and placed it on the coroner's launch."

Hana gasped, her hand rising to cover her mouth. Dominic stared directly into Marco's face, his own eyes glistening as he took in the dreadful news.

"Those *bastards!*" he scowled. Standing, he tossed his napkin on the chair as he walked to the railing, the sun warming his face as he looked up at the heavens. He lowered his head in a brief prayer, but couldn't stop the tears that came as he prayed.

Hana rose to join him, placing her hand on his shoulder.

"Michael…" she offered, "I'm so sorry."

Dominic turned to face her, then pulled her in for a hug as he gently wept.

"Carlo was one of my few close friends," he managed. "He couldn't have drowned, he was a skilled swimmer. We swam together on the varsity team."

Marco stepped forward. "I believe the Camorra sanctioned Rinaldo's death, Michael. I just encountered one of their foot soldiers on Giudecca who was involved in his abduction. The question is, why?"

Returning to the table, Dominic looked at his friends, determination now replacing grief.

"It has to be related to that confession Carlo took from Don Gambarini. He gave him knowledge of something he shouldn't have, and they wanted to silence him.

"I am not a vengeful man," Dominic said with a quiet fierceness. "But someone *will* pay for this."

AFTER MASS, Lucas had escorted Livia back to her room to freshen up before lunch with the others. Thinking back on last night's splendid evening, she realized she had forgotten about the Vivaldi manuscript until now, the one she found framed on the contessa's staircase wall. She opened the Photos app on her phone, tapping on the image to better see it. Then she got to work.

Texting Hana that she had some other things to do and would see them later, she ordered room service, then opened the music composition program on her laptop.

She had transferred the image and used her software to decode the Solfa Cipher. Like the previous two, this one also had two four-line stanzas, signed by Vivaldi at the top. It was in beautiful condition, likely the reason the contessa had it conservation-framed for display.

Now she simply had to parse the Italian fragments into English for the full transcription. What she found intrigued her:

Almeno un cardinale ribelle
e due cospiratori vaticani
condurre l'operazione Scambio
I dipinti selezionati sono preparati per il restauro
poi spedito a Palazzo Feudatario a Venezia
per la riproduzione per mano di grandi falsari
Tutto questo è dettagliato nel Giornale di Coscia
Dio perdona loro i modi corrotti, non posso

At minimum one rogue cardinal
and two Vatican conspirators
conduct Operation Scambio
Select paintings are prepared for restoration
then shipped to Palazzo Feudatario in Venice
for reproduction by the hand of great forgers
All of this is detailed in the Coscia Journal
God forgive them their corrupt ways, I cannot

Fascinating, she pondered. *This lays out the entire scheme; well, most of it anyway.*

Just then there was a knock at the door, and Livia heard a young man's voice call out, *"Room service."*

She opened the door and a smiling waiter stood there behind a service cart.

"Buona sera, signora. Your lunch?"

"Buona sera, si, grazie," Livia responded, as the young man wheeled in the white-clothed service cart. He moved it over to the window next to the desk, removed the silver cloche covering the plate, and slipped the dome onto a shelf beneath the cart.

"My bag is in the other room, just give me a moment," Livia said in Italian.

As the young man watched her leave the room, he quickly inspected the work she had been doing on the desk, then reached into his pocket for his phone, slid the Mute button on to silence the sound, then took two photos of the computer screen and her notes on the desk. He dropped the phone back into his jacket pocket.

Livia returned to the room, a generous tip in her hand. Passing it to him, she thanked him and he left the suite.

As she began enjoying her Salade Niçoise, Livia reviewed the materials again, making sure she had the proper transcription.

Michael will certainly want to see this, she thought, pleased with her work.

CHAPTER
NINETEEN

S ituated in the Apostolic Palace adjacent to St. Peter's Square, the Vatican Pinacoteca, or Art Gallery, includes many of the Church's most beloved paintings and frescoes: Caravaggio's *Entombment*, Perugino's *Madonna and Child with Saints*, Leonardo da Vinci's *St. Jerome in the Wilderness*, and Raphael's *Madonna of Foligno*, among many others. The gallery had originally been housed in a suite of rooms known as the Borgia Apartments from the 15th century until 1932 when the more controllable venue provided better protection for the precious art.

Security precautions here, as with the rest of the Vatican, were of the highest order. Guarded day and night by uniformed Vatican Carabinieri, the city's internal police force, there was little to no chance of theft even being a possibility. All galleries of this nature worldwide have few such concerns, their only real apprehensions being a masterful plot by an insider, someone who knows the weaknesses or loopholes of an institution's security systems—one reason most museum personnel are vetted with criminal background checks and, sometimes, extensive psychological profiles.

But no red flags are raised when the natural order of things proceeds as expected, when scheduled processes go according to plan.

Art restoration is one such area. Although the Vatican Museum has a full-time scientist and other staff devoted to developing custom conservation plans, for centuries Vatican specialists have outsourced restoration of painted works on canvas to the trusted experts at Feudatario Restorations in Venice. Long-established partnerships like this are highly prized in the art world, as with other commercial enterprises, where trust and faith have been mutually rewarded for years, or in this case, centuries.

The experts at Feudatario excel at both restoration and conservation of valued artworks. Restoration involves the renovation or repair of works which have sustained damage or have simply decayed over time, with the goal of returning a work to its original, undamaged state. Conservation, on the other hand, deals with preservation efforts to safeguard against future damage or deterioration.

ONE PAINTING IN PARTICULAR—THE prolific Raphael's *Madonna of Foligno*—had been scheduled for restoration work for some time. First painted in 1512 on wood panel, it was one of the many works of art that were looted from the Vatican and taken to Paris during Napoleon's siege of Rome in 1799, where, three years later, it was restored and transferred to canvas. After the Battle of Waterloo in 1815, the painting was returned to Rome and displayed in the Vatican Museum's Pinacoteca gallery.

On Monday morning two men, each wearing white lab coats and white cotton gloves, carefully removed the Raphael painting from its place on the gallery wall, stood it at an angle on a carpeted upright dolly and secured it for movement.

Wheeling the dolly into the adjacent warehouse, they took their time as they made ready the painting's shipment container, an archivally prepared wooden box with sufficient absorbent material to prevent external impacts.

Finally, the box was sealed, addressed and bar-coded, then placed aboard an armored truck equipped with GPS and two armed security guards inside.

The only ones who knew about the transfer outside the Vatican's own shipping paperwork were the receivers at Palazzo Feudatario, who were expecting delivery the following day.

CHAPTER

TWENTY

"Signore," Aldo explained to Renzo Farelli, "all I saw were pages of music, and words mentioning a rogue cardinal, two Vatican conspirators, and something called Operation Scambio. Look. Here are the two photos I took of what she was working on." He showed Farelli the images on his phone.

The young Camorra *cugine*—whose primary means of employment was as a waiter at Ca' Sagredo until he was 'made' and inducted into the clan and thus off probation—stood nervously in front of Farelli, relating his encounter with Livia Gallo.

"Send these to me, Aldo. I must inspect them more closely." The young man forwarded both images by email to Farelli.

"As you can see, there is also a very old picture of music on the signora's computer. And she had written the name Vivaldi on a notepad." The boy beamed at his work.

"Vivaldi?" Farelli repeated to himself. "What does Vivaldi have to do with anything?"

"I am sorry, signore," Aldo said. "This I do not know."

The capo's jaw worked as he mulled this worrisome situation. A rogue cardinal? Vatican conspirators? He fumed at the jeopardy their operation faced. *How could these people know anything about Operation Scambio?!*

"I need you to get me that computer, Aldo," Farelli stressed. "And as soon as possible."

"Si, signore. I will try to get it as you wish."

At a stern look from Farelli, the young man fumbled, "I mean, yes, I will get it. Today."

CARLO RINALDO'S death had cast a pall on everyone as they gathered in Livia's suite that early evening. Dominic especially was disturbed, pacing the room as he turned over the events in his mind.

"Why did they have to kill him, forgodsake?!" he asked no one in particular. "These guys are ruthless bastards without conscience, which means we could all end up the same way."

The priest sat down, dispirited. "We should just give up on this insane quest of mine. I don't want to put any of you in danger any longer. Let them have their spoils."

Marco, ever the combatant, pushed back. "Michael, Carlo's loss is regrettable, but if we stop now, wouldn't he have died in vain? Surely he would have wanted you to see this through. Isn't that why he shared the Don's confession with you? I certainly want to see it to the end now! You have a great team here who cares about you and this mission—and it's *our* mission, not just yours. We've all come too far to back out now. Screw these guys. I say bring it on."

"Marco's right, Michael," Karl said with conviction. "We've never backed away from high stakes before, and if you recall, the odds have been far worse in past situations. Count me in." He looked around the room.

"Me, too," Lukas and Hana said at the same time.

Dominic looked up, emotion clouding his face. He stood up, reaching out his hand to Marco.

"Thanks." He gripped Marco's outstretched hand, shaking it firmly.

"Thanks to all of you. I couldn't have a better team. Things just got too heavy there, but I agree—Carlo's death would have been pointless if I stopped now. So, where to from here?"

Livia figured this was the right time to bring up her discovery.

"Well, this may help. Hana, remember that framed Vivaldi piece on the contessa's staircase wall that I took a photo of? Turns out to be yet another Solfa Cipher!"

"There's *another?*" Dominic asked, surprised. He looked at Hana. "You didn't mention this before?"

"I'd forgotten about it, what with some hideous geezer wearing an ugly bird's beak mask staring at my breasts at the time."

"Oh, that's right," Livia said. "'Don Angelo Gallucci,' he said his name was."

"*Gallucci?*" Marco and Dominic blurted out at the same time. Marco spoke first.

"He's head of the local Camorra. And apparently also a friend of the contessa." He looked seriously at Dominic. "We need to be vigilant here. These people are not to be taken lightly. And they hide in plain sight. Anyone could be on the Camorra's payroll."

"Carlo mentioned Gallucci by name at the party," Dominic added, "telling me much the same thing. He said he feared repercussions over Gambarini's confession if the Camorra ever found out. Obviously they have."

Marco glanced around the room. "Well, that pretty much answers the question then. From now on, each of us must be very careful who we speak with, and never travel alone. If they can daringly take down a man as well-known here as Father Rinaldo, well, I don't need to elaborate."

"If I may," Livia continued after a pause, "getting back to the Vivaldi manuscript. This message could be of great importance;

it mentions intriguing specifics that may be helpful. I've already transcribed it." She read the verses aloud:

> *At minimum one rogue cardinal*
> *and two Vatican conspirators*
> *conduct Operation Scambio*
> *Select paintings are prepared for restoration*
> *then shipped to Palazzo Feudatario in Venice*
> *for reproduction by the hand of great forgers*
> *All of this is detailed in the Coscia Journal*
> *God forgive them their corrupt ways, I cannot*

"My God!" Dominic said. "This is a goldmine of compromising information. So the operation has had a name, *Scambio*—the Italian word for *'switch'* or *'exchange.'* And they sent paintings out for restoration from Rome to some palazzo here in Venice called Feudatario, which were then reproduced as *forgeries*? And the 'Coscia Journal' was obviously kept by Cardinal Niccolò Coscia. I wonder if it still exists today? Such a diabolical scheme! And yet somehow brilliant."

"You think this is all still going on?" Hana asked.

"If Carlo's death is any sign," Marco affirmed, "I'd say yes."

"Livia," Dominic said, "if you hadn't had the foresight to take a photo of this at the party, we would never have had this kind of knowledge. We are all indebted to you."

Livia smiled humbly and blushed. "But what to do with it now?" she asked.

"First," Marco said, "we need to find this Palazzo Feudatario, to see if it's still in business. Second, Michael, you should inform Cardinal Petrini of what we've discovered here. He needs to institute measures at his end to ensure that the Vatican's restoration outsourcing procedures and personnel are trustworthy and reliable. Having 'rogue' cardinals makes it all the more disturbing."

"And lastly," Marco finished, "I'll check with the Carabinieri tomorrow to see if they have any leads on Carlo's death. Karl, you should stay here with Michael and Hana so we're all covered."

"Sure, Marco. And Lukas can keep Livia company."

"And while Marco is doing that," Dominic proposed, "Hana, Karl and I can look for this Palazzo Feudatario.

"But for now, let's get some dinner. Who's hungry?"

All agreed in unison as they made for the door, heading downstairs to L'Alcova Ristorante.

At the same time, Aldo from Room Service had been waiting against the wall just outside the door, appearing to be leaving another guest's room on the third floor, the room adjacent to Livia's.

As he feigned holding back his service cart while the group filed out the door, he bid them all good evening as they passed him. Before the door closed shut, however, he slipped his foot inside the door jamb preventing it from closing. Nobody noticed as they walked away, chatting.

He allowed the group time to get into the elevator, and after the doors closed, he knocked on the door to Livia's suite.

"*Room Service,*" he called out. He knocked once more. Then, certain no one was inside, pushed his cart into the room.

Looking around, he noticed the laptop computer was still on the desk. He closed the cover, unplugged the computer from the wall socket, wrapped the cord around the unit, then slipped it onto the shelf beneath the cart and left the room.

AFTER DINNER, everyone returned to their rooms except for Hana, who joined Livia for a nightcap in her suite.

Livia found two small bottles of Martini & Rossi Bitter Amaro in the minibar and poured them into two glasses. They each took a seat, letting their meals settle as they savored the aperitif.

"So," Hana began, a glimmer in her eyes. "What do you think of Marco?"

Livia grinned. "I knew I wasn't just seeing things during dinner. You couldn't keep your eyes off him, could you?"

"Well, he is quite the charmer, isn't he?"

"Ah, if only I was thirty years younger, I'd give you a run for your money. Yes, he is quite the catch. Are you going to play this out?"

"I do think there's something there. If he doesn't make a move soon, I will." As she said this, she thought wistfully of Michael, and what could never be.

"Where did you just go?" Livia asked, eyeing her friend's far off look. "To Michael, by any chance?"

"Well, aren't you the mind reader," Hana said, blushing. "Obviously that could never work. But yes, if things were different..." She let it end there.

Livia smiled at having guessed Hana's dilemma. "I'd say you stand a strong chance with Marco, so—"

As she was speaking, Livia happened to glance at her desk.

"Hana! My computer's gone," she cried out, standing to look for it elsewhere in the room.

"Where could it be?! It was here before we left for dinner!"

Hana got up and helped her look around the suite, with no success.

"Call the front desk and report it's been stolen," Hana said. "And ask them to check their keycard access files."

Calling the front desk, Livia did as Hana suggested. There were no other keycards used except hers for that entire day, she was told, but they would send up the hotel's security manager right away.

CHAPTER

TWENTY-ONE

E veryone had gathered for breakfast the next morning, the main topic of conversation being one that disturbed them all.

"Who would want Livia's computer?" Dominic asked, already knowing the answer. "Maybe someone who wanted the decoded Vivaldi cipher? Which likely means the Camorra. And doubtless they have ways of getting into hotel rooms undetected. But how did they know Livia had it in the first place?"

"Having it means they must now know we understand what they're up to," Marco said, a shadow of concern on his face. "I don't like this at all. Hana, is it really necessary that you and Livia need to be here?"

Livia was first to speak. "Well, apart from getting my computer back—which doesn't seem likely now—I think I've done all I could to help out with the Vivaldi manuscripts. Besides, good luck to them trying to figure out my password.

"I should head back to Rome anyway."

"I think that's wise, Livia," Hana said. "And thanks for your help. But as for me, there's no way I'm leaving. I'm seeing this through to the end. Whatever that might look like."

Marco moved closer to her. "Are you sure that's wise?" he asked softly, his eyes searching hers. "It may not be easy going."

She placed her hand on his arm. "Michael and I have been in far worse situations than this, Marco, but thanks for your concern."

Noticing the hint of intimacy between the two, Dominic rose from his seat and moved around the room, rubbing his hands together.

"Livia, thanks so much for your help," he said. "I hope you at least enjoyed yourself for the most part. Sorry about your computer, though."

"No need for you to apologize, Michael," Livia said. "But if you do find those miscreants, try to get it back. I'll be leaving this afternoon, then."

"Hana," Dominic asked, "are you up for tracking down this Feudatario with Karl and me? Marco is going to question the police about Carlo, and I figure that's a good use of our time." Karl nodded in agreement.

Hana glanced at Marco, then turned back to Dominic. "Sure. Let's see what we can find."

It was just past noon when the rusty hull of an orange and white delivery barge eased up to the blue-striped *pali da casada* canal poles jutting from the water in front of Palazzo Feudatario. Two boatmen stepped off the barge and onto the dock. A long, wheeled utility cart stood nearby.

Two other men on the barge carefully picked up the huge 4-meter by 3-meter wooden container in transit, then all four helped guide the crate onto the utility cart while steadying the boat. It was a well-practiced, time-honored maneuver for delivering goods of all kinds throughout Venice for centuries. Three palazzos up the canal, ten men were performing the same offloading procedure for a massive black grand piano on a larger barge, just business as usual in the floating city.

Its cargo unloaded, the barge pulled away from the dock as four of the palazzo's guards wheeled the hefty crate into a freight elevator in the building, taking it to the upstairs studio for unpacking.

Don Angelo Gallucci watched as the curator and his helpers removed the painting from its secure packing material and hoisted it onto a prepared wall hanging.

Measuring 3.3-meters by 2-meters, Raphael's dramatic *Madonna of Foligno* hung before them.

"*Spettacoloso*," the curator marveled, standing back to take in the full picture.

"Spectacular, indeed," Gallucci admitted. "This is one of our finest acquisitions yet, at least in my lifetime. Take the very best care in its reproduction, Giuseppe. Give me your time estimate once you have it, will you? We may already have a buyer lined up."

"*Si*, signore," said Giuseppe. "We will do our finest work on this masterpiece."

∼

"FEUDATARIO?" repeated the hotel concierge in response to Dominic's question. "*Si*, Padre, Palazzo Feudatario is in the Dorsoduro *sestiere*, next to Ca' Rezzonico museum. They are known worldwide for their historical art restoration services.

I'll bet they are, thought Dominic. He thanked the woman, then he, Hana, and Karl went outside to hail a water taxi on the *fondomento*, the paved walkway alongside the canals. Finding one available, they boarded the craft. Dominic gave the driver instructions: "Palazzo Feudatario in the Dorsoduro, *per favore*."

The boat gently pulled away from the dock, its bow turning south under the Rialto Bridge for the ten-minute trip. All three sat on the aft seat, taking in the splendors of Venetian life on the water as the craft made its way down and across the Grand Canal, the sun warming them against the cool breeze crossing the water.

~

THE VENICE CARABINIERI headquarters near Campo San Zaccaria was quiet. Venice being a fairly safe place, there was little occupying the police's time as Marco entered the station. Two uniformed officers were sitting at a table playing Scopa, a popular Italian card game, as they waited for their services to be needed.

Even though the officers were a mere three meters away from the reception desk, Marco knocked on the counter a few times to get their attention. A few moments later, one officer cried out *"Scopa!"* as he gathered all the cards on the table. After winning the hand, he got up to greet the visitor.

"*Si*, signore, what can I do for you?"

Marco reached inside the breast pocket of his jacket and removed a small leather case with a badge and ID card, which he flashed to the officer.

"I am Commander Picard with the French Sûreté. We understand you retrieved the body of Father Carlo Rinaldo from a canal two days ago. Do you have any determination yet as to the cause of death?"

The officer inspected the credentials, then asked, "And how does this concern the Sûreté, Commander?"

"Father Rinaldo's parents are important French citizens. We are working with them to help resolve the matter of their son's death here in Venice."

"Ah, *si*, I understand now. The coroner has ruled Don Rinaldo's death to have been a drowning, plain and simple."

"But Father Rinaldo was a young man, and an expert swimmer in college. It is very unlikely he drowned. Has an autopsy been performed? Was there any evidence of foul play?"

"The coroner sees many of these deaths in the *canali* each year, signore. And what makes you think foul play might have been involved?" It was clear the officer showed little interest in pursuing other possibilities, especially with a card game waiting.

Marco took a deep breath, then exhaled. "Okay. But may I have a copy of the coroner's report, for the parents?"

The officer considered this for a moment, then sighed. He went to a filing cabinet against the back wall, rifled through the folders, found the documents he was looking for, then placed them in the copy machine. A couple minutes later, he handed several stapled pages to Marco, who thanked the officer.

Marco grinned to himself as he exited the building. *Amazing what a badge can do*, he thought. He hadn't been with the Sûreté for some time now, but kept the credentials for just such uses. He knew Italy was all about badges and seals and rubber stamps, the whole 'official protocol' thing. He also knew that Carlo's parents were not French, but Italian-American—but those guys wouldn't know that. Besides, as one of the clergy, official notification for a priest's death would have gone through the church, so the Carabinieri would not have pursued next of kin beyond that.

THE WATER TAXI pulled up to the dock at Palazzo Feudatario. After Hana paid the driver, she, Karl, and Dominic stepped off the boat and headed toward the entrance.

An obstinate guard stood in the way of their entering the building.

"Excuse me," Dominic said pointedly. "We have business here."

"Do you have an appointment?" the guard asked gruffly.

"I did not know one was needed. This is where art restoration is done, yes? We'd like to speak with the manager."

"May I have your names, please?"

"Father Michael Dominic with associates. From the Vatican."

The guard's eyes opened wider. "One moment, Padre." He turned, opened the door, and closed it behind him.

"Not suspicious at all," Dominic smirked at Karl.

"Well, I can imagine having guards if they're protecting valuable artworks," Hana said. "At least that would make sense. And guards aren't paid to be nice."

Dominic grumbled something unintelligible, folding his hands in front of him as he waited.

A moment later the door opened, and a dour older woman greeted them. "Please, do come in. We normally do not receive visitors without appointments. I am told you are with the Vatican, Father Dominic?"

"Yes, I am Prefect of the Apostolic Archive. And these are my colleagues, Hana Sinclair and Karl Dengler."

"I am Valentina Calabrese, manager of Feudatario Restorations. Please, have a seat. How may I help you?"

The four took a seat in the cozy sitting room on the ground floor of the four-storied palazzo. Hana noticed the building had a tall open atrium in the center of it, leading all the way up to a glass ceiling above the fourth floor, making for an airy, light-filled ambience. She also saw that the staircase leading up had its own glass door secured with a digital keypad. And CCTV cameras were placed in strategic positions. Security here was taken seriously.

"I apologize for not having an appointment, signora, but we would like a tour of your palazzo, if it is not inconvenient," Dominic said pleasantly.

"I am afraid that will not be possible, Padre. We do not give tours to anyone, being a secure facility for the work we do. And, being from the Vatican, you should know Feudatario has been proudly serving the Vatican Museum's restoration needs for hundreds of years. We have many customers, of course, but the Vatican is our most prized and distinguished client."

"Actually, I work in the Archives, not the Museum, so I was

unaware of our mutual relationship. May we at least see some of your work, while we're here?"

"Again, I am afraid not. You would need to get permission from His Eminence Cardinal Abruzzo. He is the Patriarch of Venice, as I am sure you know."

"I see," Dominic muttered, somewhat confused. Undaunted, he kept pushing. "What if I had permission from the Pope himself?"

The woman was startled by the challenge. Her hands slid down her dark gray skirt as she resettled herself in the chair.

"Even then, I believe approval from Cardinal Abruzzo would still be needed. I suggest you start with him. May I give you his number?"

"That's alright, I know how to reach him." He and the others stood up.

"Thank you for your time, signora. I'm sure we will see each other again soon."

After exchanging goodbyes, they left through the door they came in. The guard stepped aside to let them pass, an unfriendly smirk on his face as he did.

When they were out of earshot, Dominic said, "Next, we pay a visit to the Patriarch of Venice. Want to bet he lives in a grand palazzo himself?"

FROM HIS FOURTH FLOOR OFFICE, Angelo Gallucci watched the security camera monitor as Dominic, Karl and Hana left the building.

"What did they want, Valentina?" he asked his manager.

"A tour of the building, signore," she said. "I told him he needed Cardinal Abruzzo's permission, but he asked if the Pope's would suffice! Do you think he could do that?"

"It would not matter, though I give him credit for the bold suggestion. The priest is aware of our activities now, of that I am certain. I must speak with His Eminence. Would you get him on the phone, please?"

~

EARLIER, having said her goodbyes to everyone, Livia placed her luggage next to her on the fondomento, waiting for the water taxi the concierge had called for her.

As the boat slowly glided to the dock, a boatman jumped off the bow and secured the lines.

"Signora Gallo?" he asked.

"*Si*. To the train station, please."

Helping her aboard the vessel, the boatman collected her luggage, then signaled the driver they were clear to depart.

The boat pulled out of the dock, heading toward the Santa Lucia station as directed. Then it took a right turn onto the Rio di Roale canal, heading in the opposite direction of the train station.

"Excuse me," Livia said, pointing west to the driver. "You took a wrong turn. The station is that way."

"We are taking a shortcut, signora. The traffic is too heavy on the Grand Canal. This is a back way."

While she was talking, she didn't notice the other man coming up behind her, a strip of duct tape in his hands. Reaching quickly around her face, he slapped the tape over her mouth, then pulled her below into the cabin as she tried to scream.

CHAPTER

TWENTY-TWO

S ister Lorraine, the cook and housekeeper for the Patriarch of Venice, was in the kitchen preparing a steaming tureen of Venetian Fish Soup for Cardinal Abruzzo's lunch when the telephone rang.

Answering it, she listened for a moment, then set the phone down.

"Your Eminence," she called to him in the dining room, "it is Signor Gallucci. Shall I tell him you are taking *pranzo* and will call him back?"

"No, sister, I will take it in my office, *grazie.*"

The portly man lifted himself from the dining table with some effort, his Prada slippers softly padding the way to his office in Palazzo San Silvestro. Once there, he sat down and picked up the phone.

"*Si*, Angelo, what is it?" he asked with a long sigh.

"Father Dominic came to the studio just now, Eminence, asking for a tour. He brought the reporter woman with him. Of course, Valentina told them they needed your permission, but I'm wondering how long we can put him off. He said he might ask the Pope for access."

The cardinal considered for a moment. "Father Dominic does

have close access to His Holiness, but I doubt he would take the pontiff's time for such a ridiculous request. It is my decision alone, and since you store such pieces of value, we must make him understand that we give no tours to anyone. The Vatican is not our only client."

"I think there is a larger issue at stake here, Salvatore," Gallucci said quietly. "I do not think he wants a tour at all. His interest in Contessa Vivaldi's Giulia Lama painting is my concern. The Vatican Museum's own curator, Marcello Sabatini, was at the contessa's party too, inspecting the painting when Renzo entered the room. What if he returns to Rome and discovers the switch? It could be the first thread that unravels our entire operation."

"Let me deal with these issues, Angelo. My family has been doing this for a long time now and we have yet to face any major obstacles. I would advise you not to worry. If things get out of hand, you have ways of dealing with it. And you don't need my permission for that. Now I must go. My lunch is waiting."

BEFORE HE HAD Sister Lorraine prepare his soup, Cardinal Abruzzo had one more call to make, to Bishop Gustavo Torricelli in Rome, head of art conservation at the Vatican.

"Gustavo, this is Salvatore in Venezia. Yes, I am fine, *grazie*. My reason for calling is… well, we may have a potential problem with your Marcello Sabatini. He was here this week inspecting one of our special project pieces. Would you monitor him for me? Let me know if he poses issues about our business together."

∾

MARCELLO SABATINI SAT on the sofa in his Vatican Museum office, nervously caressing a string of rosary beads in his hands as he prayed on what to do next. Should he tell someone about his discovery? Would his career be over if he did—or didn't? How long has this been going on?

How long has this been going on? That's it… but where to start?

Moving to his desk, he turned on the computer. First, he did a database check of Giulia Lama's painting, reviewing its Condition Report and all recorded history on it since its arrival in the Vatican.

The database showed the Vatican Museum had originally purchased the piece in 1754 from the Venetian poet and noblewoman Caterina Dolfin, whose father had squandered the family fortune such that she had to sell off her personal collection to survive. It showed little activity since then, apart from the occasional special exhibition and, of course, its periodic need for restoration.

Restoration. *When and where did we send this for restoration?*

Regardless of how well a particular painting is cared for—and Vatican works of art are cared for very well—it will still suffer from the effects of natural aging and accumulating dirt and airborne pollutants. The restoration process, always handled by trained experts, repairs such paintings, including those damaged by smoke, insects, paint loss, weakened canvases, and even minor tears.

The records showed specialists performed the last restoration on *Crucifixion with Apostles* in 1967. In Venice. At Palazzo Feudatario.

Sabatini knew of Feudatario's unimpeachable reputation, and their collaboration with the Vatican for centuries, so surely there could be no problem there. Perhaps it was switched during transit? But that wouldn't give forgers enough time to do anything like the quality reproduction he had seen.

No, Sabatini thought, the only place a forgery could occur over time would be during restoration. He must look more closely into the work at Feudatario.

~

THE WATER TAXI pulled up at its dock near the Rialto Bridge. Dominic and Hana stepped off and walked the short distance to the old Church of San Silvestro, through the throng of tourists and Carnivale celebrants, until they reached the Patriarch's palazzo.

Responding to the doorbell, Sister Lorraine opened the door.

"Buona sera, sister," Dominic said, smiling. "Father Dominic and Hana Sinclair to see Cardinal Abruzzo."

"I will see if he is taking visitors, Padre. Would you be so kind as to wait here for a moment?"

The door closed, leaving Hana and Dominic standing in the sunshine on the Campo San Silvestro. Young boys rode their skateboards around the concrete square as a foursome of older couples sat under the shade of a giant nettle tree, taking in the sights of the busy Rialto.

The door opened again. "His Eminence will see you now, Padre," the nun said. "Please come in."

Sister Lorraine led them to a sitting room overlooking a small canal behind the palazzo, then left the room which, Hana noted, had the faint smell of fish in the air. The most prominent features in the room were several extraordinary Old Masters paintings. Both Dominic and Hana looked at each other, their same unspoken thoughts wondering how the cardinal could afford such priceless paintings, art works surely deserving of a museum or the Vatican's collection itself.

A few moments later, Cardinal Abruzzo entered the room, now dressed in his official clerical attire.

"Hello, Father Dominic, is it? How might I be of service?"

"Yes, Your Eminence, Michael Dominic, Prefect of the Vatican Apostolic Archive. And this is my colleague, Hana Sinclair. I trust we aren't intruding?"

"This is Venice, Father. Not that much goes on here that I can't take a little time for a fellow priest."

"I appreciate that. We're actually here with a request. I've tried to get a tour of the restoration studio at Palazzo Feudatario, but they refused, saying I needed your permission. First—and please, I don't mean to be presumptuous here, but—I don't understand how the Patriarch can even issue such permission. It is a private business, isn't it?"

"That it is. A private business, as you say. The fact is, though, I am the owner of Feudatario. It has been in my family for generations. So Signor Gallucci's insistence on getting my permission would be appropriate. He is not at liberty to do so himself. You said you had a request?"

It surprised Dominic that the cardinal owned the property. But he also knew that particular allowance depended on which order a priest belonged to, since many religious orders did not require vows of poverty. Obviously, this was the case with the Patriarch of Venice, as evidenced on the walls of the room in which they were sitting and the fact that he owned a private business.

"We were hoping you would grant us permission to tour your facility. Would that be possible?"

The cardinal paused as he stared hard at Dominic.

"Father, Feudatario works not only for the Vatican. It has valued clients from many museums and other institutions throughout Italy, and our security commitments to them do not permit such casual tours of the premises. I'm afraid I cannot honor your request, I'm sorry."

Eager to get inside at any cost, Dominic was just about to cut to the chase and explain about Vivaldi's accusations of forgery— but suddenly resisted the urge. *What if the cardinal himself is in on it?* He couldn't risk revealing what he knew just yet.

"I understand, Eminence. Of course, you're right. My apologies if I seemed too assertive."

"Not at all, Father. I understand your interest in our processes, but I am pleased you respect our policies. Is there anything else I might do for you?"

Dominic stood to leave, but a thought struck him. "A pity about Father Rinaldo's death, isn't it?"

He eyed the man for any reaction. And there it was. A slight change in his facial expression, surprise at hearing the name Rinaldo from someone who, in the cardinal's mind, probably never knew the man.

"Why… yes, it is. Father Rinaldo was, um… a good man. Did you know him?"

"Quite well, yes. We were in seminary together. I believe his death to be suspicious, and we have people looking into it."

"I was told he drowned," the cardinal said flatly, licking his lips while averting his gaze from Dominic's—both obvious signs of someone hiding a known truth.

"That's most unlikely, since Carlo was a powerful swimmer. Anyway, thank you for seeing us, Eminence. *Arrivederci* for now."

HAVING HELD her piece during the meeting, as they left the palazzo Hana spoke her mind. "That man was lying about Carlo," she burst out. "He knows something more, I'm certain of it."

"I agree, but I wasn't surprised. Abruzzo is in deep with whatever's going on here. If Feudatario is implicated, as the owner of a multi-generational company he's obviously aware of it."

"What next?" she asked.

With a cunning look in his eyes, Dominic said, "I have an idea."

CHAPTER
TWENTY-THREE

When Valentina Calabrese lifted the cover of Livia Gallo's laptop, it prompted her for login credentials.

"All we need now is your password, Dr. Gallo. Give it to me, please."

Livia sat in a metal folding chair facing Valentina, her hands and feet bound. Aldo, the room service waiter from her hotel, had removed the duct tape from over her mouth and now stood next to her. In his hand was a sharp knife glinting under the exposed light bulb hanging overhead.

"Don't even think about calling out, signora," Aldo said, trying to sound menacing. "No one will hear you, anyway." He slid the blunt back edge of the knife along her throat as an inducement.

"Go to hell," Livia snapped.

Valentina looked at her hostage in a new light. Then, with a grim smile, she rose from her desk and strolled to where Livia was sitting.

"Things can go much easier for you if you help us, Dr. Gallo. We just want to see what it is you discovered." In one swift motion, Valentina raised a hand and smacked Livia's face. "Does that help?"

Livia's head whipped to one side from the impact, her eyes widened, and she suddenly shook all over. The slap had stung but the realization that her very life rested on her responses robbed her of any remaining bravado. These same people had likely killed Father Rinaldo. Would they kill her as well?

"There's nothing much on there anyway," she said, her voice now quavering. "The password is *'il migliore dei mondi possibili,'* all lowercase without spaces."

Valentina smirked with amusement. "'*The best of all possible worlds?*' What inspired that?"

Livia felt that maybe talking would buy her more time. Had talking helped Rinaldo? She pushed away the thought. "It's a quote from the Enlightenment philosopher Gottfried Leibniz. Not exactly suitable at the moment, but I've always appreciated it. Its meaning is derived from one of his works, one attempting to solve the problem of evil in the world. Something you wouldn't know about."

Valentina let the gibe pass, then entered the password. The screen lit up. The first thing she did was disable the need for password protection. *This laptop isn't going anywhere,* she reasoned.

Still showing on the screen were images of old sheet music. As a pianist since childhood herself, Valentina also recognized music composition software. She could read the music, but the tune made little sense to her as she played it in her head.

Then she looked at the transcription Gallo had made in a word processor—and was stunned to find mention of Vatican conspirators, Operation Scambio, restoration forgers, and *Feudatario!* She quickly deduced that the pages she was looking at came from the hand of Antonio Vivaldi.

"Don Gallucci!" she called urgently to the boss. "You must see this."

Gallucci entered the room and came over to where Valentina was sitting, then glanced at the display.

"What is it?"

Valentina looked up at him with fear in her eyes.

"You know of the great 18th-century violinist Antonio Vivaldi? He seems to have exposed us—centuries after his death! Look here. These are his original handwritten musical pieces which Signora Gallo here seems to have discovered and transcribed. It looks like Vivaldi used some kind of code she deciphered, but it reveals *everything!*"

"Where did you find these?" Gallucci asked, his now pale face looking at Livia with a mix of anger and anxiety.

"That should hardly matter now," Livia spat. "Everyone knows about your operation, and they're working to bring it down. Things might go better for you if you release me. Adding kidnapping to your list of crimes only makes things worse."

Ignoring her, Gallucci looked thoughtful.

"Renzo showed me the transcriptions his man had found, but I didn't understand it actually came from Vivaldi's own hand. *Dio mio!*" he gasped. He fell into a nearby chair. "After all this time. It cannot be possible."

"You must call His Eminence, Angelo," Valentina said. "This is his problem."

"*All* of us share the problem, Valentina. Operation Scambio brings in millions each year. Restoration work alone is a pittance by comparison. But yes, Abruzzo must be informed."

"What do we do with the woman?" Aldo asked, keen to prove himself.

"I'll leave that to you, Aldo. Just do it quietly."

Livia screamed and kept screaming and struggling until the strip of duct tape was slapped over her mouth again. Aldo placed a white cloth over her nose with something wet on it. The tang of chemicals assaulted her nostrils. Then the room got fuzzy and quiet as she lost consciousness.

He said do it quietly, Aldo figured, as he slid the sharp side of the blade across her slim, pale throat.

"Eminence, we have a problem."

Don Angelo Gallucci sat in a high-backed Queen Anne chair in the sumptuous library of Palazzo San Silvestro, the Patriarch's residence. Seated across from him was Cardinal Abruzzo, listening carefully, a glass of Negroni resting in his hand on the arm of his own chair.

The cardinal said nothing, nodding his head for Gallucci to proceed.

"We just learned that the priest Dominic and his associates have discovered the special work of Feudatario, and the Camorra's involvement in Operation Scambio. Now, I should point out that they found this information encoded on an 18th-century musical composition by Antonio Vivaldi, so they may just associate this as a historical footnote. Obviously, your family's work goes back that far, and how Vivaldi found out then is anyone's guess today. But the fact remains, now others know it outside our circle.

"I would not be concerned at all were it not for the fact that Signor Sabatini's examination of the Giulia Lama painting may have encouraged further research on his part. He is an expert at such things, after all, and Renzo saw him inspecting the piece closely at the contessa's party. Though our work is sufficiently expert to fool even the most trained eye, if he gets the chance to run forensic tests on, say, the substrate or pigments used, then we may be in store for a more formal challenge."

"That doesn't mean much on its own, Angelo," Abruzzo said, waving off the Don's concern. "Did Renzo see him take actual samples from the canvas?"

"No, Eminence. Renzo left the room immediately to avoid questions they had for him, since the contessa told them she bought it from his gallery."

The cardinal took a sip of the Negroni, then lit a Toscano Antica cigar as he considered what he had just heard.

"I spoke with Bishop Torricelli, our man at the Vatican, yesterday. Sabatini works for him, so we have some control there. I doubt he will be a problem, but he will inform me should anything develop.

"In the meantime, how is the Raphael project going?"

Gallucci reacted to the abrupt change in subject with surprise and unease, wondering if the Cardinal took his full meaning of the problem at hand. But he answered nonetheless.

"It... it is a phenomenal acquisition, Eminence. And the timing of its arrival couldn't be better. Renzo has a discreet and very wealthy client in Paris ready to purchase it, no questions asked. He believes he can get twenty-five million euros for it. My team is at work on it now, and should have it finished in a few weeks. We are also accepting a Caravaggio soon, also from the Vatican. Since these are in reserve storage there, and not on display in the museums, there is little chance the replicas will be discovered. And with Bishop Torricelli's help, they'll stay in storage."

THE STACK WAS GETTING HIGHER as Sabatini printed out Condition Reports for the select Vatican paintings sent to Palazzo Feudatario over the past ten years. He had chosen not to go further back in time, focusing on just those restorations which had occurred during his tenure at the Vatican Museum. Plus, he was frightened at what he might find if he went back as far as the records permitted.

Then there was the matter of time. The stack before him would take some effort to do spot checks, let alone verify the authenticity of every piece. And he dared not tell another soul just yet, uncertain who the inside man was that had been enabling this corruption to continue.

By the time he finished, he counted thirty-four paintings that he viewed as potentially suspect. Next, he would have to go through the same laborious forensic testing as he did for the Lama painting.

Titian, Bellini, Botticelli, Gentileschi. From the hands of these men came some of the finest paintings ever made, now among the Vatican's holdings. And these were just the Italians. The Netherlands' Bosch, Spain's El Greco, France's de la Tour and so many other renowned artists appeared on his list as well. Sabatini's hands shook as he held the stack, fearful of what he may yet find.

As he walked through the storage galleries to locate the pieces he would spot check, LED torch in hand, he collected sufficient microscopic grains from each painting that would be put under the microscope and through the spectrometer processes.

That he could not share his suspicions with anyone yet added to the crushing weight of his task.

A FEW HOURS later Marcello Sabatini was back at his desk, having completed his forensic analysis of just six of the thirty-four paintings. He felt sick to his stomach.

All six were forgeries.

CHAPTER

TWENTY-FOUR

Marcello Sabatini had just put each of his three children to bed while his wife was cleaning up in the kitchen after dinner.

"I have one last thing to do, *caro mio.* But when you are done with the dishes, let's watch *Montalbano* on TV, *si?*" His wife smiled at him, nodding in agreement, then returned to her cleaning.

Meanwhile, Sabatini sat down at his computer and nervously opened a new message using his Vatican email account.

Dear Father Dominic:

I have confidentially conducted thorough forensic testing of Giulia Lama's *Crucifixion with Apostles,* along with six other paintings by Old Masters found here in the Vatican Museum's storage galleries. They had sent these to Palazzo Feudatario for restoration at some point over the past ten years.

Including the Lama, all seven here proved to be forgeries.

Over that same period I count twenty-seven other paintings that were also sent to Feudatario, but the constraints of time prevent me from testing all of them. Given the odds, however, we must assume most if not all of them to be forged as well.

I am deeply distressed by this outcome, as I am sure you will be on learning of it. I have told no one yet of my findings, but intend to speak with Cardinal Petrini about the matter in the morning.

I cannot trust anyone else here, for someone in the Vatican must be complicit in this activity—someone with the power to oversee outgoing and return shipments and validate Condition Reports.

I have prepared a package of my test results and will personally give this to His Eminence tomorrow. For now, I share this only with you, in confidence, so that you may deal with things in Venice as appropriate.

Sincerely / Marcello Sabatini

After rereading the draft email, Sabatini pressed the Send button. Relieved, he began assembling the package of test results for Cardinal Petrini.

Bishop Gustavo Torricelli's mobile phone pinged an unusual three-tone alert, one fairly new to him since he only recently had the Vatican Museum's employee spyware program installed. *Who would be working at this time of night?* he wondered.

A small notification window popped up on his screen, showing an email had just been sent by one of his curators, Marcello Sabatini—the one he had just been warned about by Cardinal Abruzzo.

Tapping the 'Review' button, Torricelli opened the outgoing message Sabatini had sent to Dominic. He grew increasingly alarmed as he read one incriminating sentence after another.

Something had to be done. Abruzzo had instructed him to handle the matter himself, obviously giving the cardinal plausible deniability should blame somehow fall in the Patriarch's direction. But what to do?

Torricelli was desperate. After some consideration, he picked up the cell phone on his bedside table, nervously tossed it around in his hands, evaluating the decision, then dialed one of the few special numbers programmed into it. A man answered, "*Si?*"

"Faustino, do you know who this is? Good. I have an immediate need for your premium service. I will send you what details I have on the subject and leave the rest to you. Yes, through our secure ProtonMail accounts. And you must do it tonight or before the subject arrives for work tomorrow morning. Details will be in the email."

CHAPTER
TWENTY-FIVE

Once a proud member of the Italian Carabinieri's elite bomb squad, Faustino Perez had been quietly discharged from official duties three years earlier as a psychological misfit and conduct unbecoming an officer of the law.

The whole affair was over a trifling matter, he reasoned, for his planting of a tiny improvised explosive device in his station's locker room was only intended as a joke to startle his friends. It was hardly bigger than a firecracker, and it hurt no one, for God's sake. Where was their sense of humor?

Sadly for Perez, he was alone in his twisted reasoning. Once his closest comrades, fellow officers now shunned him in Rome's cop bars where they all hung out after hours. His job as a night security guard for a small munitions manufacturer—easy to get since the Carabinieri would never admit it had once hired a psychopath—was a slap in the face given his unique skills. Though he was happy to have it, the pay was so lousy it forced him to take side jobs to make ends meet.

Ah, but those side jobs. They made more money for him than being a cop ever could. And with ready access to the right materials he needed, he could still employ the skills he'd trained for years to perfect. Plus, he had gained a respectable reputation in discreet circles, not only as an accomplished freelancer of those skills, but owing to his superior sniper marksmanship training, an excellent assassin.

PEREZ HAD little time to prepare for Gustavo Torricelli's job. He didn't get off work until 5 a.m. But as long as he had the package prepared, he should be able to get it in place before Signor Sabatini left for work the next morning.

He already had a passable selection of standard plumbing pipes stored in his garage and picked out a small one that would suffice for the job.

Once he arrived at the factory, with everyone gone home for the night, he began his work. First, he turned off the CCTV cameras for the areas he needed access to.

Since security guards had complete access to the entire facility, the large round keyring on his belt opened every door in the building, including the chemical storage unit. All he required was a little nitroglycerin, a good amount of ammonium nitrate and a tiny bit of collodion cotton, plus a few alligator clips. All easy acquisitions which took only minutes to locate.

Using the workbench in the back shadows of the factory floor, he carefully prepared the materials, then tightly packed the pipe, attaching an electrical blasting cap to one end while securing both ends with duct tape. As he worked, he played out the scenario in his mind: when the car key is turned completing the ignition system, the bomb would explode.

With the pipe completed, he exited the building around midnight, hid the package under the front seat of his truck, then returned to his post, turning the CCTV system back on. The entire process only took an hour.

. . .

WHEN HIS REPLACEMENT arrived just before 5 a.m., Perez clocked out, then made his way to Signor Sabatini's home in the Trastevere neighborhood just south of the Vatican. It was still dark outside, but the sun would rise any minute now. He had to act fast.

Bishop Torricelli's secure email indicated Sabatini drove a light blue Fiat Panda, a boxy little car and one very easy to break into. Sabatini would be carrying the evidence that needed to be destroyed with him when he left in the morning. Since the wide alleys to apartments on the Via Benedetta were too narrow for parking cars, the Panda was parked at the end of the quiet lane next to a Fiat Cinquecento on the passenger side.

Parking his truck behind the Panda, Perez checked for lights on in nearby apartments. Nearly all of them were still dark.

Sliding a Slim Jim lock access tool down the driver's side window panel, the door lock popped open. Perez got in, squeezed himself down onto the floor, and placed the pipe in the hollow cavity behind the dashboard. He then attached the alligator clips to points along the electrical ignition cables.

His work here was done.

CHAPTER

TWENTY-SIX

M arcello Sabatini helped his wife attend to the children's breakfast, and with his package of evidence for Cardinal Petrini in hand, kissed his wife goodbye and walked the kids down to the school bus stop near where his car was parked.

Glancing at the Panda, it frustrated him to find it tightly wedged between two other Fiats, both Cinquecento models. There was no way he could squeeze inside himself, so he decided it being such a nice day anyway, the 20-minute walk up the Via della Lungara to the Vatican would do him good.

A LITTLE LATER THAT MORNING, Dino and Gino Rizzo, 17-year-old twin brothers well known to the Carabinieri for their string of shared misdemeanors, had taken the bus from their ramshackle flat in Tor Bella Monaca, Rome's seediest district east of the city, to the working class neighborhood of Trastevere, where their search for Fiat Pandas was sure to pay off.

With twelve cars stolen every hour of every day in Italy, the Panda was the most popular for thieves to target. Easy to break into and hot-wire, the cars were promptly taken to chop shops and stripped down for their parts. It was a lucrative business for the Camorra, and the Rizzo brothers—new initiates in the organization—had their scheme worked out to an easy science. This was their way of moving up; in time, they would both become 'made men.'

into and hot-wire, the cars were promptly taken to chop shops and stripped down for their parts. It was a lucrative business for the Camorra, and the Rizzo brothers—new initiates in the organization—had their scheme worked out to an easy science. This was their way of moving up; in time, they would both become 'made men.'

The bus stopped at the end of Via Benedetto, a quiet residential street with little business traffic, where the boys got off and began walking, searching for opportunity.

They hadn't been off the bus for even five minutes when Dino pointed to their quarry: a light blue Panda sitting next to a Fiat 500 closely parked on the passenger side. Using a Slim Jim blade, Gino popped open the door lock. They both jumped into the front seats from the driver's side.

Gino pulled out a flathead screwdriver from his back pocket, jammed it into the ignition, and pounded on it with the palm of his hand. That's all it took. Now just a turn of the screwdriver, like a key, and they would be off.

Grinning, the Rizzo brothers turned to each other and high-fived their success. Then Gino twisted the screwdriver.

GIUSEPPE FRANCO, the most talented painter and lead forger at Palazzo Feudatario, started with the largest and oldest canvas they had in stock from a vast collection of such materials the studio had acquired and stored over the past three hundred years.

Trimming the canvas to a size similar to the Raphael painting, Giuseppe then affixed it to antique stretcher bars taken from other old paintings, using small iron nails appropriate for the Baroque period. Once mounted to his satisfaction, it was time to prepare the canvas.

The first step was to further age it. He prepared a mixture of diluted bleach, brushing it over the entire back of the plain-woven cotton and the wooden stretchers. Once that had dried, he mixed a compound of brown umber paint diluted with thinner, along with a little rainwater from which old cigarette butts had been soaked in for days, rubbing that mixture onto the back of the canvas to produce a more rustic appearance.

Reversing the canvas, he first brushed it with several thin layers of a white zinc dioxide undercoating as a substrate for the top layers yet to come.

Then he began the actual work. Using time-honored oil pigments—and creating those he needed using common chemicals and other natural elements available in the 18th century—Giuseppe started the long process of applying his keen eye and fine hand to replicating Raphael's *Madonna of Foligno* which hung next to him on the wall.

Having used these same processes for decades, Giuseppe Franco was considered a master among masters for the few who knew his genuine talents. Not only was he paid well for his efforts, but he truly loved his work, believing he was channeling the original artists in recreating their beloved masterpieces.

That each of his own paintings would go on to others who could not possibly appreciate them as much as he did saddened him. But this was, after all, his life's work. Maybe someday he would find the time to make one for himself, if Don Gallucci would allow it.

CHAPTER
TWENTY-SEVEN

As he sat in the Vatican Secretary of State's office waiting for Cardinal Petrini to finish his phone call, Marcello Sabatini leafed through the documents in the folder on his lap, rehearsing how he would explain the technology in lay terms.

His own phone vibrated in his pocket. It was a call from his wife, he noted. He let it go to voicemail. He would call her back later.

Petrini ended his call and hung up the phone. "So, Signor Sabatini, what news do you bring on our duplicate painting problem?"

"Your Eminence, I am afraid the matter is far worse than we had thought. While I was in Venice, I examined Contessa Vivaldi's *Crucifixion with Apostles* closely, even taking a tiny sample of the pigment for analysis here in our lab. What I discovered proved to be most shocking—the contessa's painting is authentic, but the one in our inventory is an excellent forgery. Too good. Here are the analyses to prove it." He opened the folder and removed the documents he had prepared, laying them out in front of the cardinal.

He explained to Petrini the technical components of his

forensic investigation, which indisputably proved his conclusion.

"But I have worse news, Eminence. I went back through our records for the past ten years and discovered that at least thirty-four paintings had been sent to Feudatario for restoration and returned to us. Given the extensive time involved, I tested only six of those—and *all* proved to be forgeries as well, in addition to the Giulia Lama.

"We must presume, then, that Feudatario Restorations in Venice is engaged in the business of expertly creating duplicates of our paintings, and sending forgeries back to us here in Rome. I understand that is a strong accusation, yes. But this would also imply, of course, that someone in the Vatican is involved in facilitating the operation. It sickens me to have discovered this, Eminence. What do you suggest we do now?"

By the time Sabatini had finished, Petrini was shaking with a quiet fury. He stood up and walked around his office.

"This is *outrageous!*" he shouted. "How dare these people betray the Church in such an obscene operation."

The door opened and Father Bannon, Petrini's secretary, looked in.

"Is everything alright, Eminence?" he asked.

"No, Nick, it's not. Cancel my meetings for the day. I'll explain later." He waved the man out.

As Petrini continued to walk and think, Sabatini's phone vibrated again, this time with a text message from his wife. He glanced at it.

Marcello! They have bombed our car, with two men inside it! The Carabinieri are here and want to see you. You must come home now!

Sabatini turned pale. His hands began shaking as he stood up unsteadily.

"Eminence, I... my... my car has just been bombed!"

~

EARLIER THAT MORNING, after running a couple loops around Piazza San Marco, Dominic took off west from the gothic Doge's Palace along the Riva del Schiavoni for two kilometers. Though many tourists were already out walking along the water, or having espressos and biscotti at kiosks on the fondomento, the path was wide enough to accommodate most any size crowd along with devoted runners. And there were many out this sunny morning.

Passing the Victor Emmanuel II Monument, the Church of the Pietà, and the Naval History Museum, Dominic entered the grounds of the Giardini della Biennale public gardens. After another kilometer, he passed into the quiet Sant'Elena neighborhood, with its pleasant paths lined with topiary yews and cypress trees. As he jogged through cobblestone back alleys and over quaint arched bridges crossing the narrow canals, his thoughts turned to sorting out all the facts he knew.

So... The Camorra's Don Gallucci runs Operation Scambio from Palazzo Feudatario, which is owned by Cardinal Abruzzo. Renzo Farelli owns an art gallery, and was involved with Carlo's death. He's probably also in league with Gallucci and the Camorra acting as a front for selling forgeries since he sold the original stolen Lama painting to the Contessa. And Vivaldi's message said there were two Vatican conspirators and a rogue cardinal. Of course, that was a couple centuries ago. But we know Operation Scambio is still in operation, so it must still involve at least one cardinal. Abruzzo? How could it not be! Feudatario is his family's business and has been for decades. But who would the two conspirators be in Rome? That accusation from Vivaldi was so long ago, and much has probably changed. Everything could be a lot bigger now with even more people involved than in Vivaldi's time.

By the time he approached Ca' Sagredo hotel, his t-shirt was clinging to his chest and his hair was stringy with sweat. The workout felt great, but his mind was still swirling with details he couldn't piece together.

As he headed toward the hotel's entrance, two beautiful women dressed in chic spring dresses and wearing fashionable sunglasses eyed him admiringly; one of them called out "*Che bella figura!*" as they both applauded his fit build and handsome features.

Suddenly thrust out of his own thoughts, Dominic laughed, blushed, then turned and applauded them in return as he walked backward a few steps. Italian culture can be refreshingly straightforward like that, without the pretense of false modesty. Much like how Livia and Hana had openly complimented him ... and in his mind's eye he recalled that occasion and the look right after that which had passed between Hana and Marco. *What's going on there?*

After showering, Dominic checked his email before meeting with Hana and the others to plan their next steps.

Finding a message from Marcello Sabatini, he opened it. As he read it, a tingling sensation made its way up his spine. *This was bigger than I'd imagined!* he thought. It was time to call Cardinal Petrini. He dialed his direct line at the Vatican.

"Michael, I was just about to call you. Have you heard what's happened?"

"Yes. I just read Marcello's email about the forgeries, Eminence, and I have much to tell you as well."

"No, not that. Marcello had a bomb placed in his car this morning, likely by the Camorra, the Carabinieri told him. Marcello was here talking with me when it happened. Two young men were in the car when it exploded, both of them known to the police as small-time Camorra operatives involved in a car theft ring. Either they were stealing the car or setting the bomb. Either way, clearly the bomb was meant for Marcello.

"Michael, both he and I believe this is related to the forged paintings operation coming out of Feudatario. Since you haven't spoken with Marcello yet, here's what we know...."

Petrini gave Dominic all the facts Sabatini had given him,

including the forgeries coming back to the Vatican, with the originals likely being sold discreetly by galleries run by the Camorra in Venice and possibly elsewhere.

"Mostly these are well-known paintings," Petrini added, "so someone must carefully vet the buyers, knowing they are purchasing an original work that belonged to respected institutions. Which means they would never be able to display them, else they would be recognized and exposed. But as we know, many private art collectors will do anything to gratify their most potent desires."

"Well, that doesn't account for the contessa, though," Dominic said. "She certainly believes her acquisition of the Giulia Lama was legitimate, otherwise she wouldn't have hung it in such a conspicuous place and so proudly explained its background."

"Perhaps that's just an oversight on her part, or she did not know the true provenance of what she was acquiring," Petrini added. "In any event, I'm surprised the Camorra hadn't noticed it and taken some kind of action. Marcello said the contessa's Carnivale party looked to have many of their people in attendance. Wouldn't they be more concerned? In fact, that painting is part of what started all this!"

Dominic thought back to something Sabatini had told him. "As I understood it, that painting had been in the Vatican's storage unit for many years, since the Lama wasn't sufficiently prominent for exhibition. Maybe they also use the works of lesser known artists to sell to buyers unaware of the work's potential origins. Taking the gallery's word for legitimate provenance."

The magnitude of the problem brought a pause to their conversation.

Then the cardinal noted, "Marcello left to attend to this bombing incident, but he said his next move would be to see what paintings are scheduled for restoration at Feudatario, and elsewhere, since we can't be fully certain other restorers aren't in on this as well."

At that point Dominic reviewed with Petrini their activities in Venice, including discovery of the Vivaldi ciphers, the probable murder of Father Rinaldo, Dr. Gallo's laptop being stolen, the historical outlines of Operation Scambio, and their unproductive meeting with Cardinal Abruzzo.

"Abruzzo," Petrini growled. "He's a piece of work, arrogant and self-seeking. Hardly a virtuous man of the cloth, in my opinion. If it weren't because he's the Patriarch of Venice, and not simply another cardinal, it would be easier for the Holy Father to just move him elsewhere. But there is a long tradition in the Venetian Patriarchy that even I may not be able to impose on."

"In the meantime, Eminence, what are you going to do internally there? How to find out *who* is coordinating this activity in the Vatican?"

"I think once Marcello has done a bit more research, we may have more to work with in that regard. I'm putting a security man on him immediately. He's already in fear for his life. But now that he's told you and me, that danger may subside. I imagine he was only a threat to them until he could share what he knew. They will already know they failed to stop him from seeing me today. I'll let you know what he comes up with.

"Meanwhile, you and the others take good care there, Michael. I want nothing to happen to you. Get back here as soon as you can."

CHAPTER
TWENTY-EIGHT

Cardinal Abruzzo trembled with rage as he stood looking around the room. Angelo Gallucci, Renzo Farelli, Giuseppe Franco, and Valentina Calabrese all sat stiffly in the Patriarch's library in Palazzo San Silvestro, waiting for Feudatario's owner to unleash his wrath.

"Not only have we shown our hand without resolving the situation, in a terrible twist of fate we lost two loyal boys in that now senseless explosion. And Sabatini is still alive! As a result, Bishop Torricelli tells me that Petrini is now aware of Operation Scambio! Heads will roll in the Vatican soon, possibly Torricelli's first, a tragic loss to us if he's discovered. And it's only a matter of time before everything my family has worked for generations to build comes tumbling down upon us all. *This is unacceptable!*

"Angelo, I want your team to take care of these people nosing around Venice. This Father Dominic and his friends can only cause more trouble for us. I suggest whatever you do, it's discreet and permanent. Make sure their bodies are taken out into the Veneto Lagoons beyond Burano and weighted down in the waters there. Or whatever it is you people do for such things. 'Concrete boots' I believe our friends in Sicily call them."

"It's 'concrete shoes,' Eminence," Gallucci rectified. "And

141

that's an unfounded legend. Nobody uses them. It takes too long for the concrete to dry with the person standing in—"

Abruzzo slammed a fist on his desk. Gallucci clamped his mouth shut. Abruzzo scowled at the Don, unaccustomed to being corrected, especially for such minor semantics. After a moment's silence in the room, he continued, "We need to move our current project from Feudatario to someplace safe, lest they attempt a raid on our studio. Renzo, is your gallery large enough to accommodate secure work on the Raphael? That is my chief concern at the moment."

"Yes, Eminence, we can handle that. I will have to clear space for it, but we could have it ready in two days' time."

"Good. Now, as for what to do with Rome...."

THE VATICAN MUSEUM'S records room was tightly packed with gray and black filing cabinets of varying sizes, some with key locks, others with combination dials, most others unsecured. Marcello Sabatini knew right where to go for the records he sought: the restorations section.

Opening the cabinet containing documentation for artworks that were sent to or scheduled for restoration by Feudatario, he pulled out several thick folders and laid them on the spacious reading table behind him.

Pulling out a chair for the time-consuming project, he began his work, starting with the most recent dates.

He was unsettled to find that just this past week one of the Museum's most highly prized Raphael paintings had been shipped to Venice. He set that shipping document aside. Next up for restoration, in fact the very next week, was a priceless Caravaggio that had a small tear in a lower corner. He put that aside, too. There was no way he would allow that painting to leave the Vatican until they sorted this matter out.

Working his way backward in time, he came across the six

forgeries he had previously discovered. Though he already had forensic evidence in hand, he pulled those out as backup for Cardinal Petrini and the Art Squad's review. Italy's dedicated squad of the Carabinieri entrusted with protecting the country's artistic treasures would have to be called in on this matter.

As he sat there thinking of the bold daring such a project entailed, especially involving the Vatican, it occurred to him that more prominent institutions might also be involved, since Feudatario serviced other museums and galleries throughout Italy. It would be a delicate task informing them.

He would contact his colleagues at those organizations and advise them of his discoveries—in confidence, of course, since no institution wanted adverse publicity like this. And this was the worst kind of publicity imaginable.

His first order of business would be to demand return of the Raphael.

SABATINI CALLED his friend at the Uffizi Gallery in Florence, home to many of Italy's finest artworks: Giotto, della Francesca, Botticelli, da Vinci, Michelangelo and Caravaggio, among so many others. All prime bait for an operation as sweeping and repulsive as Feudatario's.

"Ciao, Giancarlo, this is Marcello Sabatini from the Vatican Museum. Yes, I'm fine, *grazie*. But I call with an important matter of some discretion, and I need your full attention. Is this a good time?"

CHAPTER
TWENTY-NINE

I t was midnight, and after watching the building from the rear alley for an hour, Marco determined that only a single guard was on duty, sitting at the reception desk on the ground floor, glued to his cell phone and drinking coffee.

All seasoned rappellers, Marco, Karl and Lukas made quick work of scaling the back of the building to reach the roof above the fourth floor. While it provided abundant natural light for the studio beneath it, the large, angled eight-paned glass ceiling proved to be the best way to break into Palazzo Feudatario.

Lying on the red brick roof tiles, the three men peered over the glass panels, watching for signs of any activity in the studio before they began their work. The room was dark and empty.

Karl, the most talented at picking locks—skills taught to him by his fellow Swiss Guard Dieter Koehl and a gypsy he had encountered in earlier adventures—got to work on the locking hasp of one window. With some effort, he finally disengaged the hasp; the hinged window popped open. No alarm sounded.

Tying off their rope to a sturdy chimney on the roof, each man rappelled down into the studio, quietly dropping onto the floor. Spotting two CCTV cameras in opposite corners, Marco removed a powerful Class IV laser beam penlight from his jacket, aiming it at each camera while remaining in the shadows.

He passed the green laser beam over the entire circular lens of each camera, knowing the action would burn the CCD sensors, creating dead pixels on the recorded image. They were now clear to proceed with their work.

The entire fourth floor studio was a massive room filled with easels and canvasses in various stages of restoration. A wide variety of specialized tools, pigment jars, solvents, thinners, and scores of brushes were spread across many tables.

Each man slipped through the cluttered moonlit room searching for their prize. A few moments later, Lukas let out a light whistle, motioning for the others to join him.

And there it was. Surrounded by many other paintings hanging on the high wall, Raphael's *Madonna of Foligno* held a prominent place.

As they had expected, standing next to it was a massive easel with a nearly finished duplicate of Raphael's masterpiece. Marco took out a small LED torch from his jacket to better examine the forgery. Comparing the two paintings, he was startled at how perfectly matched they seemed to be. To his eye anyway. Whoever the artist was, he excelled at his work. He took out his iPhone, snapped photos of both paintings along with several shots of the studio, then pocketed the phone.

Then, reaching for his belt, Marco pulled out his Gerber LMF Combat knife, raised it high above his head, then swiftly brought it down, ripping a long gash from the top of the canvas to the bottom, destroying the forgery. Though moved by its artistic competence, he had no qualms about doing so.

THE GUARD on the first floor had just set down his coffee cup on the counter when he fell silent. He was certain he'd heard something upstairs, a sound echoing through the tall open atrium. A kind of ripping sound.

Unlocking the digital keypad on the stairway door, he pulled out his Glock 19 and quietly made his way up the staircase.

NEEDING further evidence to press their case with the Vatican, Karl and Lukas found filing cabinets behind the main door to the studio and rifled through various folders, seeking sales documentation for past orders and restoration consignment invoices. If they could find buyers' names and addresses, they could turn it all over to Italy's Art Squad for further disposition.

Just then the door to the studio opened and the guard burst in, his Glock raised and aimed at Marco standing in the moonlit center of the room next to the easel. Pointing his flashlight at him, he got a good look at the Frenchman's face just before Karl, moving swiftly from behind the open door, dove for the guard's gun, then suddenly twisted, taking the man face down on the wooden floor. With the wind knocked out of him, the Glock fell out of his hands, skidding across the floor. Karl quickly moved on top of him into a *shime-waza* judo position, a strangling technique intended to render his opponent helpless. His right arm circling the guard's throat, Karl flipped him over, pulling his own arm in tighter, applying pressure to the man's neck. The guard's arms and legs flailed about, but Karl's powerful arm clamp made it impossible to escape.

Fifteen seconds later, the man lost consciousness. His struggling ceased.

Karl heaved the man's heavy body off him and stood up, gasping for breath.

"Are you alright?!" Lukas asked, his hands on his partner's shoulders.

"I'm fine, Lukas," Karl said, panting.

"Well, it seems we now have the run of the place, at least while he's out," Marco said. "See if you can find those documents, then let's get out of here. Be looking out for that

Coscia Journal, too, while you're at it. We need that as the ultimate proof."

Karl and Lukas stuffed as many seemingly relevant folders as they could into their backpacks until they were filled. They all looked around the studio for anything else that might be useful, but there was nothing that looked like a journal of any kind, something they would likely keep in a safe, anyway.

Finding nothing more of interest, each man shimmied back up the rope's ascender clamps. Back out onto the roof, Karl closed the hinged glass window behind them.

WHEN THE GUARD regained consciousness a few minutes after his attackers left, he called Angelo Gallucci to report the break-in. He dared not call the Carabinieri, for obvious reasons. The guard failed to notice the damage to Giuseppe's Raphael canvas, but said the thieves had been looking at folders in the filing cabinets, and as far as he knew, that was the extent of it. He also said he got a good look at one man before he was subdued from behind and would recognize him again. Though angry, Gallucci said there was nothing to be done now. He would be there first thing tomorrow.

When Giuseppe Franco arrived at the studio in the morning, however, he was devastated, reduced to tears when he found the destruction of his painstaking work on the faux Raphael. Nearly a full week of long days and weary nights vanished in the slash of a blade. *Who could do something so vulgar to such a profound work of beauty?!*

Don Gallucci had no doubts at all about who had done this. He was now more determined than ever to rid himself of Dominic and his meddling friends.

Taking out his phone, he made a call.

CHAPTER
THIRTY

Housed in a four-story Baroque palazzo on the Piazza Sant'Ingazio, across from the Jesuit Church of St. Ignatius, Italy's *Tutela Patrimonio Culturale*, a special unit of the Carabinieri known as the Art Squad, is headed by Colonel Benito Scarpelli, a precise man in his sixties who, before the current post he has held for some twenty years, worked as curator for antiquities at Sotheby's in London.

The phone call he had just gotten from Cardinal Petrini was unwelcome, though hardly surprising, news. Scarpelli had worked with the Vatican many times before, being the repository for some of the world's most valuable artworks. But forgeries replacing originals in the Vatican's own museums? That was a new one. He needed to assign one of his best men to this case, someone expert in Old Master paintings with an eye for detecting the unique signatures of the most capable forgers. And there was only one man for this job: Special Agent Dario Contini.

Contini was a seasoned expert in extracting vital details of how and when a painting had been created. Using a variety of methods and specialized equipment, he could pick out constituent chemicals used on the canvas, identify old and modern pigments and binders, and even determine how many layers of paint and washes of color had been applied.

He was also an inveterate gum chewer, favoring the spicy tang of anise in Black Jack chewing gum. He was convinced it helped his mind focus on the task at hand.

Contini had worked with Marcello Sabatini before, the two of them sharing similar idiosyncrasies in their respective fields. But as Sabatini had now recused himself from this case out of fear for his life, as Colonel Scarpelli had informed him, Contini was now on his own.

Cardinal Petrini had couriered over Sabatini's package of evidence he had assembled, so he began with that. To ensure for himself that Marcello's findings were accurate, Contini put the extracted sample from Giulia Lama's painting through his own routine inspections.

The one device he knew had not been used yet in Sabatini's work was a Fourier-transform infrared microscope, an expensive and uncommon piece of equipment used to obtain an infrared spectrum of absorption while collecting high-resolution data over a wide spectral range. As he had surmised, the sample grain provided from the Contessa's version of the Lama painting proved to be authentic for the period. So Contessa Vivaldi's painting was indeed the original. His mind eased, he accepted Sabatini's remaining determinations about the other six forgeries in the Vatican's inventory, deciding now to move on to the broader investigation of Feudatario to understand how deep and wide this operation might be.

And since the Camorra was involved, he would need his own security detail. From experience, he never took chances with the Italian Mafia.

Conscripting two capable agents to join him, he had his assistant book passage on the next train to Venice.

∽

"SIGNORA CALABRESE, I must insist that our Raphael be returned to the Vatican at once," Cardinal Petrini said to Feudatario's manager on the phone. "We have grave concerns about your services at the moment. I have two Swiss Guards in Venice now; they will assist you with the repacking and return of the painting this afternoon.

"Whether we do further business with your firm remains to be seen."

"But, Your Eminence, is there some reason I can give our owner as to your reasoning in this matter?" Valentina Calabrese asked. "Is there some way we might make other accommodations for you?"

"That won't be necessary. And as I said, we simply have private concerns. Kindly do as I ask. My men will be there at ten o'clock tomorrow morning. *Arrivederci.*"

Calling Dominic now, Petrini waited for him to answer.

"Michael, I need you to have Sergeant Dengler and Corporal Bischoff go to Palazzo Feudatario at ten tomorrow morning to oversee the repacking and return of our Raphael painting. We cannot take a chance those scoundrels will try to replicate it. I've arranged for an armored truck in Mestre to meet them at the Tronchetto."

"As it happens, Eminence, we've already taken care of that. We discovered they were in the process of forging a copy. Marco Picard from Baron de Saint-Clair's security team is with us here, and he and the Guards, um… mitigated the situation. You don't want to know the details."

Petrini knew better than to ask. "Please thank them for me, Michael, and yes, it's best I don't know the ways and means of your operations. When might you be returning?"

"Frankly, there is still much to be done here. I was just told that Colonel Scarpelli of the Art Squad is sending Dario Contini, their best forgeries expert, to Venice to give us a hand. We also now have some of Feudatario's files on past restorations and

Hana and I will go over those with Agent Contini. I'll keep you apprised of our activity."

∼

IT WAS A NEARLY full moon when Marco and Hana were seated for dinner at the Gritti Terrace that evening. With views of Punta della Dogana and the Santa Maria della Salute Basilica across the majestic Grand Canal, the moonlight shining off sleek black gondolas as they glided through the water made for a perfect setting. One gondolier began singing a romantic aria as he gently rowed his craft, with two lovers bundled together beneath a red blanket as they took in their dream tour of Venice.

Marco had ordered a bottle of Bruno Rocca Barbaresco before they arrived, which the server had already opened to breathe and poured just after they sat down.

"I must admit I was surprised that you asked me to dinner," Hana said, her hand brushing back her chestnut brown hair, "but I was hoping you would."

"And *I* hope your grandfather won't mind," Marco confessed, grinning. "I *am* supposed to be doing my job here, you know, keeping you out of harm's way."

"And who says you aren't? For what it's worth, I couldn't feel any safer than I do right now." She smiled.

Their eyes met, and Marco raised his glass. "To one who halves my sorrows and doubles my joys."

Moved by his chivalry, Hana smiled a bit nervously, then took a long draw on her wine for fortification.

"I hope you don't mind, but I've ordered for us already," he said. "I spoke to the chef earlier and asked him to prepare his most special off-menu choices. For you he's preparing duck breast with orange fregola and carrot puree. Does that sound appealing?"

"My God, you've thought of everything! Yes, that sounds divine. And what are you having?"

"He insisted I have his beef sirloin with artichokes, shallots and Amarone sauce. What could I say but, *oui?*"

"You Frenchmen sure know the way to a girl's heart."

"Speaking of which, I have a little surprise after dinner. I rented one of those classic mahogany boats to cruise the Venetian canals under the moonlight. It seems such a perfect night for it. I will be your chauffeur for the evening, *mademoiselle.*"

Hana's hands trembled slightly as she reached for her wine glass. *This may be an endless night...* she mused, sighing.

The server brought their meals, and as they enjoyed the food their conversation ranged from where and how each grew up to their lives before they met. It had been a long time since Hana had any romance in her life—apart from her undeclared longing for a certain unavailable priest—and she found Marco's company refreshing and hopeful.

And while he was also enjoying his time with Hana, Marco, ever-vigilant to his surroundings, was aware they were being watched. As they were eating, he noticed the guard Karl had taken down at Feudatario was walking in the shadows on the fondomento along the canal, occasionally glancing in their direction. Another man was with him; both were smoking cigarettes as they ambled along the walkway. Later, he noticed they had gone from one end and back again to the restaurant. It was obvious their presence was not coincidental.

WITH DINNER FINISHED, Marco and Hana walked hand-in-hand to the boat rental service on Fondamenta Cannaregio, not far from the restaurant. Having already planned beforehand, Marco escorted his date to their waiting Aquariva Super, an elegant 40-knot runabout with mahogany deck panels, maple inlays, and sumptuous ivory leather seating. It was a stunning classic, one of Italy's finest.

Looking around, it seemed they had lost their followers, but experience and intuition kept Marco's guard up. He started the powerful engine, revved it a bit, then backed away from the dock, heading out onto the Grand Canal. With a posted speed limit of just seven kilometers per hour, they slowly cruised the waters, taking in the gorgeously lit palazzos and weaving their way between gondolas and other watercraft. Marco turned into one of the smaller canals heading into the interior of the island for a glimpse at the real Venice most tourists never see. With no alley lamps and only the moonlight to guide them, it was an ideal romantic setting.

As they cruised the quiet Rio De La Madalena canal in the Cannaregio *sestiere*, Marco heard the low, powerful thrum of another boat's engine nearby. Under pretense of looking back to chat with Hana, who was sitting behind him, he noticed a black Chris Craft Corsair following about fifty meters behind them. Turning right onto the Rio di Santa Fosca canal, a few moments later the following craft also turned, still on their tail.

Marco had a plan.

At the end of Santa Fosca, he turned left onto Rio De Noal, which would soon take them out into the wide Laguna Veneta, where he could open the boat up to full speed and make for the outer islands, Murano and Burano.

Asking Hana to join him at the helm, he showed her the controls and let her take the wheel. Rio De Noal was a wider canal with no other traffic, so there was little trouble she could encounter during the brief lesson. He taught her how to steer and how to throttle, which is all she needed to know for what he had in mind.

"Now, don't be alarmed," Marco said tersely, "but the reason I'm teaching you how to drive is that we are being followed. *No! Don't turn around...* They've been watching us since dinner. One of them is the guard at Feudatario that Karl tangled with. I have a plan once we get to Burano island, but all it will require is that you know how to keep control of the boat. That's it. I'll do the rest."

Hana's every sense was now on full alert. Her date was about to take a dramatic turn she had not expected.

As they cleared the jetty into the lagoon, Marco urged her to throttle up, and the engine evenly roared into action. Ten knots, fifteen, twenty, twenty-five. At thirty knots, they were at a decent speed, slicing through the calm water.

The Chris Craft followed suit, chasing them at speed a hundred meters back.

Passing San Michele island, they cruised past Murano on their way to Burano. Like Venice, these upper islands also had small inner canals. If Marco's plan worked, they would be in the clear. But there would be combat, of that he was certain.

Reaching canal Rio di San Mauro, the southwest entrance to Burano, Marco took over the helm as they slowly entered the residential waterway. He would wait until they were midland before making his strike. All he needed was a bridge. Looking at the onboard map, he found one, the 'Love Viewing Bridge,' crossing the approaching turn at Rio Assassini. He smiled at the name of the canal—'River of Assassins'—a most fitting location for what he had planned.

Heading east now on Rio Assassini, the bridge was at the end at a sharp north turn in the canal. He explained the details of his plan to Hana.

As their boat turned north and out of view of the Chris Craft, Marco took off his jacket then dove into the water. Swimming to the fondomento, he hoisted himself out and ran back onto the bridge, crouching low on the north side. As instructed, after turning Hana put the boat into neutral, letting it coast up the quiet Rio Pontinello.

As it approached the low bridge, the Chris Craft slowly turned north. Marco took out his Gerber combat knife and grasped it firmly. As the boat gradually emerged beneath him on the north side, Marco, poised on the bridge railing, jumped down and landed on top of the man not driving. One slash across the throat put him down.

Surprised, the driver let go of the wheel and turned to take on his opponent. As he reached for his shoulder pistol, Marco was too fast, gutting him with the Gerber as he held the falling body. At slow speed, the boat collided with two other craft docked along the canal. After checking both men for IDs and pocketing what he found, Marco righted the craft and used it to catch up with the Aquariva.

As prearranged with Hana, she put the boat back into gear, then guided it to the end of the small canal and out into the open Laguna Veneta. Marco followed her in the Chris Craft. When both boats had cleared the jetty, Marco led the way, speeding north toward a group of sparse, unpopulated islands east of Burano. Hana followed close behind him.

Finding a hidden cove on the far side of one unpopulated island, Marco tossed the anchor overboard, then wiped his fingerprints from the wheel and other areas of the boat he might have touched.

Hana pulled her boat next to the Chris Craft, and Marco leaped across the gunnels and onto the Aquariva.

Moments later they were back out into open lagoon waters. Marco throttled up to full speed, heading south.

Still panting after the encounters and shivering from his wet clothes, Hana handed him his jacket and wrapped a blanket around him while he drove.

She looked at him with serious but admiring eyes. As he stood there meeting her gaze, he pulled her into a firm embrace. They kissed long and passionately as the boat sped across the open lagoon and back to Venice.

CHAPTER
THIRTY-ONE

After his run early the next morning, Dominic showered and dressed. Not having heard from Hana last evening —she was probably working on her Carnivale story anyway—he decided to drop by and invite her for breakfast.

He knocked on the door to her suite, a welcoming smile on his face. A few moments later the door was opened by Marco, naked but for a white bath towel wrapped around his taut waist.

"Hey, Michael," he said cheerfully, raking back his long wet hair with a well-muscled arm. "Hana's in the shower but should be out soon. Want to join us for breakfast?"

Speechless, Dominic's smile turned awkward as he simply stood there, staring at Marco. *Damn, this guy is ripped. But, what's he doing in Hana's room?* His mind had yet to process the full meaning, it happened so unexpectedly.

"I, uh… yeah," he stammered. "Breakfast. Sounds good. I'll uh… see you down there."

"*Tres bon!* Ciao, then," Marco said, closing the door.

Dominic stood in place for a few more moments. Unaware there might have been a stronger connection between the two, he didn't know how to feel about this fresh development. Anger?

Protectiveness? Or was it, God forbid, jealousy? His reaction was visceral, deep. Almost primitive. Hana was *his* friend. But of course, that's where it ended. It had to. He just didn't think that... *Oh hell, what is it I'm thinking, anyway?!*

KARL AND LUKAS were already seated at a large table in the restaurant, waiting for the others to show up for breakfast. Dominic joined them, asking the server for coffee as he sat down.

"Are you okay, Michael?" Lukas asked. "You look like you've seen a ghost!"

Deep in thought, Dominic looked up abruptly. "No, it's nothing. Just thinking."

A few minutes later Hana and Marco were walking toward the table, her arm wrapped around his. He pulled out her chair, then took a seat next to her. Both were smiling self-consciously.

The rest of the table fell silent. Whether in surprise or admiration, it was hard to tell. Except for Dominic, who looked sullen. And since he was a man without pretenses, it showed.

Hana picked up on it immediately, but decided it was best to focus on the previous night's activity.

"Wait till you hear what happened to us last night," she said soberly to the group. "Marco and I were cruising the Grand Canal in a speedboat when he noticed we were being followed...."

She continued the tale, omitting the romantic dinner, until everyone at the table, including Dominic, was fully engaged by the adventure.

"I'd rather not go into detail about the fate of those men," Marco interrupted when Hana got to that part, "but they won't be bothering us any longer. They were clearly out to do us harm. The driver pulled his gun on me and was prepared to take me down right there. I believe we are all being targeted now, so watch your backs. I mean it. I took their IDs and will have them run through Interpol's database, but it's pretty clear to me they were Camorra."

"So you actually had a boat chase across the lagoon with the bad guys?" Karl asked, wonder on his face. "Like in a James Bond movie?"

"And *I* was driving," Hana claimed with pride. "It's the most excitement I've had since, well, our escapades in Argentina with that evil Dr. Kurtz." She looked admiringly at Marco, who was with them there and where they first met.

"I just remembered, I've got some work to do," Dominic suddenly said, standing up. "Karl, you and Lukas are picking up the Raphael this morning, right? Let's regroup when you're done and figure out our next moves. I'll see you guys soon." With a slight wave, he walked away from the table, heading toward the elevators.

"Is he alright?" Marco asked.

Hana looked at him knowingly. Leaning in to whisper to him so the others wouldn't hear, she said, "This may sound strange, but I have a feeling he's bothered by seeing you and me together. Michael and I are pretty close. And after all, he is a man. Just one with restrictive vows, which I'm sure bothers him. Frankly, it's not right that the Church still holds to that archaic custom."

"I agree," Marco whispered back. "But if he were in such a position, he'd have to fight me for you. And I wouldn't want to hurt a good friend like Michael."

Hana blushed and smiled. But her troubled gaze traveled the now empty hall where her dear friend had just rushed off.

SHARPLY AT TEN O'CLOCK, Karl and Lukas appeared at Palazzo Feudatario to ensure that the Raphael was packaged up and ready to go. The orange and white barge was moored at the dock, with four men waiting to receive the freight. The armored truck hired from Mestre—the last city before crossing the causeway into Venice—was already waiting at the Venezia Tronchetto parking lot near the train station for transport of the painting back to Rome.

Valentina Calabrese gave the two Swiss Guards a cool reception when she opened the door to them, but no other staff appeared to be around. The box had been sealed and brought down by elevator to the reception area.

Karl had one request. "Signora, please, before we sign for receipt, would you kindly have the crate reopened so that we may ensure the painting is as delivered?"

Though she knew this to be a protocol for such high-value goods, she sighed audibly, then picked up the phone, calling for one of her men to bring down the tools to open the crate and reseal it.

After that business was done, and everything seemed in order, Karl instructed the freight team to move the crate onto the barge. Twenty minutes later Karl and Lukas jumped aboard, and the barge slowly made its way up the Grand Canal to the Tronchetto. The painting was carefully hoisted into the armored truck, and with their job finished and the Raphael on its way back to Rome, Karl and Lukas took a vaporetto back to the Ca' Sagredo.

BACK IN HIS SUITE, Dominic paced the room. He couldn't suppress the unease in the pit of his stomach. Though he suspected the nature of that unrest, he was reluctant to acknowledge it. Catching his reflection in the mirror over the desk, what peered back wasn't the man he knew himself to be. It was someone smaller, someone miffed by pettiness. He didn't like that guy very much.

I chose this life for a reason. I knew what I was giving up. Let it go.

She will always be in my life, just not in that way… Marco is a fine man. They're good together.

He figured the best use of his time now would be to focus on something that thoroughly absorbed him. A project that would take his mind off the emotions that were haunting him.

The files from Feudatario were the logical diversion he needed. He opened the first folder on top of the tall stack.

As he examined each invoice, restoration detail sheet, and Condition Report for the various paintings Feudatario had taken in, one common name kept appearing: Eldon Anton Villard. *Why is that name familiar?* Dominic pondered. *Ah… the French billionaire.*

A titan in the luxury goods market, Eldon Villard owned several chic fashion houses, a prominent yacht manufacturer, and one of the largest private jet leasing companies in the world, among other diversified assets including large stakes in economic freeports based in Geneva, Luxembourg, and Trieste.

But apart from his ranking on the vaunted list of Forbes billionaires, he was most envied for his historically prestigious art collection. Villard's movements in the art world signaled important benchmarks in the industry, and his presence at international auctions ensured wildly competitive bidding, with the hammer usually falling in his favor. The value of his art collection had been estimated at over three billion euros, the largest accumulation of fine art in private hands.

Any desirable work of art Eldon Villard wanted, he got.

And from the records Dominic was rifling through, it appeared Villard had also commissioned a thriving restoration business with Palazzo Feudatario.

But what was not clear from these papers was whether Villard was the consignor for restorations, or the ultimate purchaser of paintings which had been restored. Dominic imagined these must go through some gallery instead, who were specially equipped for such transactions.

A gallery like Renzo Farelli's Studio Canal Grande? he wondered suspiciously.

Inspecting the documents more closely, there it was—the initials "SCG" next to Villard's name on numerous project consignment forms.

It was time to do a little gallery shopping. Surely Hana would be up for that.

CHAPTER

THIRTY-TWO

Toshi Kwan, the eager young technical lead for the Vatican Secret Archives' digitizing lab, was examining the illuminated pages of a magnificent Book of Hours from a 15th-century psalter when Cardinal Petrini walked in.

"Do you have a few minutes, Toshi?" Petrini asked.

"Of course, Eminence," Kwan replied, standing up. "How can I help you?"

Petrini's attention was drawn to the object of the technician's focus. "What have you got here?"

"This? Oh, it's a codex from the workshop of Jean Bourdichon, a miniature masterpiece we believe once belonged to either Pope Pius VI Braschi or Cardinal Francisco Zelada, who was prefect of the Pontifical Library in 1798. As you can see, there are two coats of arms, one here on the cover, the other on the back. But it has no title or name otherwise attributed to it. Fortunately, this copy survived Napoleon's pillaging of the Vatican in 1799."

As Kwan flipped through the pages, Petrini found it contained a calendar of Church feasts, extracts from the Four Gospels, Mass readings for major feasts, the fifteen Psalms of Degrees, and other common psalter illuminations.

"This is truly beautiful work. I really must take more time here, enjoying the gifts we have. You are quite devoted to your work, aren't you, Toshi? I envy you the experience. So much more joy than my job entails...." Petrini's mind drifted a moment, then his expression turned somber.

"The reason for my visit is unrelated to your fine work here, but as you are an IT expert—as recommended to me by Father Dominic—I have a request. You do have administrator access to the Vatican's computer network, yes?"

Kwan nodded.

"I want you to find anything related to Marcello Sabatini from the Vatican Museum. Email, text messages, file storage... whatever you can find, I'd like to know about it. How long do you think this might take?"

Kwan thought for a moment, then replied, "Probably only an hour, maybe less."

"Good. Please call me at once with your findings. And Toshi, this is confidential. Keep this between us, yes?"

FORTY-FIVE MINUTES later Kwan called Petrini's office. Father Nick Bannon answered the phone, then put the call through to his boss.

"What did you find, Toshi?" Petrini asked.

"Eminence, I've discovered something you may not like hearing, unless of course you've already sanctioned it.

"Go on."

"It appears Bishop Torricelli, head of the Vatican Museum's art restoration department, has installed spyware on his staff's computers. It's a rather odious program and highly intrusive, since it sweeps for and stores employees' personal data: email, text messages, internet browsing history, personal contact information—the bishop has built a significant database of material he shouldn't have access to, in my opinion anyway."

Petrini listened in silence, his anger growing as Kwan continued.

"But since you mentioned Signor Sabatini, he seems to have been especially targeted. In fact, I found a confidential email sent from Sabatini to Father Dominic in Torricelli's private folder, discussing forged paintings in the Vatican. You are mentioned— apparently Sabatini has already met with you on this matter?— and he says he is 'deeply distressed' by the situation. Is that what you were looking for?"

"That's exactly what I needed, Toshi. Thank you. Please email that letter to me now, if you will." Petrini hung up the phone, furious. He tapped the intercom to his secretary.

"Nick, get me the phone records of Bishop Torricelli's office as soon as you can, including his personal cell phone, for the past two weeks. You have my personal authority to do so."

Bannon called the Vatican switchboard. Speaking to Sister Teresa, the supervisor of the six nuns on duty, he passed on the Secretary of State's request. Since the Holy See owns its own phone company—the Vatican Telephone Service, a complex telecommunications and data network infrastructure designed and maintained by members of the Society of St. Paul—it took only a matter of minutes to acquire Petrini's requested documentation. Sister Teresa promptly emailed the package to Father Bannon, who printed out the call sheets and brought them into the cardinal's office.

Scanning each page, Petrini swiped a yellow highlighter across certain lines he found of interest, but two stood out as uncommonly frequent—and one of them was most disturbing.

Torricelli had made multiple calls that past week to Cardinal Abruzzo, the Patriarch of Venice. That might not have been so unusual, since Petrini knew Abruzzo's family owned Palazzo Feudatario, and Torricelli was in charge of the Vatican's art restoration business. Still, he found it suspect, since Abruzzo didn't handle day to day details of the business.

But the next name he found to whom several calls had been made was a complete shock.

Don Angelo Gallucci. The head of the Veneto Camorra clan.

A vision of deadly flames whipping through a car consumed Petrini's mind.

The bomb in Sabatini's car!

A studio full of forgeries!

All connected!

Was Torricelli involved in either of these operations? Was *he* the modern-day Vatican mole of Operation Scambio? And what about Abruzzo?

Petrini was staggered by the possible extent of involvements here. He needed to consult with Dominic about what he'd found.

Then another thought struck him. He glanced at his watch, then called his secretary again.

"Nick? Where's that armored truck? The Raphael should have been here by now."

CHAPTER

THIRTY-THREE

Having crossed the causeway out of Venice, the armored truck and its high-value cargo had passed through Mestre, then turned northeast—away from Rome and its intended destination of the Vatican. Its GPS tracking technology had been intentionally disabled.

On orders from Don Gallucci, the driver and guards—all on the payroll of the Camorra-owned armored truck agency—had instead headed toward the end of a narrow strip of Italian territory lying between the Adriatic Sea and Slovenia. Raphael's *Madonna of Foligno* would find its new home in the freeport of Trieste, and no one outside of Gallucci's intimate team would know of its existence there—except for the Raphael's new owner, Eldon Villard of Paris.

Freeports are, by and large, the province of the global ultra-wealthy elite, who store their priceless treasures there in complete anonymity and maximum security while their owners enjoy tax-free privileges, since, while stored in its secure environment, all goods are considered "in transit." Despite their physical presence in the host country, all such goods are deemed outside the Customs territory, thus deferring all duties and tax liabilities until the objects leave the well-protected property when they change ownership.

But few things ever left the freeport zone; indeed, there were even special luxury suites where owners of the objects could display, buy, and sell their objects freely, without taxation and in complete secrecy, which continue to remain in the privileged shelter afforded by the zone. Beyond its legitimate business, the Trieste Freeport—like similar economic free zones in other countries—also had the reputation of being an ideal place for transferring and storing black market artifacts, and the plunder gained from extensive money-laundering operations worldwide. Much of this exclusive inventory had been sitting there simply appreciating in value for decades. And few people would ever see it.

AFTER THE ARMORED truck left Venice, Giuseppe Franco gathered his tools—easel and paints, special pigments and solvents, brushes and other specialized implements—and packed his bags for an extended stay in Trieste to restart his work on the Raphael forgery in a special studio arranged at Don Gallucci's request. With nothing else to divert his attention from the task at hand, Giuseppe was a quick study in his work. He should have the painting reconstructed within a few days.

IN HIS OFFICE at the Vatican Museum, Bishop Torricelli's phone rang. Noting the Caller ID, he saw it was from the Secretary of State's office. He took a deep breath and prepared his response to what he knew would be asked of him.

"*Pronto*," he answered with a pretense of irritation.

"*Buona sera*, Excellency," Father Bannon said. "I am calling on behalf of Cardinal Petrini, who is asking as to the status of the armored truck carrying the Raphael. Can you give me an update?"

"Oh, the *nerve* of those people in Venice," he snarled, feigning anger. "Apparently the paperwork was prepared incorrectly, and when it left Venice it was dropped off at the airport there and sent on a flight to *Moscow!* Can you believe it?!" Torricelli fervently hoped he would.

Nick Bannon was apprehensive. This wasn't the kind of information he'd expected to deliver to his boss. He knew what the response would be.

"And when will this be sorted out? When will the painting be returned to Rome?"

"Given the bureaucratic delays Russians have in such matters, I expect we would see it back here in about two weeks. Hopefully."

"Two weeks?!" Bannon reacted as Petrini would have.

"It is beyond our capabilities to make their procedures move any faster, Father Bannon," Torricelli said with mock sympathy. "Please tell His Eminence I am terribly sorry, but it's out of my hands."

Bannon thanked the bishop and urged him to keep him apprised of the situation, ending the call.

Then he told the boss.

ANGELO GALLUCCI'S scheme had worked. With the authentic Raphael now safely stored in Trieste—under pretense of it being quagmired in Russia—and with Giuseppe now able to work on it free of interruptions, they had bought the precious time they needed.

But they now knew this reproduction had to withstand scrutiny when it was returned, since the Vatican was clearly harboring suspicions of authenticity.

Giuseppe Franco had no such fears. He was confident his

work was equal to or better than the Master's. Although he regretted the destruction of the replica he had already been working on at the Feudatario studio, he felt all the more energized to produce a forgery this time that could withstand any scrutiny.

Where Giuseppe might normally use such pigments as his meticulously hand-ground ultramarine—an ingredient not available until the late 19th century—he would instead use cobalt blue, a pigment in use since the 9th century, modified with other oil colors and solvents to achieve the same cast and hue as the original. It was more difficult to work with than the ultramarine but provided the authenticity to withstand greater scrutiny later.

As he began his work in the makeshift studio at the freeport, Giuseppe's first step was to prepare the canvas. He thought back to one of his historical predecessors, Terenzio da Urbino, a 17th-century conman who scavenged for shabby old canvases and frames, cleaned them up as best he could, then actually turned them into forged "Raphaels."

Giuseppe had brought with him several large, old worthless paintings from the same era, ones that Feudatario had stored in its sizable antiquated inventory. Each had been removed from its frame and rolled up for transit. Choosing one larger than the Raphael, he cut the canvas down to approximate the correct size, then scraped off all the existing paint until he reached the initial pale white substrate found beneath the original picture. He then mounted it to stretcher bars taken from one of the older pieces, trimmed accordingly.

Laying down a new foundational layer for the appropriate period, he would once again use his masterful skills to replicate Raphael's every brushstroke and nuance of color and shadow. After less than a week's effort, when he expected it to be done, he would bake a novel blend of hand-ground colors, along with lilac oil and Bakelite, in an oven at 200 degrees Celsius for about three hours. From experience, he knew this last layer would allow the final painting to appear radiant, with a surface that would react as expected to the traditional alcohol test, emulating the constituent oil chemicals of an Old Master rather than modern oil paints.

Toward the end, he would coat the painting with several layers of varnish, then when that had dried, roll it on a cracking cylinder to give it the veneer of ancient craquelure, the common minuscule cracks found on most old paintings; being Italian, these would have to give the impression of tiny bricks. To enhance the impression, he would coat the surface with India ink, which would then soak into the cracks, heightening the effect after cleaning off all other traces of ink from the varnish.

Lastly, he would rough up the canvas at various points, simulating the Raphael's slight abrasions and other apparent damage over time. Then he would remove the original from its frame, mount the forgery, using the exact frame from the original Raphael, including the original iron nails hammered into their same holes. The original would be remounted on another frame, however, one still representational of the era. The new owner won't care about the frame—it is the original canvas they would be paying millions to own.

Having performed this process numerous times before over many years without challenge, Giuseppe was certain his channeling of Raphael would produce a painting of remarkable identity to, if not better than, its original.

CHAPTER

THIRTY-FOUR

With his two bodyguards in tow, Agent Dario Contini of Italy's Art Squad strode into the Ca' Sagredo hotel like a man on a mission.

Splendidly dressed in a navy blue Armani blazer over a crisp white shirt, with a red Ferragamo tie and tan slacks, his compact frame was bookended by the two larger agents, whose shoulder-holstered weapons were discernible only to the trained eye.

Approaching the front desk, Contini announced himself—flashing a shiny gold badge as he did so—and asked for Father Michael Dominic's room.

"I will call the Padre to see if he is in, signore," the woman at the desk said. "One moment."

"I did not ask that he be called, signora. I asked for his room number."

Realizing the man's badge carried weight, she broke protocol and told Contini what room Dominic was staying in. As he and his team walked to the elevator, she remained on the phone, if only to alert her guest to the presence of official men paying him a visit.

When Dominic answered the phone, she relayed the

information. The priest thanked her and prepared for Contini's arrival.

"AND THAT'S PRETTY MUCH ALL of it," Dominic said, after regaling Contini with their exploits over the preceding week. The agent sat through all of it, listening intently while chewing his Black Jack gum and scribbling in a small Moleskine notebook he carried in his breast pocket.

"You say this painting is now in Moscow, sent there by accident?" the agent asked, his voice tinged with suspicion.

"Yes, apparently there was some mix-up in the Bill of Lading. I don't have all the details, but you could call Cardinal Petrini's office in Rome to see if they have further information."

"And your colleague, Dr. Gallo. Has her computer been retrieved yet?"

"No, I'm afraid not. But we have to assume the Camorra's involvement in its theft, which means they know everything we know about their operation... which we believe raises the stakes for all of us."

"I would not be too concerned about that now, Father. The more people who know, the less likely they would be to move to eliminate them. I would guess, however, that the gears of their machine are moving pretty rapidly now.

"I assume you were unaware that the Camorra owns the armored truck agency the Vatican used to transport the Raphael?"

Dominic was stunned to hear this. "No! But as I said, the Vatican made those arrangements. If that's the case, though, I doubt the painting would be in Russia."

"Yes, that would be my presumption as well," Contini said as he stood to look out the window. "Which likely means they still intend to reproduce the painting, wherever it is. They are probably doing so as we speak, in fact."

There was a knock on the door. Opening it, Dominic let Marco and Hana into the room, then introduced everyone.

"Since Marco's here now, he can give you more details on his encounter with a couple of Camorra goons he met up with," Dominic said, looking the Frenchman in the eyes.

Not appreciating having that particular door opened, Marco gave Dominic a dark look in return. *Two can play that game*, he thought, accepting the challenge of an alpha moment.

"Well, Hana and I were having a nice romantic dinner at the Gritti Terrace, you know, getting to know each other better...," he glanced back at Dominic for a moment, "when I noticed two men watching us from the fondomento." He continued the story, changing only the ending.

"And after a bit of a scuffle on their Chris Craft, one of them caught me off balance, pushing me into the canal. That's when they took off, heading back to Venice. We haven't seen them since." Marco placed a protective arm around Hana for good measure. Instinctively, she leaned into him. With one last look at Dominic, the commando simply smiled.

Contini felt the atmosphere in the room tense, but paid it no heed. "I wish these matters had been brought to our attention earlier."

"Yes," Dominic nodded, with a glance back at Marco, "thugs following citizens certainly should have been reported—"

"No," Contini interrupted him, looking directly at Dominic. "The duties of my office are clear, as you well know, Father. Forgeries. Which should be brought to the Art Squad as soon as suspected."

Dominic felt his face redden. He didn't dare glance toward Marco. The Italian Art Squad had been invaluable to him and Hana at previous times; it was certainly an oversight not to have informed them much sooner.

Contini tore a piece of paper out of his notebook, held it to his mouth, then spit his gum into it, tossing the wad into a trash bin.

"Such canal incidents should be reported to the Carabinieri. I am not here to investigate such things but to best determine whether a painting is genuine or a forgery, then take appropriate action as needed.

"Shall we go have a chat with Signor Farelli at his gallery?"

CHAPTER

THIRTY-FIVE

B ack aboard the police boat, Dario Contini directed the
uniformed officer driving to take them to Renzo Farelli's
posh Studio Canal Grande, on the ground floor of a
palazzo across from the Rialto.

The day was sunny and warm, and the piazzas were packed
with tourists of all nationalities. Several cruise ships had
dropped anchor in the lagoon earlier that morning, ferrying in
thousands of new arrivals who packed the shops and walkways,
eager to find mementos for their visit, partake of the famous
Venetian cuisine, or just tour the many art galleries and
museums.

Studio Canal Grande was one such destination, and befitting
its location at the foot of the Rialto Bridge, it was a natural draw
for those with a discerning eye for fine art. And today it was
packed.

Contini and the others entered and, while standing just inside
the door, the agent looked around the spacious, airy gallery. He
spotted security guards at various points, spotlessly dressed in
dark suits with coiled earphones, many of them standing next to
the most valuable paintings on the walls, most likely meant to
keep people from touching the rare works.

Looking at the art itself, he spotted works by Donatello, Brunelleschi, Bosch, Vasari, and Bellini, but mostly more contemporary and certainly lesser known artists.

As the others trailed behind him, Contini moved to a grim Hieronymus Bosch triptych to scrutinize it more closely. Titled *The Crucifixion of Saint Wilgefortis*, the oil on oak wood featured three panels depicting the crucifixion of a female saint before a rowdy crowd of spectators. Contini knew of the historical legend for the poor woman's fate: once a beautiful young girl, she was forced by her father to marry a Muslim king, but she prayed against it, pleading with God to lose her beauty and thus become unattractive to her intended. Miraculously, she grew a beard. And though the marriage was called off, her father had her crucified as punishment for her prayers.

Contini had seen this painting before, in the Palazzo Ducale in Venice, and later at the nearby Gallerie dell'Accademia di Venezia. That it was now here in Farelli's gallery made him curious, but he also knew galleries often traded art works for exhibitions and special events. Still, he peered at it up close, instinctively looking for any obvious signs of forgery.

Turning to the guard standing next to the work, he asked if Signor Farelli was in the gallery.

"*Si*, signore. He is in his office."

Contini flashed his badge and asked to see the owner. The guard, surprised by the man's official state rank, spoke into a concealed microphone in his jacket cuff.

Having received instructions in response, the guard said, "If you will follow me, signore." He led Contini to the back of the gallery, creating a path for the others to follow through the crowd of visitors. Reaching a private office, the guard knocked on the door.

"*Entrare*," said a voice from inside. The guard opened the door, letting Contini and his team into the office, then returned to his post.

Renzo Farelli looked up from whatever had been occupying

him on his desk to see six people file into the spacious office.

Farelli stood up, forcing a welcoming smile above the bulky knitted gray scarf encircling his neck.

"Ah, Padre Dominic, Signorina Sinclair, it is good to see you both again. And you have brought quite the delegation with you."

Contini wasted no time on subtleties. He pulled out his badge, raising it to Farelli's eyes.

"I am Special Agent Dario Contini with the Italian Art Squad, signore," he said. "We are here to discuss certain matters of importance with you. May we sit?"

"I wish you had called for an appointment, signore," Farelli said, looking at his watch. "I have a scheduled meeting here shortly... I—"

"This will not take long, I assure you."

Slightly disoriented and clearly exasperated, Farelli gestured for them all to take seats. Dominic, Hana, and Marco sat on a wide sofa while Contini took a seat in front of Farelli's desk. The two agents kept standing on either side of the door.

Contini pulled out his Moleskine notebook and turned to a page.

"Signor Farelli, this is simply an interview regarding certain subjects we will get to in a moment, but as an official of the state, I must caution you that any answers you give are subject to laws of perjury. Are we clear on that?"

Farelli shifted uncomfortably in his chair. "Yes, I understand. I have nothing to hide."

"Good to know," Contini asserted. "Now, are you associated in any way with Don Angelo Gallucci of the Veneto Camorra?"

"Everyone knows who Don Gallucci is, signore."

"I asked if you are associated with him."

"We do not have a personal relationship, no." Farelli gulped noticeably. He reached for the coffee cup on his desk, taking a sip of the now cold brew.

"Earlier this week a Raphael painting was transported from

Palazzo Feudatario destined for the Vatican, but it has apparently been shipped to Moscow in error. Are you aware of this?"

"Yes, word of such things travels fast in Venice, but I do not recall who told me."

"And when were you told?"

Farelli threw out his hands in a gesture of frustration. "Signore, I do not recall who *or* when."

"Were you involved in the disappearance or death of Father Carlo Rinaldo?"

Dominic sat up straighter, waiting for a response.

Farelli was adamant. "No, signore, neither of those things."

"One last question. Are you aware of something called Operation Scambio?"

Farelli sat back in his chair and steepled his fingers. "What was that name again?"

"Scambio. Operation Scambio."

"No. That does not sound familiar. Should it?"

Contini noticed Farelli look around the room at the others, avoiding his interrogator's eyes as he responded. The agent pulled out a stick of Black Jack, unwrapped the foil paper, and slid it into his mouth. As he chewed in the otherwise silent room, he looked Farelli in the eyes.

"If you are certain, signore, then that is all for now," Contini said, closing his notebook and returning it to his pocket. "I assume you have no plans to travel outside of Venice soon? Good. I may be back."

Contini had given no time for Farelli to answer the question, stating it more as a fact.

"A word of caution, Signor Farelli," Contini said, rising from his chair. "The Camorra appears to be running some kind of game here in Venice at the moment, much of it dealing with art works by Old Masters. Since that is your business, I would urge you to contact me if you encounter anything suspicious. *Sputa il rospo, si?*"

Marco whispered to Hana to translate Contini's exclamation. "What does he mean by *'spit the toad'*?"

"It's an old Italian idiom meaning *'Speak up!'*" she whispered back. "But the *way* he asked it implied a warning."

Farelli stood nervously as everyone left the office. Once the door was closed, he picked up his cell phone with trembling hands and made a call.

~

"I HAVE some work to do back at the hotel," Hana said to Contini as they all boarded the police boat. "Is there any further need for us to accompany you, Agent Contini?"

"No, signorina, thank you for your time. When are you all planning to leave Venice?"

Dominic looked around at the others, then answered for them. "We don't have a specific timeframe as yet, though we were thinking of going down to Florence for a day to speak with people at the Uffizi and Galleria dell'Accademia. But if we do, we'll come back here after that."

"If you do go," Contini said, "I would like to join you in Florence. Those two museums have had dealings with Feudatario Restorations as well, and I would like to see the works returned to them after restoration."

"Sure," Dominic replied. "That's what we were planning as well, and it would be good to have an expert with us since Signor Sabatini has removed himself from this investigation."

Just then the officer driving the boat, who had been listening to the police scanner, pulled Contini over to him, whispering something in his ear. Contini's face took a dark turn. Then he looked at Hana.

"Signorina, we have just received terrible news about your friend, Dr. Gallo," he whispered. "It seems a fisherman found her body in the lagoon off Murano. The Carabinieri would like to speak with you."

CHAPTER

THIRTY-SIX

Hana stared blankly at Contini, as if she hadn't understood what he said. *No, that can't be right. Livia just left for Rome a couple days ago. There must be some mistake.*

Both Dominic and Marco rushed to either side of her as her legs gave out, her mind unable to adjust to both the news and the boat rocking in the waves. The impact of the news finally registering, her eyes glistened, then tears flowed down her cheeks.

"Hana, here, sit down," Dominic urged, guiding her to the aft bench seat in the boat.

"It's my fault," she sobbed, her hands covering her face. "She would be alive now, if not for *me*. Who would do something so awful to such a lovely woman?"

Marco and Dominic looked at each other, already knowing the answer.

"I take responsibility for this," Marco said assertively. "Knowing the risks, I should have accompanied her to the train station. *Merde!*"

"This is not your fault, Hana," Dominic agreed. "You know nothing would have kept Livia away from holding that Vivaldi material in her own hands, the reason she came to Venice in the first place. And she made such a substantial contribution to our work here. It was a high point in her life, she told me. You can't take this out on yourself."

"Let's go back to the hotel, Michael," she said, sniffling. "I need some time alone before speaking with the police."

BOTH DOMINIC AND Marco escorted Hana back to her suite at the Ca' Sagredo. Before they left, Marco checked each room in her suite and double checked the locked door behind them, saying they would return in an hour or so to take her to the Carabinieri station.

Meanwhile, they both went down to the bar to talk over their next moves. Dominic texted Karl, asking that he and Lukas join them.

A few minutes later all four men were seated at a table, a bottle of beer set on cardboard deckels in front of each of them.

"Art isn't really my world," Dominic began. "The Secret Archive has little to do with the Vatican Museum, and yet I find myself mired in matters relating to it. If Marcello Sabatini hadn't backed out, he'd be here in my place. But someone needs to look out for the Vatican's interests, and since I'm here, that's me."

"And where you go, we go," Karl said, taking a long draw on his beer. Then, glancing at Lukas, he added, "Oh, I just spoke with our commander, who approved our extra time here. Cardinal Petrini stressed to him the importance of our mission."

"One person we haven't considered in all this yet is Eldon Villard. He appears to be the most prominent and frequent buyer of Feudatario's 'restorations.'"

"You mean one of the wealthiest men on the planet is now involved?!" Karl asked, stunned by Dominic's comment.

"I kept finding his name as the ultimate buyer or restoration consignor on all those files you took from Feudatario. I'm not sure what that means for our purposes, but I thought I'd toss it out."

"Maybe Hana's grandfather might help us get to him, if we need to," Marco suggested. "They run in the same circles."

"Good point," Dominic said, absently flipping his deckel on its sides. "Baron Saint-Clair has powerful connections."

"In the meantime," Marco said, "Michael, will you take Hana to the Carabinieri? I have a little business to attend to."

"Anything we should know about?"

"It's probably best you don't."

Karl, sensing something dangerous in Marco's eyes, wanted in. "Need any help, Marco? Lukas and I are ready and willing."

The commando thought for a moment. "No, this is something I need to take care of myself, thanks. You should stay with Hana and Michael."

THE SUN WAS STARTING to set as Marco spent the past hour idling the boat in the shadows across the canal from Palazzo Feudatario, watching for any personnel movement. He had seen Don Gallucci leave with two guards a half hour earlier, and the building had remained quiet since. He decided it was time to move.

Maneuvering the Aquariva up the canal a bit, then motoring across the water so as not to be seen, he tied the boat to a public dock a couple palazzos away from Feudatario. Fastening an Osprey silencer onto the business end of his specially-fitted Glock 17, he jumped over the railing and made for the palazzo.

There was one guard at the door, a brutish fellow with his back to Marco as he approached quietly on foot from the eastern walkway. Using the butt of his pistol across the back of his head, the guard went down with a thud.

Marco tried the door. It was unlocked. Entering the foyer, he heard two voices in a nearby room, one a woman's, the other that of a young man, laughing. Raising his Glock, he rounded the corner and entered the room.

Valentina and Aldo looked up, surprised. Neither of them moved.

"Who are you, and what are you doing in here? This is a private residence," Valentina said, anger in her voice.

"It doesn't matter who I am," the Frenchman said tersely. "What does matter is that a friend of mine was murdered by you people, and I'm here to find out who did it."

Valentina instinctively glanced over at Livia's laptop, still sitting on the desk. Marco caught the turn of her head, then noticed the computer's African Padauk cover. He turned knowingly to Valentina.

"Well, look here. Caught red-handed with the evidence. Would you care to explain how you obtained Dr. Gallo's laptop?"

Marco then looked up at the young man. "*You...* You work at the hotel. So it all comes together now, *oui? You* stole the computer from Livia's room."

Without thinking it through, the impetuous young Aldo reached for a letter opener on the desk next to him and lunged at Marco. A slight but confident swing of the Glock and pull of the trigger, and Aldo fell onto the floor, a bullet hole piercing his forehead. The letter opener flew into the air, landing with a clank on the floor next to Valentina's feet.

She screamed. Marco swung the pistol in her direction, aiming for her own head.

"Now, tell me what you know about Dr. Gallo's murder."

Though shaken, the woman spoke with determination. "You do not know who you are dealing with. Take the computer if you want and get out of here, while you still can, or you will end up the same as your friend."

"*Merci,*" Marco said, "that was all I needed to know. This is for Livia." He pulled the trigger, and the muffled spit of the Glock found its mark.

Valentina's body remained upright in the chair, but her head fell backward, her open eyes staring up at the ceiling.

Marco moved to pick up both spent cartridges from the floor, then walked over to the desk, picked up the laptop, looked around the room for anything else of interest, and left through the front door. The guard was still out cold.

Walking casually down the fondomento to the Aquariva, he unfastened the cleat lines, then cruised back to the hotel.

CHAPTER

THIRTY-SEVEN

I t only took Giuseppe Franco several days to finish his Raphael masterpiece. Isolation in the Trieste freeport's studio and his virtually nonstop dedication to the task also made it among his fastest forgeries. Even he could not distinguish between the copy and the original. It was his finest work yet, he marveled. *Don Gallucci will be pleased.*

Phoning the *capintesta*, Giuseppe asked what he was expected to do next.

"There's been a change in plans. Keep the copy there in the freeport, Giuseppe," Don Gallucci said. "That will be transferred to Monsieur Villard at his freeport in Luxembourg, while the original will be returned to the Vatican. Things are too exposed for us here just now, and we cannot take the risk of being discovered on this one. If the forgery is as good as you say, Villard won't know the difference.

"I'm meeting with Cardinal Abruzzo now, but when I get back, I will have Valentina arrange for an armored truck to pick up the Raphael this afternoon. You return to Venice as soon as you can. We have an extraordinary Tintoretto coming in from the Uffizi that will be your next project."

Calling his office to relay the instructions, there was no

answer. Assuming his staff was away, he'd take the matter up with Valentina later.

Meanwhile, owing to the change of who would get which painting, Giuseppe had to restore the original frame back onto the authentic Raphael. For the copy, he had it wrapped in an Italian 17th-century Sansovino frame, with gilded surface and ornamentation in the form of overlapping scrolls, volutes, and cherubs, suitable for the time period and the Veneto region of its sculptor, Jacopo Sansovino.

Signor Villard should be quite happy with it.

"Good news, Eminence," Cardinal Abruzzo said to Cardinal Petrini after calling the Secretary of State. "Your Raphael *Madonna of Foligno* will be on its way back to you soon. We pushed through the Russian bureaucracy and have liberated the painting from Moscow. An armored truck will deliver it to the Vatican tomorrow."

Petrini was nonplussed. "Thank you, Salvatore. Our curators will inspect it most carefully on its arrival. Oh, and would you provide me with the freight paperwork as well? I want to ensure that such mistakes can be prevented in the future."

Petrini assumed his ploy would be received unexpectedly by Abruzzo. If the Moscow transfer was legitimate, there should be no problem. If it was a ruse, he expected some sort of obfuscation on delivering the bills of lading and customs documents.

"I... yes, I will, uh, do what I can to get that for you, Eminence. Unfortunately, the truck has already left, but I will ask my assistant to make those arrangements for you. Is there, um, anything else?"

"No, that is all for now, Salvatore. *Arrivederci.*"

Father Bannon was sitting across from the cardinal as he pressed the speakerphone's off button.

"I don't trust that bastard, Nick. He has turned against the Church, I'm sure of it. Keep an eye out for that paperwork, will you? It may be key to testing his loyalty or betrayal in this matter."

"Of course, Eminence," Bannon said. "But for what it's worth, I agree with you. Cardinal Abruzzo knows his tenure as Patriarch is secure, but his actions reveal those of a rogue provocateur. He inspires a lack of confidence in his actions."

"Let's keep watch on him, Nick. As for his collaborator Bishop Torricelli, I have plans for him, too."

CARDINAL ABRUZZO TURNED to Don Gallucci, who had been listening on speakerphone to the conversation.

"Obviously he now knows about Operation Scambio, Angelo," Abruzzo scowled. "I want you to create whatever paperwork might be necessary to prove this 'Moscow transfer' concoction. Make it look good, then have it sent to the Vatican."

"I'll have Valentina get right on it, Eminence."

"In the meantime, perhaps we should lie low for a while. If Petrini puts a magnifying glass on our activity, that won't end well."

"We do have Tintoretto's *Leda and the Swan* coming in from the Uffizi this week. It's a big prize, Eminence, one we've wanted to get our hands on for some time now, and the restoration needed is long overdue, anyway. Let us work on that, then we can put things on hold for a bit. The Uffizi will wonder why we cannot take it on otherwise. That might cause other kinds of problems on its own."

Abruzzo looked agitated. "Alright, just this one for now. Of course, you can take in others for legitimate restoration, so business keeps coming in, but as for Scambio, we need to take a break until Father Dominic and his people have left Venice and things have cooled down."

"I agree. They cannot stay here forever, and we dare not make things messy for them. I think you get my meaning...."

Abruzzo gave Gallucci a knowing look, but chose not to acknowledge the intent of his meaning.

"We will speak again soon, Angelo. *Ciao*."

As Don Gallucci's launch pulled up to the dock at Palazzo Feudatario, he noticed there was no guard standing at the door. Then he looked at the ground below the light, seeing Nico laying there.

"Looks like we've had company," he said to one of his men who was tying off the boat. "You, check to see Nico's condition when you're done."

The other man cautiously drew his pistol as he and Gallucci approached the entrance. Opening the door, the guard went in first, clearing the way for the Don to enter. Passing through the foyer, he entered the office. Staring at the scene, he lowered his weapon.

"Boss," he said, turning to face Gallucci, "you're not going to like this."

CHAPTER

THIRTY-EIGHT

D on Angelo Gallucci looked at the bodies of his two employees, furious their palazzo had been breached. "Show me the recording," he demanded of the guard.

Opening the tall black Gardall safe in his office, Don Gallucci checked to make sure the ancient, highly incriminating Coscia Journal was still intact. It was. At least they didn't get that.

Watching the CCTV recording, Gallucci saw it was just one man, the one they call Marco. He saw Aldo lunge for the commando, then Aldo go down after one shot from the Glock. Then he watched and listened as Valentina argued with him and Marco taking her out the same way. The last words she heard were, "This is for Livia." He then walked over to the Gallo woman's laptop, tucked it under his arm, looked around, and left the office.

Don Gallucci sat at his desk, considering suitable retribution.

∾

THE NEXT MORNING Trenitalia's Frecciargento *Silver Arrow* pulled out of the Santa Lucia station in Venice for a two-hour rail journey through the northern Italian countryside, bound for Florence.

Sitting in a first class car, Michael Dominic, Hana Sinclair, Marco Picard, and Dario Contini had gathered in a wide booth with a table between them, on which had been laid out interior maps of both the Uffizi Gallery and Galleria dell'Accademia di Firenze. His two security agents sat in nearby seats. After buying bottled water for everyone, Karl and Lukas sat in a seat further forward in the car.

"From the details you found in Feudatario's files," Contini explained, "I have marked the locations of those paintings we must examine. This will save us a bit of time, I think." He had slashed red 'X's along certain walls in each of the many galleries, halls, and pavilions of each institution.

"I have called ahead to the directors of each gallery, informing them of our arrival and mission. They will be most cooperative."

"I'm still not sure why it's necessary that we come along," Hana said, "not that I ever mind visiting Florence." It being a warm day, she drank thirstily from her water bottle.

"Well, first," Dominic said, "Agent Contini might need help from the Vatican, which I can more easily accommodate. Second, look at this as a great story idea—*Historical forgeries through the centuries!* Not that the Church wants that kind of publicity, but you could surely work around the more sensitive parts, if you were so inclined. And last, who doesn't want unrestricted access to two of the foremost art galleries in the world?! I have to admit, it's that last part that intrigues me most. Amazing how many doors a badge can open." He looked at Contini, who smiled self-importantly.

"Besides," the agent added, "the more proof we have, the faster we can shut down those scoundrels at Feudatario. They've been getting away with this for far too long. It would be good to see them all find a new home in Rome's Regina Coeli prison."

"Where they can join our old nemesis, Cardinal Dante," Hana

said with some satisfaction, referring to the former archbishop of Buenos Aires who had been incarcerated as a result of their last adventure together.

"From what I recall," Dominic said, "Marcello Sabatini had already notified the curator at the Uffizi, Giancarlo Piovani, about Operation Scambio. He's probably the one we should speak with there."

"Yes, it was he with whom I spoke," Contini confirmed. "We will meet with him first."

~

BEGUN in 1560 as a repository for the vast personal art collection of Cosimo I de Medici and his family—along with administrative offices for Florentine magistrates at the time—the Uffizi Gallery is one of Italy's most prominent museums and undoubtedly its most popular.

Home to an immense and comprehensive collection of Florentine paintings from the Late Gothic, Renaissance, and Mannerist periods, the Uffizi's needs for restoration were frequently outsourced to qualified specialists known for their dedication to preserving the finest of the finest.

After the taxi bus dropped them off at the entrance to the gallery on the banks of the Arno River, Dominic and the others walked through the grand façade on Piazzale degli Uffizi and on into the grand atrium, where they were met by Signor Piovani, the chief curator.

"Let us go to my office upstairs," he offered.

"Michael," Karl said, "Since you're in good hands here, Lukas and I are just going to explore the museum, if that's alright. Call us if we're needed?"

"You bet, Karl, have fun."

Leading the others down the West Corridor, Piovani walked them up the great 16th-century marble Buontalenti Staircase to the second floor, then past the Barocci and Lombard Rooms, the

Tintoretto and Veronese Halls, and across the second corridor to the administrative offices overlooking the river.

Dominic, Hana, and Marco's heads were spinning, trying to take in the stunning works of art they passed despite the speed Piovani was traveling, hoping they might have time to see more of the treasures after their meeting.

After introductions were made, they each took a seat in the curator's office, then Contini began.

"It is my understanding, signore, that you have been in contact with Signor Sabatini at the Vatican regarding this Camorra operation they call Scambio. Is that right?"

"*Sì*, I have spoken with Marcello. This is all very disturbing, since we have done business with Feudatario Restorations for decades. In fact, I have only learned today that we just shipped Tintoretto's *Leda and the Swan* to Venice yesterday for some minor work. On its return, I shall inspect it most carefully myself to ensure it is the authentic one we sent."

"May we see these paintings on which Feudatario has done work in the past?" Contini presented a list of some twenty artists and titles. "We got these names from their own records, and I would like to make sure you have the originals and not the forgeries."

"Of course, signore. We will begin with the Titians."

Piovani led them through various rooms and smaller galleries dedicated to each artist, where Contini, wearing white cotton gloves, inspected various sections of each selected piece closely with a magnifying loupe and a blacklight pen, lightly touching the paint in certain sections to ensure nothing rubbed off on his gloves, and generally looking for telltale forgery flaws.

"If you have not yet had these X-rayed, signore, I would suggest that you do so at once," Contini suggested, "and while you are at it, put tiny grains of the paint through spectroscopic analysis. It would be a wise investment of your time, I assure you."

Signor Piovani swallowed hard as he nodded, the obvious insinuation from Contini's words disturbing.

Looking down the hall, Hana excused herself to use the ladies room.

"I'll go with you and find the gent's," Marco said. "They must be next to each other."

"I know what you're doing, you know," she said, looking into Marco's eyes.

"No, really! I do need to use the men's room... but I still have a job to do." He smiled at her as they turned back toward the west corridor and down the stairs to the entrance and restrooms.

Dominic watched them walk away arm in arm and took a deep breath. *I've got to let this go... What the hell's wrong with me?!*

With their footsteps echoing down the marble hall, Hana took in the ancient statuary and Renaissance paintings as they walked, while Marco instinctively looked at people. Not being peak tourist season yet, the museum was sparsely occupied.

Turning the corner to the restrooms, Marco stopped in his tracks. Looking toward the entrance of the museum, he recognized a man he had seen before heading to the door. Before exiting, the man turned and looked directly at Marco, then ran outside.

It was the guard from Feudatario who Karl had taken down!

"I'll be right back, Hana. I think I saw someone I know." Rather than run and draw attention to himself, Marco walked hurriedly toward the exit.

THE HOUSEKEEPING STAFF had been cleaning the ladies' room as Hana approached the doorway. The maid had parked a large rolling janitor's trolley just outside the door as she was coming out.

"You can go in now, signorina. I'm finished," she said, avoiding Hana's eyes.

As Hana entered the room, her phone rang. It was her

grandfather, Armand de Saint-Clair. As she made her way to a stall, she answered it.

"*Bonjour*, Grand-père! So lovely to hear from you. Can I call you ba—"

Just as she was about to open the lavatory door, someone in the next stall was coming out. Before she said another word, she was grabbed from behind by a man, pushed inside the cramped stall, and a cloth with the distinct smell of chloroform was pressed firmly over her mouth and nose. Trying to fend off her attacker, she let go of the phone, which clattered to the floor. She flung her arms futilely to escape as darkness enveloped her mind. In ten seconds she hung limp in the stranger's grip.

The maid quickly came back in rolling the trolley in front of her. She and her male accomplice picked Hana up and squeezed her body in the lower section, which was hidden by cloth drapes on all sides. Wheeling the bin out of the room, they headed down the hall to a door marked *Privato*. Using a key from a ring on his belt, the man unlocked it, then pushed the trolley through, closing the door behind them. They were now in the maintenance area, with a loading dock on the outside wall.

The woman ran to an exit door next to a truck ramp and opened it. A white delivery van was waiting for them just outside, its engine rumbling. The man took Hana's body out from under the trolley, tossed her over his shoulder, then placed her in the back of the van. Both of them jumped in behind Hana and slammed the door shut. The vehicle started up and made its way out of employees' parking lot, losing itself in the heavy traffic of Florence.

EXITING THE MUSEUM, Marco raced after the Feudatario guard, who had just turned a corner. Running as fast as he could, he finally reached the corner, only to see a green Peugeot SUV speeding away. No one else was in the vicinity. The car had obviously been waiting, motor running. *Merde! MERDE!*

Have I been played?

Racing back into the Uffizi, Marco ran toward the restrooms. He pounded on the door to the ladies room.

"Hana?" he shouted. "*HANA?!*" No answer. He opened the door and asked if anyone was in there. Again, no answer. Pushing his way inside, he slammed open every stall door. Hana wasn't there. But he found an iPhone on the floor in one stall, the glass face of it covered in cracks. He picked it up and pocketed it.

Running back through the museum, taking the steps two at a time back upstairs to where they had left Dominic and the others, he finally found the group. Gasping, he asked, "Has Hana come back here?"

Dominic looked surprised. "No, last time we saw her was when you two left."

Breathing heavily, Marco cursed again, hands on his hips, walking in tight, frenzied circles.

"They have her, Michael... The bastards took Hana!"

CHAPTER
THIRTY-NINE

Pierluigi Falco snapped open a vial of smelling salts under Hana Sinclair's nose. Awakening with a jerk of her head, she turned away from the acrid smell of ammonia and groggily opened her eyes.

"What happened? Where am I? Who are you?"

"You can call me Pierluigi. As for the other questions, we'll have time for those," Falco replied softly with a vague lisp. "First, sit up and have some water."

Hana pulled herself up from the bed she had been lying on. The youngish man standing over her was of average height and bony thin, with sparse blond hair and a sallow, pitted face. He seemed kind enough. But then she remembered this wasn't where she was supposed to be.

"So, I assume you're part of the Camorra, and that I've been kidnapped?" she asked almost matter-of-factly. After smelling the water, she took a sip.

"Kidnapping brings up such crude images. Let's just say you're our guest here for a while."

"How long is a while, Pierluigi? And where is 'here'?"

"So many questions, and such a clever girl," Falco said, feyly cocking his head and smiling mischievously. "I can't tell you *that* now, can I?"

What a strange creature, Hana thought. She looked around the room, which was decorated in purple themes, with whimsical furniture and crazed wall hangings, an orange lava lamp on the nightstand and bookshelves packed with creepy dolls of every nationality. Hana felt like a captive in Alice's Wonderland.

She also noticed the windows had bars on the outside, and she was in a building three or four stories up. Maybe this was an asylum.

"Now you just relax here for a while and I'll bring you a nice dinner later on," Falco singsonged. Wriggling his fingers as he waved back to her, he left the room, then closed and locked the door from the outside.

"I NEVER SHOULD HAVE LET myself be drawn out like that," Marco said, punishing himself for leaving Hana unprotected.

"While I wouldn't argue with you on that," Dominic said, "now is not the time for self-recrimination. What does your instinct tell you they might do to her, Marco?"

The former Green Beret paced the room, thinking.

"I expect this might be in retaliation for something I did at Feudatario yesterday. Without going into details, I retrieved Livia's computer and got in some payback for her murder. But they know we mean business now."

"Oh, great," Dominic sniped. "And look what 'meaning business' has gotten us into now."

"Michael, I truly am sorry. But insulting me won't help matters. Let's try to work this out together, alright?"

Dominic reddened, then softened his tone. "Alright. Sorry. So now what?"

"I have to think that bringing harm to Hana will not further their interests. Quite the opposite, it will bring down an army of hurt on them, and they know that, given the authorities are helping us out. No, I think something else is at play here. We'll just have to wait and see, hoping they contact us. Florence is a big place, and Hana would be impossible to find here."

There was something about what Marco had just said that struck Dominic as familiar, but he couldn't quite place it. *What was it? What's so familiar?*

Then he remembered.

"*Marco!* Hana might still have an AirTag in her wallet! We tested this about a year ago and it came in handy during a similar emergency. Hana had been kidnapped by the Ustasha, and we used an AirTag to find her!"

"What is this AirTag?" Marco asked.

"It's an ultra-compact disc, a tracking device developed by Apple that carries Bluetooth and ultra-wideband signals. You can affix them to most any object you want to keep track of, and locate them from any distance using the 'Find My' app. All the tag needs is *any* iPhone within a ten-meter range to relay its low-energy encrypted signal, even a phone belonging to someone else in a crowd! The tag then sends its location signal to the home device—that would be *my* iPhone—using iCloud and, as you French would say, *et voila!* The tag is found. Hopefully Hana still has it in her bag, and they've let her keep it."

"Well, what are you waiting for?!" Marco urged him excitedly. "Open your iPhone!"

Just then, Dominic's phone rang. Surprised at the timing, he looked up at Marco, then answered it on speaker so they both could listen.

"Is this Father Dominic?" the voice asked.

"It is. Who's this?"

"My name is irrelevant. But I imagine you know by now that we have your friend, Signorina Sinclair. Be assured no harm will come to her as long as you do exactly as I ask."

"And that is...?"

"She is the granddaughter of Baron Armand de Saint-Clair, chairman of Banque Suisse de Saint-Clair in Geneva, yes?"

"I'm sure you already know she is," Dominic snapped. "So what's your point?"

"We are holding your friend in exchange for two million euros. It should be a simple matter for the baron to arrange, in small denominations, non-sequential. You have twenty-four hours. Keep your phone near you, Padre. We will call back then with further instructions." The caller hung up.

Dominic's fingers raced to locate the Find My app, then tapped on it to open. He punched the menu option for "*Hana's Wallet*," then waited for it to find the signal.

It showed the last known location was at the museum, in the restroom most likely, and the time shown was about fifteen minutes ago.

"Well, this means one of two things. First, no one near her has an active iPhone—at least not yet. Second, she may have previously removed the AirTag from her bag. Though I can't imagine her doing that, since she knows it's come in handy more than once. Unless she's changed bags."

"Didn't you say she kept it in her wallet?"

"Yes."

"Well, women may change bags frequently, depending on the outfit, but the wallet usually remains the same," Marco asserted confidently. "But you could not be expected to know that. After all, you are not French."

Dominic sighed and rolled his eyes. "I also happen to be a priest, one with little experience in women's handbag etiquette."

Marco regarded him, then nodded. "*Oui.* That makes sense too."

"We just need to keep checking back, hoping someone with an iPhone comes near her bag."

"I don't know that I have the patience for that," Marco agonized. "I'm still kicking myself for such a foolish rookie mistake."

"Again, no argument from me," Dominic said, then quickly added, "but it isn't like I haven't also made serious mistakes. We just go on from here." He wanted to resent Marco's error for other reasons beyond his failure at protecting his best friend but the tension between them served no purpose. Nothing mattered at the moment but saving Hana.

"I suppose I'll have to call the baron and get things moving." Marco said. "But if we do find Hana's location, be prepared for battle. Let's get Karl and Lukas prepped, too. Good thing they came with us."

Dominic's phone rang again. "Speak of the devil, it's Armand. You should take it."

Marco snatched the phone from Dominic's hand, answering it.

"Baron, it's Marco. Yes, Michael is with me here. I'm sorry to report I have some bad news." He listened to the baron say he had just been speaking with Hana when the line went dead. Marco then related the events and the kidnappers' demands, asking how he would like to handle the situation.

"Well, of course money is not an issue. I'll arrange for that immediately," Saint-Clair said tersely, "but how could you let this happen, Marco? I trusted you to protect Hana from just this kind of thing!"

"Sir, you know I will do everything in my power to get her back. Michael and I have a plan but it depends on technology and logistics; I won't go into details, but if it works, I will personally handle the situation and bring Hana back safely. We also have two very capable Swiss Guards here to help us out. You must trust me, Baron. I will not fail you." With a mixture of fury and embarrassment, Marco's face was glistening with a light sheen of sweat as he paced the room while speaking.

The baron was just as apprehensive. "I will have two million euros wired to the BNP Paribas bank in Florence when we're finished here. It will be in my account there, accessible in your name, Marco. Do whatever it takes to get my granddaughter back safely. Based on what she's already told me, I assume you're dealing with the Camorra?"

"Yes, sir. Though they did not identify themselves, that's my assumption as well. We've been causing them quite a few headaches this past week. But despite that, kidnapping is one of their more principled businesses. Once payment is made, they're known for always returning the victim."

Marco failed to mention that he'd killed many of the Camorra's own assets lately, and there *was* a chance of retribution killing despite the ransom payment—though he hoped they conducted this particular job as they normally would. The Mafia's honor was at stake, after all. If word got around that their victims were killed after payment was made, that lucrative business would dry up faster than spit on a Sicilian sidewalk.

"Let me know the minute you have more news, Marco. I'm counting on you." The baron ended the call.

Dominic kept checking the Find My app to see if any iPhone had come near Hana's AirTag tracker, with no luck yet.

CHAPTER

FORTY

S et in the fashionable upmarket district of Muette in Paris's 16th Arrondissement, on the west bank of the River Seine, Eldon Villard's 40-room villa was home to one of the world's foremost art collections.

The 18th-century mansion boasted a quintessentially Parisian setting, with a façade built from locally sourced limestone of the kind that was used on the exteriors of Notre Dame Cathedral and the Louvre, with grey slate tiles on the mansard roof, and tall casement windows with splendid views of the Eiffel Tower just across the river.

But this villa was specially rebuilt only with art in mind. Every room was constructed such that its interior layout was secondary only to the walls, on which were hung many of the world's finest paintings, a pristine collection valued in the multi-millions of euros. Apart from impressive security technology and on-premises guards, the villa was also protected by a state-of-the-art fire extinguishing system, one that sucked oxygen from the atmosphere rather than using water which would damage works of art.

Eldon Villard had a keen eye and an unquenchable passion for the Old Masters, which he often bought and infrequently sold. But his larger collection was securely maintained at the expansive freeport complex in neighboring Luxembourg, where —like most high-net-worth individuals who use freeports for such purposes—he was free to buy, sell and trade pieces without the burdens of taxation or Customs duties, or the inquisitive pursuits of law enforcement authorities.

A tall aristocratic sort favoring Fioravanti bespoke suits and Louis Vuitton Richelieu wingtips crafted from waxed alligator leather, Villard's business enterprises constantly took him around the globe, where he would check in with his favorite galleries for the latest treasures they held aside exclusively for his approval. His private jet of choice getting there was a gleaming silver Gulfstream G650ER, allowing him to fly almost halfway around the world before needing to refuel.

The jet had just taken off from Le Bourget in Paris for the Friuli Venezia Giulia Airport in Trieste, where Villard would view one of his most prized acquisitions yet—Raphael's *Madonna of Foligno*. As he sat in the main cabin nursing a flute of Louis Roederer Cristal champagne, a superior 2013 vintage, he reviewed the Condition Report and provenance records of the piece. He was well aware that it had come from the Vatican, making him even more covetous. How Renzo Farelli's Studio managed that bit of expropriation was not his concern. The painting would always remain in his private storage locker —actually more an interior series of small steel-reinforced luxury warehouse suites—in the Luxembourg Freeport anyway, so no one would ever see it but him. At 57, Eldon Villard had made it. He could have and do anything he wanted.

~

The Frecciarossa *Red Arrow* sped Renzo Farelli from Venice to the Trieste Centrale station in just under two hours, during which time he had immersed himself on the Condition Report of the Raphael. He needed to speak fluently about the painting when he met Eldon Villard.

From the train station, Farelli was picked up by a dark limousine sedan and taken to the Trieste Freeport, where he was greeted by its director, Pietro Meloni, while they both waited for Villard's plane to arrive.

"He should be here within thirty minutes or so, Signor Farelli. In the meantime, would you like a tour of the freeport?"

"No, thank you. But I would like to see the painting while we're waiting. Can you take me to it?"

"Of course, please follow me, signore."

Meloni led him through a maze of gently lit hallways lined with state-of-the-art brushed steel doors, each equipped with biometric handprint identification panels and retinal scanners. The walls of each spacious storage room were composed of half-meter thick steel-reinforced cellular concrete, with fire suppression and prevention equipment that reduced the oxygen ratio in each room. Since air normally contains around 21% oxygen, the system lowered this to around 16% percent oxygen, preventing fires from even starting.

Meloni stopped in front of Vault 42, held his hand up to the ID panel and rested his chin on the retinal scanner support. There was a confirming acceptance tone, then the smooth grind of heavy bolts retracting, and the steel door silently swung open.

Stepping into the room, Meloni ran his hand over a wall panel that initiated a slowly rising beam of custom LED lighting, illuminating the stunning Raphael hanging on the center wall with custom LUX levels enhancing every color and shadow of the piece. This room was clearly designed for displaying art of the finest quality.

Impressed with the freeport's attention to detail, Farelli walked into the room and stood in awe of the painting before him. He knew, of course, that this was Giuseppe's forgery, but it was thoroughly indistinguishable from the original. His trained eye examined every area of the piece, satisfied that Villard would be quite pleased with his purchase.

And at 25 million euros, it would be the Camorra's largest sale yet.

The sound of footsteps approaching made Farelli turn back toward the door. Entering the room were four people, three men —two of them obviously personal security guards—and a woman, presumably an assistant. The easily recognized Eldon Villard stepped up to Farelli, holding out his hand.

"Signor Farelli, I presume?"

"*Oui*, Monsieur Villard, it is a great honor to meet you," Farelli gushed. Then, turning with a flourish of his arm, he presented Raphael's *Madonna of Foligno*.

"Is she not spectacular in every way?" he asked, clasping his hands.

Villard took in a deep breath, gazing at the painting. He stood in front of it for a few moments, then walked from side to side, viewing it at different angles.

"There isn't a better word to describe it," he said in almost a whisper. Then, decisively, "I shall take it. Signor Meloni, would you be so kind as to make arrangements for it to be moved to my jet? It will go directly to my vault at the Luxembourg Freeport, so please ensure the paperwork reflects that it is in transit only between freeports."

"We have already prepared the shipping container, Signor Villard, and all papers have been completed, as your assistant requested earlier. We will have it delivered by armored van to your jet within the hour."

"Is there a conference room where Signor Farelli and I might have a conversation in the meantime?" Villard asked.

"Of course, if you'll follow me..." Meloni waited until everyone had left the room, then secured the door.

The freeport director led the group back toward the entrance of the building and into a lavish conference room overlooking the waters of the Gulf of Trieste. While the security detail waited outside the door, Farelli, Villard and his assistant went inside and took seats.

"Signor Farelli," Villard began, "I well appreciate the risks you have taken to deliver such a fine piece to me, and I am more than grateful. However, a man in my position needs to be sure there will be no repercussions from certain parties as to my personal involvement in this matter. Are we in agreement?"

"Yes, absolutely, signore. As far as anyone is concerned, you are invisible to the transaction."

"Good. Then the matter is settled. I will have the funds wired to your Swiss account immediately. My assistant has the details." He motioned to the woman sitting across from him, who nodded, then picked up her iPad and executed the transaction.

"If there is any issue at all," Villard continued, a grave tone to his voice, "we will speak again."

He rose from his chair, shook Farelli's hand, then left the conference room. With a quick wave to Meloni, his entourage swiftly left the building and got into a black Mercedes limousine waiting outside the entrance.

Renzo Farelli was shaking with a mixture of joy and trepidation. Joy at the sheer size and smoothness of the transaction; trepidation at the consequences should Eldon Villard ever discover he had just paid 25 million euros for a forgery.

CHAPTER

FORTY-ONE

Pierluigi Falco had already spent nearly ten hours guarding his hostage, and as it was almost 8 p.m., his shift was about to end. He had spent the last couple hours preparing his grandmother's favorite recipe for Fettuccine all'Amatriciana—handmade noodles in a rich tomato sauce with aged pancetta topped with freshly shaved Pecorino Romano cheese—especially for his honored captive.

"I will leave you soon, signorina, but Hugo will take good care of you until I return tomorrow. I hope you enjoy the pasta." He placed the bowl on a table in Hana's room.

"It smells great, Pierluigi, thank you," Hana said with little enthusiasm. With his wriggling finger wave, Falco left the room.

A few minutes later, Hugo, the replacement guard, slammed the door as he entered the apartment on the third floor of Altamonte Suites in downtown Florence, a building owned by the Camorra, who leased out most of the apartments but reserved a few for their own use as safe houses.

As usual, Hugo had his iPhone flush to his ear, engaged in a prolonged argument with his girlfriend. Falco sighed as the young man entered the room, squabbling, this being a common occurrence. It was as if those two thrived on chaos in their relationship, he mused.

Falco signaled to him to stop talking for a moment. Hugo obliged, holding the phone to his chest.

"I have just fed her, and if you're hungry, there's more on the stove. I'll see you tomorrow."

Hugo waved him off, then returned to animatedly discussing the problems of the day with his girlfriend.

UNBEKNOWNST TO HUGO, his iPhone was now inside the ten-meter Bluetooth circle of Hana's bag. The moment he entered the apartment, the AirTag had recognized an iPhone, which instantly transmitted the AirTag's location to a secure server on iCloud, where it would wait until the Find My app on Dominic's host device initiated a search request.

DOMINIC, Marco, Karl and Lukas had just finished dinner at their hotel when, after multiple checks with no luck, Dominic tried the Find My app once again.

This time a tiny picture of Hana appeared at a specific location on a map of Florence, showing the location of the AirTag in her wallet.

"*Got it!*" he cried out excitedly. "She's in a building called the Altamonte Suites."

"So," he asked, looking at Marco, "what's our plan?"

Marco thought a moment, then opened Livia's laptop, launched the Google Earth software, entered the address shown on the app, then enabled the 3D option. The software flew to the given location, angling so as to show surrounding buildings from the front, sides, and back. Using the rotational tools, he viewed the building with an eye toward access and escape.

"It's only three stories tall. We'll wait until dark, say a couple more hours when most people are going to sleep, then if there are no guards outside, we can try entering through the front door. If that's locked, Karl can try to pick it. Our last option would be to go in from the roof. Will that app guide us to where the AirTag actually is, Michael?"

"Yes, it'll show the actual distance counting down the closer we get to it."

"Perfect. OK, let's gear up. I'll arrange for a rental car with the concierge, then we'll go monitor activity at the building until the time is right."

CHAPTER
FORTY-TWO

Under cover of darkness, Faustino Perez lay prone on the secluded rooftop across the street from an upscale residential building. His Austrian-built Steyr SSG 69 sniper rifle with silencer and Kahles Wien ZF69 scope properly aligned, he waited for the *Go* signal from his client, Don Angelo Gallucci.

He was glad to be back in Florence, though he rarely performed assassinations in his hometown. But this was a high-profile contract, an Italian magistrate, with a large payday attached to it. Admittedly, it was much more gratifying building bombs—the infinitely sinuous intricacies of working with C-4 and Semtex wiring, blasting caps and cell phone igniters were his passion—but since he was also in great demand for his Italian Army-trained sniper skills, why not take the easy money, too? Lately the Camorra had been his primary client; a mutual trust had developed over time. And since they seemed to have unlimited funds, they never complained about the high fees his work demanded.

The text message arrived. *Proceed when ready.*

Relaxing his body, he peered through the scope again, finding his target in the crosshairs, sitting in a wingback chair, reading a newspaper by the fireplace in his library. He took a deep breath, held it, then gently squeezed the trigger. He watched as a wide splatter of blood soaked the newspaper. Then the man's head fell to the side.

He broke down his rifle, repacked it in its foam casing lying next to him, shrugged the pack onto his shoulder, then casually walked to the rooftop exit door, went down the stairs and exited the building.

Once back in his van, Perez got another text from Gallucci: **Payment waiting at Altamonte. See Hugo**.

Hugo. What a sad excuse for an operative. Echoes between the ears and anger management issues. I'll see him after a celebratory drink.

MARCO HAD PARKED the rental car across the street and a building down from the Altamonte Suites, and for the past hour he, Dominic, Karl and Lukas sat watching the entrance, checking for unusual activity or the appearance of anyone they might recognize or who appeared suspicious. They saw nothing out of the ordinary.

Dominic checked his Find My app. A large arrow on the display pointed to the northwest corner of the building—approximately 100 meters away from their current location—as the last recorded position of the AirTag. Once they got closer, the app display would change.

"Everyone ready?" Marco asked. Karl and Lukas checked their SIG Sauer pistols and gave Marco a thumbs up. "Michael, take this Taser in case it's needed." He handed him the electroshock weapon, showing him how to operate it.

"I don't imagine killing anyone would be your first choice, and this will only cause temporary paralysis. But regardless, you stay behind us when we go in. If there's any action, I want you to wait outside the door until I call 'Clear.' Understood?"

Dominic nodded. "Thanks for obliging me, Marco, not to mention the Sixth Commandment."

"Alright, let's go."

Leaving the car, they walked in pairs, staying in the shadows, until they reached the front door of the Altamonte. It was locked.

But, ever-prepared, Karl had brought his lock picking kit with him. As the others gathered around, shielding him from view beneath the entryway light, he first inserted a tension wrench, then a high hook pick, identifying each pin starting with the rearmost. He lifted and set each of the binding pins, hearing a soft click as each one set. A few moments later, he turned the handle.

They were in.

Since they were on the ground floor, they first had to walk the halls there until Dominic's app indicated their distance from the tag identifying the suspect apartment. They needed to be within its ten-meter Bluetooth range.

The ground floor showed no change on the app.

Heading to a door marked with the image of a man walking upstairs, they entered and ran up to the next floor. Repeating the same process, apartments on that floor showed nothing on the app as well. Back to the stairs and up to the top floor.

As they proceeded up the hallway, the arrow on the app display jumped to life, now pointing directly ahead, about nine meters.

They approached the last suite in the northwest corner of the building, weapons drawn, tensions high. The Find My app confirmed the AirTag was on the other side of that door.

Marco gently tried the door handle. It was locked. They heard the TV inside was on and the volume was unusually, and helpfully, loud. Marco whispered to Karl to try picking the lock so they didn't have to break down the door, alerting others in the building.

Karl went at it, using the same quiet, efficient process as before. Within a minute, the mechanism was unlocked.

With Karl and Lukas standing on either side of the doorway, their silenced weapons raised at head level, Marco turned the knob, opened the door a crack, and peeked inside.

What he saw surprised him. He closed the door silently.

"All I see is two old people with their backs to us, a man and a woman watching television!" he whispered. Then, looking at Dominic, "Are you sure this is the right place?"

The priest checked again. "Yes, the AirTag is in this apartment. No doubt about it."

"Well, in we go, then."

With that, Marco opened the door, aiming his pistol at the older couple in the living room. Karl and Lukas followed him closely, their pistols sweeping the rest of the apartment and down the hall. The old woman was knitting something, while the man was engrossed in an Italian football game. They both looked up, surprised.

"Who the hell are you, and what are you doing in my home?" the old woman demanded.

"Our apologies if we're mistaken, signora," Marco said, "but we're seeking a friend of ours who has been kidnapped, and we believe she's in this apartment."

"Well, as you can see, it's just me and my husband watching television. Now get out of here before I call the police!"

Unconvinced, Marco called out, "Michael, could you come in here?"

Dominic walked through the door, the Taser hanging from his right arm, slightly hidden behind his leg.

Turning to the priest, Marco asked, "Could you check your app to locate Hana's bag?"

Just then the old woman stood up, set her knitting down while mumbling and adjusting her shawl—then furtively reached into the sofa cushion crack and pulled out a silenced Glock 17. Lifting it and aiming it expertly at Marco while his head was turned, she fired off a shot, hitting the commando in the left shoulder. He fell back against the wall, then went down.

Dominic instinctively raised the Taser, swiftly aimed it at the old crone, and pulled the trigger. A stream of wires with sharp barbs at their ends flew across the room, striking her on the chest, sending a 50,000-volt electric shock throughout her frail body. Falling onto the sofa, she flopped around like a fish out of water, then went still, jerking periodically.

Dominic ran over to Marco while Lukas kept his pistol aimed at the old man, who didn't seem at all concerned about the woman. Karl, meanwhile, went down the hall, searching for others in the apartment. It was empty.

Reaching for a kitchen towel, Dominic clenched it firmly against Marco's upper arm where the bullet went in. There was a slug embedded in the wall above him. The bullet obviously passed through soft muscle tissue, which the priest took as a good sign. Marco just needed antiseptic and patching up for now. And maybe a swig of whisky.

"How's it feeling, my friend?" Dominic asked. "Are you able to move?"

Clearly in pain but conscious and alert, Marco simply nodded.

"Get what you can out of the old man," he said. "It's clear now they're in on it. Is the AirTag here?"

Dominic stood up and looked around. He spotted Hana's bag sitting on the kitchen counter.

"Yes, I see it over there. So she's got to be here somewhere."

He picked up the woman's Glock and walked over to the old man, pointing the gun in his face.

"Listen carefully to what I'm about to tell you. Though I don't want to hurt you, I will not hesitate pulling this trigger unless you tell me exactly where our friend Hana Sinclair is. Right now."

The old man looked up into the solemn face of a man who truly meant what he said. He shrugged his shoulders as if he couldn't care less.

"I don't know who the person is they have next door—I

assumed it was a woman because of the purse—but Hugo is guarding someone there now. There is a bookshelf in the hallway with a hidden door behind it, connecting the two apartments; just slide the bookshelf to the left. The door should be unlocked."

"Are there any more weapons here? Other people next door besides Hugo?" Lukas asked.

"Not that I'm aware of," the man said feebly.

"Marco, you rest up until I get back," Dominic advised. "Meanwhile, Lukas, you watch these two and monitor the door. Karl and I will take care of this Hugo and find Hana."

Dominic moved to the front door, locked it, then motioned for Karl to take the lead in finding the bookshelf in the hallway.

HAVING DOWNED two shots of tequila at a bar, then driven to and parked outside the Altamonte, Faustino Perez picked up the intercom phone and rang Hugo's apartment. Answering, Hugo buzzed him in. The assassin got into the elevator and punched the button for the top floor.

THE HIDDEN DOOR connecting the two apartments was unlocked. Karl turned the handle, his gun raised and ready. Standing behind him, Dominic could hear his beating heart pound in his ears, instinct holding him back, the rush of adrenaline for finding Hana pushing him on.

With a thrust of the door, both men burst into the room. A young man, presumably Hugo, was sitting on the sofa watching TV and eating a bowl of pasta. Taken unawares, Hugo glanced at the pistol laying on the table in front of him.

"Don't even think about it," Karl said as he moved swiftly in front of Hugo, his SIG Sauer pointed at his chest.

"We're only here for your hostage, Hana Sinclair," Dominic warned. "Tell us where she is and no harm will come to you."

Resigned to his predicament, Hugo pointed to the hallway. "Last room. The key is above the door frame."

While Dominic went to fetch Hana, Karl moved to retrieve the pistol sitting on the table in front of Hugo, tucking it behind him in the small of his back.

Then he heard a quiet rapping on the door: two taps, a pause, followed by three more taps.

"Get up, quickly," Karl commanded in a whisper. "Open the door and let whoever it is inside, but if you even make a funny face you're dead, got it?"

Hugo nodded fearfully. He rose from the sofa, and Karl grabbed his collar, shoving him to the entrance. The Swiss Guard stepped behind the door, his SIG pressing against the young man's back.

Hugo opened the door. "Faustino, I—" Karl pushed the gun deeper into his back as a warning.

"It's about time," Perez said, as he walked into the room. Karl slammed the door and, pushing Hugo onto the new arrival, raised his pistol to cover both men.

Surprised but showing no signs of fear, Perez instinctively raised his hands.

"Both of you, step back carefully," Karl said, "and no sudden moves. Put your hands behind your head, lace your fingers and face the wall, a meter apart." Then he shouted, "Michael! I need you out here now!"

HAVING UNLOCKED the door down the hallway, the priest cautiously opened it, peering in, prepared for danger in case it was a setup. Instead, he found Hana sitting on a bed. She looked up, completely surprised to see Michael Dominic standing in the doorway. She leapt up and ran toward him, hugging him fiercely, not wanting to let go.

"My God, Michael, how did you ever *find* me?!" she asked,

her voice muffled in the curve of his neck. "I was sure I'd never see you again!"

"We'll get to that later. Right now, we have to get you out of here. Are you alright? Did they hurt you at all?"

"No, I'm fine. I've been treated well, in fact." Tears of emotion pooled in her eyes.

Just then Dominic heard Karl calling him, sensing urgency in his voice. With Hana behind him, he raised the Glock, and they both proceeded back out down the hallway and into the living room.

Seeing two men facing the wall, he said, "Well, I see we have company." Looking at Karl, he said, "Now what?"

"Good to see you, cousin," Karl said to Hana, smiling. "Would you mind checking the kitchen for a box of plastic wrap or twine? Anything we might use to tie these two up."

Hana ran into the kitchen, opening drawers and cupboards, finally finding an extra large box of plastic wrap and a roll of duct tape. Pierluigi kept a well-stocked kitchen, she thought.

She handed both items to Karl. "Michael," he said, "keep your eye on the new guy while I tie up Hugo. Hana, bring two of those chairs over here."

Hana dragged two chairs from the dining table into the center of the living room.

"Hugo, you first. Get over here and have a seat."

Karl handed his pistol to Hana while he first checked Hugo for weapons. Finding nothing, he wrapped the plastic film around the man, making sure he was held fast to the chair. Then he moved the other chair directly behind Hugo's.

"Hey, new guy. Faustino. Your turn now." He frisked him for weapons, finding both a pistol and a combat knife, liberating both from the assassin.

"Now take a seat. Michael, keep your gun carefully trained on this one. He has military written all over him."

"You have a good eye, boy," Perez purred. "But you really should kill me. I'm not one to forget something like this."

"Don't tempt me," Karl said, "but I doubt our paths will cross again."

"Never say never," the assassin advised. "You have just cost some very determined people a great deal of money. I'd be watching my back if I were you."

Karl continued wrapping the continuous roll of plastic film around Faustino and Hugo so many times that neither man could extract himself without help. He also wrapped their lower legs as an extra measure. By the time he was done, the box of plastic wrap was half empty.

"We'll use the rest to tie up the old folks next door."

"Are you both able to breathe alright?" Dominic asked with genuine concern.

"My, such a caring soul. You must be the priest I've heard about," Perez said. "I won't forget your consideration when I'm sent to kill you all."

Those were his last words as Karl gagged him with the duct tape.

Just then Marco walked into the room, the blood-soaked towel on his shoulder stained bright red.

"*Marco!!*" Hana cried out. "What happened?!" She ran to him, reaching out to tenderly inspect the wound. Then she kissed him and ran a hand through his hair.

"I'm ashamed to admit it, but I was shot by someone's unpleasant grandmother in the other apartment."

"This looks serious," she said. "We need to get you to a hospital."

"No, there will be too many questions we can't answer," he cautioned. "I'll make a call and find a doctor who can offer more discreet help."

"Okay, let's get those other two taken care of and get out of here," Karl suggested. "Marco, would you stay here and keep an eye on these guys until we're done?"

"My pleasure," he said. "In the meantime, I'll make that call." Marco took a seat, his pistol next to him on the table while he called an old colleague in Florence for a sub rosa medical referral. Hana stayed with him.

Dominic and Karl returned to the first apartment, where Lukas was standing over the older couple. The woman had recovered from her Taser infliction and was sitting placidly on the sofa, mumbling to herself, her shawl around her shoulders. She looked unhappy.

"Did you find Hana?" Lukas asked.

"We did," Dominic replied, "and two guys are tied up in the other room. Now it's time for this pair."

"You two, over here," Karl demanded, putting two table chairs back to back in the living room.

The old couple complied, each slowly taking a seat. While Dominic kept his gun trained on them, Karl began surrounding them both with the plastic wrap. A few minutes later, they were completely secured.

"Would you like to keep the TV on so you have something to watch until someone finds you?"

"Yes, please," the old man muttered. "Otherwise, I'll just have to listen to her constant bitching." The old woman grumbled, cursing the situation.

"We can fix that," Karl said as he gagged both of them with strips of duct tape.

"Okay, Lukas, can you get Marco and Hana from the next apartment? It's time to leave."

Dominic looked around the room, seeing if there was anything unusual warranting special attention. Apart from retrieving Hana's bag, he found nothing.

With all five now gathered together, they left the apartment, locking the door behind them. They took the elevator down.

"There's a private doctor a few miles from here who can take care of this wound," Marco said, inspecting his shoulder. "We'd better head there now.

"So, really, how *did* you find me?" Hana asked the team.

Dominic smiled at her. "Remember that AirTag we tucked

into your wallet last year, when we found the Magdalene manuscript?"

"Yes!" Hana exclaimed. "I'm glad now, but frankly I'd forgotten all about it."

"I've got to call your grandfather, by the way, and tell him you're okay." Marco said.

"My grandfather? What does he have to do with this?"

"He put up two million euros for your ransom, which fortunately we won't need now."

"Good grief," Hana said, clearly surprised. "I should give him a call myself. Thanks, everyone. I'm so grateful to count you all as friends. Even you, cousin." She smiled at Karl. "Now, let's get Marco to that doctor."

CHAPTER
FORTY-THREE

After Dominic and his friends had abruptly left the Uffizi Gallery in order to find Hana, Agent Dario Contini continued his preliminary analysis of the museum's paintings, with disturbing results.

Of the twenty paintings on Feudatario's list, he had deemed eighteen of them suspicious. Giancarlo Piovani, the curator, was fraught with anxiety, for a legitimate review of these paintings had gone through the hands of several noted authorities and passed muster. But, both Piovani and Contini reasoned, the artist who had performed this work was of such superior skill that now every painting was subject to skepticism, not a comfort to institutions that paid millions of euros each year for the presumed works of Old Masters. And most of these had come from Venice, either through one of the many fine art galleries like Renzo Farelli's, or following restoration by Palazzo Feudatario.

Contini found a similar range of suspicious works at Galleria dell'Accademia di Firenze, recommending that the management there—as he asked of the Uffizi—carry out a series of forensic tests to better identify those which met the strict manifestations of ancient work, or whether there was even a hint of modern deception.

Dario Contini felt a rush of exhilaration. He was closing in. The thought of solving a nearly three-hundred-year-old series of historical art crimes would secure his rise on the Italian Art Squad.

The only thing he needed now was that elusive Coscia Journal, believed to contain every known transaction of Feudatario's restorations and forgeries since 1740.

But because of Italy's tough laws seemingly sympathetic to criminals—thanks to the Mafia's long-held influence over the legal system—he did not have sufficient evidence yet to convince a magistrate to order a search and seizure warrant. So he would improvise in the meantime.

For that, he needed Father Dominic's help. He had to convince the priest and his team to help him find and gain the Journal by any means.

ON THE TRAIN back to Venice early the next morning, everyone was exhausted from the previous night's adrenaline rush of rescuing Hana.

Marco had been patched up by the private physician he'd been referred to, and though his arm was in a sling with Hana tending to his every need, he felt fine.

Karl and Lukas had dozed off under the hypnotic rhythms of the speeding train, leaning against each other in a shared seat.

Dominic sat alone in the back of the car, considering their next actions. After calling Contini and filling him in on last night's activity, he agreed with the agent that the Coscia Journal mentioned by Antonio Vivaldi was crucial to obtain. Though they already had enough proof to arrest those affiliated with Feudatario Restorations—and possibly Renzo Farelli for his own complicity in the murder of Father Carlo Rinaldo, if they could link him to that crime—they needed that historical evidence showing to whom forged works of art had been delivered over the centuries, and clues as to where they might be now. Camorra clans were legendary for respect of their history, and maintaining records of each clan's own legacy was the obligation of every leader.

Chances were good that the journal was held by each *capintesta* as leadership changed hands through the ages. Which meant Don Angelo Gallucci must now have possession of it, surely locked away some place safe.

ELDON VILLARD SAT in the custom Horween leather swivel armchair he'd had designed for viewing his priceless art collection in his own climate-controlled Luxembourg Freeport vault. The lilting strains of a Mozart concerto played softly through his custom Sonos sound system as he savored a crystal flute of Veuve Clicquot Le Grand Dame Blanc.

In the center place of prominence, Raphael's spectacular *Madonna of Foligno*, which he knew to have been created in 1512, hung before him. The painting featured the Virgin Mary sitting on heavenly clouds, embracing the infant Jesus, surrounded by cherubic angels. On the ground looking up was the kneeling nobleman Sigismondo de' Conti along with St. Jerome, who stood with his lion peering out from the shadows behind him. St. Francis of Assisi knelt on the left, with John the Baptist standing next to him. Between both groups appeared a small angelic child, with the towers of the village of Foligno far in the background.

Villard's vast affluence afforded him many pleasures, but art was his consummate passion, one he enjoyed in complete solitude. That this one secret, sacred space was known only to him—and owned solely by him on a prepaid 50-year lease— gave him a feeling of profound power over his ultra-wealthy peers, not to mention the countless institutions who would fight for possession of even one of his pieces if they had known he possessed them. Especially the Raphael.

Someday he really would have to tell someone about this place, if only to ensure that it was discovered and dealt with properly after his death. Until he did, it was his secret alone, one he relished like no other.

As he sat there admiring the Raphael's beauty, something about it triggered a mild alert deep in his mind's eye. It seemed remarkably fresh for a five-hundred-year-old painting. Standing up, he approached the canvas. Using the remote control for the unit's lighting, he raised it to full brightness, peering closely at the overall wash of color. Taking an LED penlight from a nearby table drawer, he held it to the right side, raking the light over the surface at an angle. He did the same thing from the left, looking for alterations or signs of fresh restoration. It *seemed* fine. Still, there was just something… off.

Instinct has served me well throughout my life… Let's get you authenticated, Madonna.

He slid a phone out of his pocket and made a call.

CHAPTER

FORTY-FOUR

With phone in hand, Angelo Gallucci paced his office in Palazzo Feudatario, furious over Hana's rescue and forfeiting the ransom money from Armand de Saint-Clair.

"How *could* you have let this happen, Faustino?" he demanded of the assassin. "You are paid too well to allow mistakes like this."

"They were well organized, *padrino*, and we were outnumbered, though the old woman put a bullet through the Frenchman, so one of their strongest is at least temporarily incapacitated. They took all of us by surprise. It will not happen again.

"I did, however, attend to that other business satisfactorily. The judge will be of no concern to you any longer."

"Yes, you did well there," Gallucci gruffly acknowledged. "That's one less problem-maker in the courts."

"How would you like me to handle the priest and his people now?"

"I will be in touch with you on that. Please remain available in the coming days." He ended the call.

As the newly appointed *capintesta*, Gallucci feared he was off to a terrible start. Not only had this latest plan failed, Operation Scambio had been exposed, his palazzo had been breached, confidential files were taken, and several of his operatives had been killed or were missing. The only thing that had gone right was the sale of the Raphael, even though that had been touchy.

He was losing control. Perez's premium services would be needed again. But first, he must meet with Cardinal Abruzzo and inform him of his plan.

~

"As Vivaldi's notes imply, Father Dominic, Cardinal Coscia's Journal is key to everything now," said Dario Contini, as the two sat in the lounge at Ca' Sagredo in Venice. "We must extricate it from the Camorra. To have a register of all sales of forgeries over the centuries would give us valuable leads tracking down these priceless paintings. And I don't doubt for a moment that it is still being kept updated. In fact, that journal may be the most important record of art history in all the world. I cannot think of another like it.

"Granted, many of the paintings may be lost by now," Contini admitted, "but given that the nobles of the time—the only ones who could afford such luxuries, apart from the Church—were the likely procurers, the customs of their houses would lend themselves to hereditary guardianship through the ages. And the Vatican would have a substantial stake in such knowledge, too, since the Church itself had commissioned a great many works."

"How do you propose to get the journal, Dario?"

"I was hoping you would ask," Contini said, a coy smile forming as he spoke. "Given our arcane laws, there is nothing I can do at this point without more compelling evidence. But that ancient journal would clinch it. You have some accomplished resources at hand—Signor Marco Picard and the two Swiss Guards, and yourself, of course—so with proper encouragement, perhaps there are ways you can act where my hands would be tied..." He left the suggestion hanging in the air, hoping Dominic would pick up on his implication of extralegal activity.

He watched as Dominic bit his lip in thought.

"I understand your predicament now," said the priest, "but this might be better directed toward Marco, who, shall we say, has less restrictive aptitude in terms of creative solutions to such matters. I'll take it up with him."

"*Bene! Molto bene,*" said Contini, smiling widely now.

IN HANA'S suite at the Ca' Sagredo, Marco lay shirtless on her bed as she changed the dressing on his shoulder wound. Since the old woman's bullet had passed through his fleshy deltoid muscle tissue—above the bicep and just outside the subdeltoid bursa—it wasn't that serious an injury, needing only time to heal. There would be scars, but as Hana could see glancing over his toned body, it was clear he'd had many other injuries from past battles.

"You put yourself in harm's way a lot, don't you?" she asked with a mix of concern and admiration.

"It *is* my job," he said, laughing. "What else would you expect of a career soldier?" He looked deep and lovingly into her pale green eyes, not expecting an answer.

She slowly leaned down and kissed him, a long, passionate caress of his lips beneath hers. Sitting up, she ran her fingers across his smooth chest as they gazed at each other in silence, the only sound being the baritone strains of a gondolier outside an open window to the Grand Canal.

It had been a long time since Hana had someone to care for like this, and she savored every moment with the man she had once pushed away as being too obsessed over her well-being. Her grandfather meant well, assigning Marco to her for protection, but it took a while for her to accept him. Now it had become something more. Something much more.

CHAPTER
FORTY-FIVE

With Valentina Calabrese now dead and no one else yet vetted to do the confidential bookkeeping, that work fell to Giuseppe Franco, as he had done from time to time in the past.

He dreaded this menial drudgery, so beneath his talents as a painter of masterpieces. But as his work was always done in secret—for most of the staff assumed that Feudatario only performed restorations and nothing more—only he knew the more sensitive areas of the business. And there were several paintings yet to record in the ancient Coscia Journal. At least he considered that a historical privilege.

The previous *capintesta*, Don Lucio Gambarini, trusted Giuseppe above all others, and treated him like a brother. In fact, he was the only trustee apart from Gambarini, and now Gallucci, to have the combination to the Gardall safe in the *padrino*'s office.

Since Gallucci was now meeting with Cardinal Abruzzo, no one else was in the building. Giuseppe entered the office, went to the safe, and opened it. Looking inside he found the usual tall stacks of euros piled to one side, a mound of Italian bearer bonds, a Glock 19, and, on its own shelf high in the tall black safe, a brown leather satchel containing the leather bound Coscia Journal.

Pulling down the hefty case, he laid it on the Don's desk, then took a seat. Giuseppe had not had to handle this kind of task for a year or more now, but there was always a thrill connected to the experience. The further back one went, the Journal's thick pages featured fine calligraphic handwriting, from times when penmanship was taken seriously as its own personal art form. Every page was filled with intricate details of each painting and its related transactions by each restorer or copyist going back to the 18th century. So many masters had gone before him; Giuseppe was currently the last in a very long line of the best forgers the world had ever seen, albeit anonymously. In that, he took great pride. It was only in this book that the real painters' names were known, names which the world would never come to learn. In that, he felt a sense of sorrow.

He had entered the basic details of the Raphael and two other paintings he had worked on which had yet to be recorded—the artist's names, the paintings' names, the subject of each, their dimensions, and the kinds of work that had been performed. Now he just needed the sales transactional data, which was also kept in the safe.

Returning to the Gardall, he pulled out a dark red folder containing Don Gallucci's private details of each sale. He sat back down and opened the folder, extracting the form for the Raphael's secret sale to Eldon Villard.

Giuseppe was impressed, but not surprised at the name of the buyer. Of course, he knew who Villard was. Anyone alive knew his name. But what made Giuseppe sit bolt upright in shock was when he saw the price paid for *his* work: €25 million!

And since these were private under-the-table transactions, no taxes had been paid, so this was pure profit.

He considered his own salary, €70,000 each year, nearly three times the average salary in all of Italy. And though he lived comfortably on that, his immediate reaction viewed it as a pittance compared to the outrageously priced fake Raphael. *His Raphael!*

He did not realize paintings were going for such extravagant prices now. He thought back to all the past canvases he had painstakingly created. The Camorra was making a fortune on his own back!

Something must be done about this, he thought. *I should get a percentage of the proceeds, at the very least! Even one percent isn't too much to ask...there is no one else who can do what I do... I am indispensable. They need me!*

I must speak with Don Gallucci.

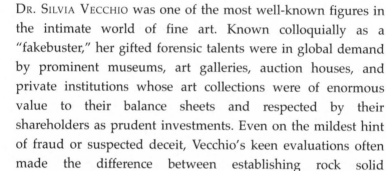

Dr. Silvia Vecchio was one of the most well-known figures in the intimate world of fine art. Known colloquially as a "fakebuster," her gifted forensic talents were in global demand by prominent museums, art galleries, auction houses, and private institutions whose art collections were of enormous value to their balance sheets and respected by their shareholders as prudent investments. Even on the mildest hint of fraud or suspected deceit, Vecchio's keen evaluations often made the difference between establishing rock solid authenticity, or determining a recently sold work by an Old Master to be an excellent fake, thus declaring it all but worthless. She did all this by eye and gut instinct; if doubts shadowed any painting she was inspecting, she would have it subjected to traditional forensic testing. And her instincts usually proved correct.

Bound on a healthy retainer to Eldon Villard for years, when she received his call to inspect the Raphael, she rescheduled her immediate commitments, as were the terms of her contract with the billionaire. Having had his assistant email Vecchio the painting's Condition Report and associated documentation, the next day he sent his private jet to pick her up in Rome and deliver her to the Luxembourg Freeport.

On her arrival by his private limousine, she was greeted by Villard's assistant at the entrance, then escorted to Vault 42. She carried with her a Pelican case outfitted with specialized tools and solutions essential to her analyses.

"A pleasure to see you again, Monsieur Villard," Vecchio said without emotion as they shook hands. Her eyes were immediately drawn to the object of her visit, hanging in its place of honor beneath perfect lighting. Setting down the case on a wooden table against the wall, she approached the painting.

"May I offer you a glass of champagne, Silvia?" Villard asked.

"No, thank you, monsieur. I prefer to work without such influences. Perhaps after I spend some time with your *Madonna?*"

It did not escape Villard's notice that she didn't say *The* Madonna. Vecchio was precise in her language and analysis, blessed with a nearly instant prickle of recognition as to the veracity or falsity of paintings. It caused him some initial unease.

Opening her Pelican case, she withdrew a MacBook Pro and a portable USB optical microscope equipped with a macro lens. Setting it up, she selected various areas on the painting and peered into the lens, looking at grain size for mineral pigments while determining if there were retouches intersecting the craquelure.

Stepping back from time to time to take in the overall painting, she stared at the sections she'd just analyzed, moving her eye around the entire canvas, making visual observations of adjoining areas, then going back in for closer microscopic examination.

Returning to her tools, she extracted an X-ray Fluorescence Gun, an ingenious non-invasive device for analyzing specific elements on objects of, in the assumed case at hand, precious cultural heritage. Performed in fractions of micro-seconds with each burst, the X-ray beam reacts with atoms in the paint pigments by displacing electrons from the inner orbital shells of the atom. In several samples, she detected *no* presence of lead— an obvious sign that modern synthetic coloring agents had been used. The artist—a very good one, she admired—must have been under pressure to produce this piece quickly, cutting corners by not using appropriate period materials which an artist of such mastery as this surely must have had.

While her back was turned to Villard, he could not see her frowning at the results. Turning around, though, she maintained a stolid poker face. She efficiently returned her tools to the Pelican case and snapped it shut.

Looking directly into Villard's expectant blue eyes, Vecchio smiled grimly and said, "Now would be a good time for that champagne, monsieur, so we can discuss this forgery of yours."

FORTY-SIX

The sun over Venice had set long ago. The *scirocco*, a warm moist air mass from the Sahara, blew over the chilly waters of the lagoon, and a wet fog had descended over La Serenissima as the temperature dropped. The palazzos along the Grand Canal were vague shadows in the dark. Apart from the mournful wail of foghorns in the distance, all other sounds were muffled.

Hana and Marco had gone out for a late dinner. Though his arm was no longer in a sling, Marco still favored it, pushing through the pain to encourage mobility of the damaged muscle tissue.

Karl and Lukas went to Lupo's Pub, their new favorite hangout near Harry's Bar where they could have a few beers and play darts, and though they invited Dominic to come along, he told them he'd rather stay in his room and take in some reading and prayer.

Although he was accustomed to solitude, even embracing it most of the time, a feeling of loneliness had crept over Dominic in the past few days. With his friends paired up and enjoying each other's company, the realities of being a priest—especially a young and vital one, with an engaging personality—were hitting him especially hard here in the enchanted city known for romance. These were the rare times that tested him most, and he prayed especially hard that he not be consumed by his wandering thoughts.

A good time for a run, he thought.

Changing into a tracksuit and slipping into his Saucony running shoes, Dominic was already feeling better, having decided to act, to do anything but sit in his room and allow his mind to fester.

Taking the stairs down instead of the elevator, when he reached the lobby he reset the step counter on the TAG Heuer strapped to his wrist—a gift from Cardinal Petrini on his ordination—and after a series of stretches, headed toward the Rialto and the San Marco *sestiere*.

SMOKING A CIGARETTE, a man loitering in the shadows outside the Ca' Sagredo watched the priest leave the hotel's entrance, do some stretching on a bench, then take off running toward the Rialto Bridge. Taking out his cell phone, the man speed-dialed a special number.

DOMINIC'S PATH took him across a small bridge over the Rio dei Santi Apostoli and into the San Marco district. Rather than run the fondomento along the waterfront, he decided to take in the back alleys and smaller walkways. There would be less foot traffic there and he could enjoy Venice's interior charms, where the people lived and shopped away from the more touristed areas.

Running on cobblestones was a bit of a challenge, but the Sauconys were made for rough trails, so he had few problems handling the paths. Taking a northern turn, he happened upon a stunningly gorgeous church, Santa Maria dei Miracoli, with a colored marble colonnade and a semicircular pediment topping the façade, clearly one of the better early Venetian Renaissance churches he had seen. He stopped, caught his breath, noted a small sign that the church was open until 10 p.m., then entered the building.

Passing through the narthex and on into the nave of the church, Dominic was transfixed by its quiet beauty. A series of towering arched stained glass windows on both sides of the nave, strategically lit from the outside, cast radiant beams of color criss-crossing the wide interior, giving the appearance of a static concert light show.

Toward the back on a side aisle was a stand of votive candles. Genuflecting on the marble floor of the main aisle and making the sign of the cross, he turned to the candle stand, dropped in a couple euros, then lit one of the votives, saying a silent prayer for his lost friends, Carlo and Livia.

After a few more minutes admiring the sacred interior, Dominic pushed open the heavy door to head back out and continue his run.

"Father Dominic, I presume?" ventured a voice in the fog. Looking up, Dominic saw the misty figure of a man standing about ten meters away from him as he emerged from the sanctuary. He was holding something metallic in his right hand, a glint of light shining off it as he confidently bounced it off his left palm: up, down, up, down.

It was a short but menacing dagger.

Dominic recognized the man instantly from the Altamonte Suites in Florence. The one Karl called Faustino.

"I told you we would meet again," the voice goaded, a wicked smile visible even through the dense fog.

Dominic quickly calculated his path and timing. The man was wearing hard-soled boots; Dominic was convinced he could outrun him. He just had to get past that knife. Hopefully, the assassin wasn't a skilled knife thrower.

"Why don't you come a little closer so we can have a chat?" Perez coaxed.

"I think I'm quite comfortable here, thanks," Dominic said, ready to move in either direction if the man pounced.

As he slowly paced one way, Perez calmly mimicked his movement, staying directly in front of him.

"Is there anything in particular you wanted to 'chat' about?" the priest asked.

"Oh, I'm certain we could find some common ground. But I doubt you'd appreciate the conversation as much as I w—"

Before he finished the sentence, Dominic bolted to his left and took off running as fast as he could. Perez followed suit, but the older man had clearly not dressed for a foot race.

Dominic sped north on the path alongside the church, taking serpentine steps every couple meters—hoping a thrown knife might miss him—then veered off at a fork into the residential area of San Marco, grabbing cobblestones with every forceful step.

Perez was still behind him, a good eight meters distance between the two.

Dominic looked for a dark alley he could duck into. Anywhere away from light and which had easy access. Spotting one, he darted into it, sprinting at full speed. Reaching the end, he turned right, fleeing up another cobbled path through the thick fog. He could hear Perez's footsteps still following him, a muffled echo off the tightly packed buildings lining the narrow walkways.

Heading south now, Dominic saw the lights of St. Mark's Square casting a bright, murky halo around the vast piazza somewhere ahead. Moving in that direction—where even at this hour there would be people milling about—he made his best time yet. His heart was pounding furiously, the effects of fear combined with exertion taking a toll on his stamina.

He made it to the piazza and chanced looking back. Astonishingly, Perez was still in pursuit, but the distance between them had spread. The assassin was a good hundred meters back now, but still running with determination, the knife still pumping up and down in his hand.

Dominic raced across the piazza and down to the waterfront, step after pounding step, turning right towards Harry's Bar and along the fondomento.

Just as he passed Harry's, Karl and Lukas were coming out the door of Lupo's Pub, laughing arm-in-arm. Looking up, they were surprised to find Michael, running toward them, out of breath, drenched in sweat, fear and desperation on his face.

"*Karl!*" Dominic cried out, panting with every word as he stopped and held onto his friend's shoulder. "That Faustino guy from Florence is behind me with a knife! He should be here any second!"

Karl reacted instantly, no questions asked. "We've got this. Come on, Lukas."

The two of them took off, jogging in the direction Dominic had come from, their heads down, Karl laying out their strategy to his partner as they slowly ran. Seven seconds later, Perez rounded the corner. Seeing Dominic in the distance, stopped on the fondomento and bent over panting, he picked up his pace, intending to run around the two men approaching him.

To his surprise, the two joggers separated slightly as they approached him, leaving a space between them for him to pass. *Better yet*, he thought, grinning.

Before he knew it, Faustino Perez was flying through the air face down, each of his legs having been tripped by the two joggers on either side of him.

As if in slow motion, Perez gaped at the cobbles closing in on his face, his arms and legs flailing in the air behind him. He turned his head to one side instinctively, but any thoughts of getting his arms out in front of him in time were pointless.

His face smashed directly onto the cobblestones. The rest of his body tumbled over on top of itself, his entire weight now thrust onto his neck, which snapped with a loud crack as he toppled to the ground.

Death was instantaneous.

SEEING THE MAN FALL, Dominic ran back to Karl and Lukas as the latter two were staring down at Faustino Perez's crumpled body, surprised by the effectiveness of their plan but satisfied with the outcome.

"We'd better get out of here before anyone sees us," said Dominic. "But first..." Despite the assassin and the circumstances, the priest said a quick prayer for Faustino's soul. Then the three of them took off running back toward St. Mark's Square, vanishing in the fog.

Once they were clear of the scene, they slowed to a walk.

"So, what happened!" Lukas urged. "Why was he chasing you?"

"To *kill* me, I suppose!" Dominic huffed. "Didn't you see that knife he was gripping? The bastard chased me all across the San Marco *sestiere* from the Miracoli church to here. We probably ran a good half-mile through the twisting narrow alleyways and campos and piazzas. The guy was relentless."

"Good thing you're a nimble runner, Michael," Karl said, clapping his friend on the back. "At this rate, the Camorra will have fewer people to send after us. Marco would be proud!"

"Let's just figure out a way to get that Coscia Journal and get out of here," Dominic said. "I never thought I'd say this, but Venice is starting to lose its appeal."

CHAPTER

FORTY-SEVEN

G iuseppe Franco sat nervously in his studio at Palazzo Feudatario, considering how best to approach Don Gallucci with his plan. He had never asked for a raise, much less demand a modest percentage of the exorbitant fees they were getting for *his* work. It was simply a matter of fairness, after all. Surely the man would see that.

He glimpsed the *padrino* sitting in his office when he came in that morning. It was now or never, he thought.

Taking the stairs down to the ground floor, Giuseppe's heart began racing the closer he got to Gallucci's office. *Stay strong! You can do this. They need you…*

He rapped on the *padrino*'s door, which was open. Gallucci, focused on some paperwork, glanced up.

"*Si*, Giuseppe? What is it?"

"*Buongiorno*, Don Gallucci," he began. "Do you have a moment to discuss a matter of some importance to me?"

Gallucci was instantly alert. He knew the tone of that voice and what question might come of it: "… *to me*" was the giveaway. He put down his pen, leaned back in his chair, and lit a cigarette.

"Of course, come in. Take a seat."

Giuseppe sat down, tiny beads of sweat on his face betraying his confidence, even though the room was moderately cool.

"I've been meaning to speak with you as well, Giuseppe, and this is as good a time as any. Your work here has been exemplary, and I want you to know how grateful our clan is, how grateful *I* am personally. And so I'd like to increase your salary to €85,000, effective immediately." He waited for a reaction.

Giuseppe was shocked that Don Gallucci had nearly read his mind. But it wasn't exactly what he'd *had* in mind. Though he was happy to accept the raise, he still felt his services were worth more.

"Don Gallucci, that... that is most kind of you," he stammered, sweat now dripping from his forehead. "However, I would like to offer a proposal. When I was entering the accounting and condition details in the Coscia Journal the other day, I noticed that my Raphael had sold for twenty-five *million* euros! And I thought... well, that *is* a great deal of money. And surely the *padrino* would value my unique services enough to give me a share of each painting I create going forward.

"I had in mind a figure of just one percent, Don Gallucci, which you must admit is quite reasonable." His hands shook as they lay on his lap, the fingers of one hand rubbing against those of the other.

Gallucci slowly leaned forward, blowing smoke into Giuseppe's face.

"I am afraid we must disagree on what you think is 'reasonable,' Giuseppe. *You* are not the one taking the greatest risks here. You sit up there in your comfortable studio, doing what you love most in the world, and yes, taking due pride in your work. But the greatest risks are mine, and those of others in our clan. Do you realize what is involved in acquiring these pieces in the first place? Especially from the Vatican or the Uffizi or other prominent institutions?! Incalculable risks! And you suffer none of that.

"No, I am afraid I cannot agree to your wishes. I am sorry.

You were just given a sizable raise, one that I'm sure was unexpected. That should be sufficient and you should be grateful for it. Now, is there anything else?"

Giuseppe was gobsmacked. He had badly overplayed his hand.

"N... no, padrino," he said haltingly. "Thank you for your time. And oh, yes, for that, um, raise, too."

Giuseppe stood to leave, but his legs weren't cooperating. He stumbled getting out of the chair, turned to straighten it, glanced at Gallucci and left the office.

BACK IN HIS STUDIO UPSTAIRS, Giuseppe fumed over the confrontation. *Merda!! He should have accepted my proposition. I am not a greedy man, but look at what they are getting for my work. I am not respected here at all by these greedy bastards.*

Perhaps I should have a talk with that priest I met at the contessa's party. I could work directly for the Vatican. Surely they would pay considerably more than the measly "raise" I was just offered for my ability to restore their art while keeping the work in-house. And I would not subject myself to further risks as I do here. What was his name...? Ah, yes. Father Dominic.

CHAPTER
FORTY-EIGHT

I t had been just eighteen hours since Silvia Vecchio had confirmed that Eldon Villard's Raphael was, well, not a Raphael, as she bluntly put it to him.

Villard himself had only one man to blame for this. Renzo Farelli. Farelli was the one who set up the deal, vouching for the painting's provenance and authenticity. And it was Farelli with whom Villard would take up the matter. He would get back his €25 million and never deal with the man again. And once word got out he was a swindler—and Villard would make sure word got out—Renzo Farelli would never again be trusted by anyone. Villard's repudiation alone would ruin him.

His assistant had arranged for a Zoom web conference with Farelli to start in a few minutes. While waiting, he'd had coffee delivered to his office and was dressing a cup with cream and sugar when the conference began.

Renzo Farelli appeared on the screen as Villard took his first sip.

"Good morning, Signor Villard," the dealer said, sitting at his desk, smiling. "I hope you are well this morning?"

Villard set down his cup, then placed his palms on the desk and leaned forward into the webcam until his face filled Farelli's screen. Involuntarily, he backed up in his chair, intimidated by the billionaire.

"I am not at all well, Renzo, something I have you to thank for. I'm sure you are familiar with Dr. Silvia Vecchio, the impeccable fakebuster? At my invitation she paid me a visit last evening, spending a good deal of time on the purported Raphael you sold me. Turns out it's a forgery, Renzo. A very good one, but a forgery nonetheless. I expect you to make arrangements to have it picked up and returned in exchange for a full refund of what I paid. I will be generous and give you forty-eight hours to do so."

Farelli was aghast, his worst expectations having materialized. Panicking, he desperately struggled to fortify his transparently weak position.

"But signore," Renzo pleaded, "that is simply not possible! The piece has excellent provenance and comes to us, as you know, from an unimpeachable source. Is it possible Dr. Vecchio was wrong in this instance?"

"No," Villard said flatly. "I believe she is correct. Your people must have returned the original to the Vatican, and sold me the forged copy."

Farelli's mind was racing to save the deal. He tried a different tack.

"Nevertheless, Signor Villard, if that were the case— assuming that even after the most scrupulous examination, the piece's authenticity still remains open to doubt—do you not see it as a thoroughly presentable work of art as if the painting were indisputably genuine?"

Villard thought about Farelli's twisted logic for a moment. He had to give the man credit for trying. "A clever but unconvincing rebuttal, Renzo, but how *dare* you try to pawn off a fake for that kind of money! I paid for a *genuine* Raphael, I expected a genuine Raphael. I have no wish to argue the matter further. Please see to my demands immediately. And do not expect any further business from me, nor others whom I might influence. Good day." Villard punched the End button, and the Zoom conference window vanished.

Devastated, Farelli lowered his head, his face falling into open hands. Twenty-five million euros, gone in a flash—five million of which was his commission! And his reputation would be shattered after this affair. *Merda!* He ripped the scarf off from around his neck, which was now suffocating him as he fought for breath.

Then there was Don Gallucci to deal with now. He would be raving mad, especially following the string of losses the clan had suffered recently. Should he even mention it to the *capintesta*?

No. He should run! Just take his money and run. With no future remaining once Eldon Villard was done with him, what else could he do?

At his age, he could retire comfortably with what he had. There was no way he'd return that five million, either. He would have to find a place out of the reach of the Camorra, and Villard for that matter. A country without extradition. Vanuatu, maybe, or Samoa, or the Solomon Islands. Someplace tropical.

Sadly, he would have to leave his beloved Le Serenissima forever.

But he would be rich. And alive.

CHAPTER
FORTY-NINE

S ince Father Carlo Rinaldo's death, St. Mark's Basilica desperately needed an additional priest to celebrate Mass until they could replace the fallen Rinaldo. Owing to its popularity as the most visited church in all of Venice, multiple services were offered every day: Morning Prayers, Eucharistic Adoration, the Rosary, Vespers, and three Masses. There simply weren't enough clergy to handle the daily demands at the moment.

Which is why the procuratoria of St. Mark's had contacted Father Dominic, on the chance he might be available to serve as the principal celebrant for Sunday's midday service. As before, he gladly welcomed the opportunity, especially at the end of what had been a grim and challenging week. He yearned for the blessed respite, the spiritual renewal Mass always brought him —and to clear his mind of the tawdry secular issues he'd burdened himself with over the past few days.

As he was now presiding over the liturgies in the great basilica—the polyphonous sounds of the lofty pipe organ accompanying the rituals—Dominic noticed the congregation was larger today, with many familiar faces he had encountered over his past two weeks in Venice, both pleasant and unpleasant.

For the moment, though, they were all children of God, with personal judgments suspended.

WITH MASS HAVING ENDED, Dominic was back in the sacristy, changing into his personal clothing while the altar servers and sacristan managed the cleansing and storage of the sacred vessels and vestments.

There was a knock on the door. One of the younger altar boys opened it.

"*Buongiorno, ragazzo,*" greeted an older bespectacled man. "May I speak with Father Dominic, please?"

On hearing his name, the priest looked up, then walked across the room to receive his visitor. "I'm Father Dominic. How may I help you?"

"Padre, please forgive this interruption. My name is Giuseppe Franco. Is there a place where we might..." he looked at the others in the room, then lowered his voice "... speak privately? It is a matter of some importance."

"Of course. We can take a walk outside," Dominic whispered back. "Haven't we met before? You look familiar."

"*Si,* padre. We met briefly at Contessa Vivaldi's Carnivale party."

"Oh, I remember now... you work at Palazzo Feudatario."

"Yes. I have been there for quite some time," Giuseppe said tenuously.

Given the attempt on his life by Giuseppe's employer, Dominic was wary. *What does this man want of me? Should I be concerned?* On the other hand, he *was* the lead restorer at Feudatario. Despite the possible risk, Dominic had many questions for him.

"If you don't mind, Padre, rather than taking a walk outside —where we would surely be seen together, presenting problems for both of us—might we instead find a less public place?"

Dominic thought for a moment. "How about the confessional? You can't get more private than that."

"*Perfetto!*" Giuseppe replied, clearly relieved. In fact, his entire demeanor changed as he realized just how perfect Dominic's suggestion was, for he was about to disclose things that could be told to no one else—and the seal of the confessional would ensure that what he revealed remained between the two of them.

Dominic escorted the man out of the sacristy and back into the main basilica, then across the transept to the embellished oak confessional booth against the back wall. As the priest stepped inside the center compartment and closed the wooden door, Giuseppe entered the penitent's side stall and pulled the curtain closed. Dominic slid open the latticed partition separating them.

"Padre, I think it is appropriate that I make a full and proper confession first, then we can speak more informally, for what I am about to confess will certainly require God's absolution."

Not surprised at all—for Dominic suspected Giuseppe's hand in the forgery scheme—he was more than happy to oblige the man. Finally, he felt he was getting somewhere.

"Of course," the priest said encouragingly. "Go ahead."

Giuseppe made the sign of the cross. "Bless me, Father, for I have sinned…"

SO FAR, Giuseppe's litany of sins were of the venial variety, nothing that would deprive his soul of receiving divine grace— but nothing that would be of much use for Dominic's purposes, either. And although he felt slightly duplicitous in his expectations during such a sacred rite, he was anxiously awaiting disclosure of the meatier mortal sins—specifically as related to the more larcenous activity he was sure the man was involved in.

"… And last but not least, Father, and the reason I needed to speak with you in the first place, I have been wholly complicit in creating forged copies of Old Masters paintings—very rare and expensive works of art—on behalf of my employer, who either sells them as originals, or replaces the original with the forged copy under the guise of restoration. Mind you, I was unaware of the extent of this situation until recently while in my employer's office, assisting with the books. Though I have not had a hand in that activity, it has been ongoing for many years, and I am heartily sorry for my own role in this shameful deception."

There it was! The door was now open for further discussion after the Sacrament of Confession was concluded. Dominic dispensed the man's penance, asking him to step outside the confessional and sit in the pews while performing it, then return to the privacy of the booth to continue their conversation. Giuseppe prayed an Act of Contrition, after which the priest absolved him of his sins. Giuseppe then pulled open the curtain door, leaving the booth to say his penance.

Meanwhile, as he sat in the dim isolation of the confessional, Dominic's mind was racing. *Why had Giuseppe come forward to me? What compelled him to do so now, and in this particular manner? What were his reasons for taking part in the elaborate scam in the first place? And most important of all—where is the Coscia Journal, and can he get hold of it for us?*

Finally, he would get his answers. Dominic began praying himself, thanking God for delivering this repentant man to him at the perfect time needed by both of them.

FINISHING HIS DEVOTIONS, Dominic glanced at his watch. Fifteen minutes had passed. Surely by now Giuseppe would have finished the modest penance given him. Leaning forward, he opened the door a crack to make sure the man was still there. He was, sitting in a pew a few meters away, his head bowed in prayer.

But there was something odd about his posture. It looked like he was sleeping.

Dominic stood up, opened the door, and walked toward the penitent.

"Giuseppe?" he whispered. No response.

He stepped closer, not wanting to interrupt a man in prayer but concerned in a way he couldn't quite put his finger on.

And then, even in the dim light of the basilica, he saw the blood.

Giuseppe's throat had been slashed from ear to ear. And around his neck hung an upside down crucifix.

CHAPTER
FIFTY

After notifying the Carabinieri of Giuseppe's murder, Dominic gave last rights to the man in the quiet of the church before it would be packed with police. He remained at the scene of the crime until the authorities were done questioning him.

Naturally, he could not divulge what was said during the victim's confession, and though the officers themselves were Catholic and respected both the sacrament and the priest's sacred vows, it irritated them nonetheless. They suspected, correctly, that the answers to some of their questions lay in what the dead man had confessed.

Meanwhile, Dominic had texted Hana and Karl, asking for them all to meet him at St. Mark's Basilica while he was being interrogated. They needed to talk.

He met everyone just outside the basilica as each group arrived. Since they were already in the vicinity, he suggested they take a table at Quadri, a restaurant on the piazza across from the basilica, where he could fill them in with what little he could without revealing Giuseppe's confession.

Finding a spacious outside table under a wide umbrella, the

five sat down and ordered beers while looking over the lunch menu.

Meanwhile, Dominic told them what he could about the painter's death, which was nothing much apart from how he found him while waiting to have a further discussion outside the bounds of confession.

"The police said the inverted cross was surely a signal of the Camorra's involvement, which is no surprise," Dominic said. "In hindsight, I should probably have encouraged our conversation *before* the confession, but too late for that now. Suffice it to say we're on the right track.

"I also spoke with Dario Contini the other evening. He intimated that should we use whatever means necessary to get the Coscia Journal, he would back us up. I think he meant all options are on the table, especially gray areas he might be unable to pursue himself."

"Spoken like a true cop who just wants to get the job done. Bravo for him," praised Marco, ever the commando. "So, what do we have in mind?"

Everyone sat in silence, taking thirsty draws on their beers as they considered the options.

"What about just walking in, armed to the teeth, and demand they give it to us?" Karl proposed. "We have already dispatched many of their people, so there may not be that many more to deal with now."

"Still too risky," Hana said. "It would be deemed a holdup, caught on camera, plus someone might get shot."

"I think that's the point of using guns," Karl replied with a smirk. Sitting next to him, Hana punched his shoulder.

"What about fire?" Marco asked, his eyebrows raised with interest. "I would think Don Gallucci would do anything to protect that Journal, making sure it left the building with him. At which point we would be there to liberate it from him. It would also put a dent in their illicit business."

The others looked around the table, appraising Marco's suggestion. No one made a counter argument.

"Interesting," Dominic said, feeling a little guilty even considering something so drastic as arson. "Maybe if you confined it to his office..."

Marco didn't miss Dominic's use of the pronoun *you*, but understood the priest's dilemma.

"For what must be obvious reasons," he said gallantly, "I think Michael should be excused from making decisions on our course of action. I will take personal responsibility for everything. Karl and Lukas and I can handle this."

"Oh, and just because I'm a woman means I can't be involved?!" Hana asserted with a twist of her head.

Marco couldn't resist the bait. "You *could* pour the champagne after we men have accomplished our mission..." Now she punched Marco's shoulder. The bad one. He grimaced, then laughed and reached over to give her a kiss.

"Actually, we could use a driver for our getaway boat," he added seriously. "I've still got the Aquariva standing by and we'll need your help."

"Then count me in, too," Hana said with a satisfied smile.

The waiter came to their table to take their lunch orders. After everyone had chosen their meals, Marco continued.

"So, here's what I propose..."

FIFTY-ONE

T he sun had gone down several hours earlier and the more active boating traffic had dissipated for the day. The few craft out now were several candlelit gondolas gliding late night tourists under the romantic moonlight of a warm spring evening.

Sitting in the Aquariva across the now placid waters of the Grand Canal, Marco, Hana, Karl and Lukas had been watching Palazzo Feudatario with binoculars for the past hour. There was no guard at the door this time, and from what they could tell Angelo Gallucci was in his bedroom on the third floor, just below the studio, not asleep yet but apparently reading. They did spot one guard sitting in the reception foyer, doing something on the computer, but they were certain there would be more somewhere in or near the building. No one else had been seen through the tall arched windows of the palazzo on any of its four floors. The studio, over which they would again enter, was dark and empty.

As before, Marco quietly guided the Aquariva across the canal, docking the boat two palazzos down from Feudatario. The three men stepped onto the dock with their gear and backpacks and took the pathway to the rear of the buildings, keeping in the shadows as they walked to their destination. Meanwhile, Hana guided the boat back across the canal to their previous watch post, waiting for the appropriate time to retrieve the team.

While Marco and Karl prepared their gear and surveyed their route up the building, Lukas stood guard behind the palazzo. Having climbed the route before, they knew where the drain pipes and window ledges were for safe handholds and footholds. The gear in their backpacks would be needed once they were on the roof and inside—ropes to lower themselves into the studio, and the flammables to start the fire.

They began their ascent. It only took a few minutes to reach the roof, and once there they rested for a minute or so before opening the skylight window. Marco's shoulder was stressed, but it was manageable. Pain was not new to him; he just pushed through it.

Karl edged his way quietly across the roof to work on the lock, with Marco following. The last thing they wanted was anyone hearing their footsteps below, even though the fourth floor appeared to be vacant.

But this time, there was a problem. Presumably because of their last breach, Gallucci's people had beefed up access through the skylight with steel bars criss-crossing the entire eight-panel glass ceiling! There was no way they'd be able to get through this way now.

That meant trying to enter through one of the arched windows on the back of the building, a more challenging feat since footholds were so narrow. Though both men were experienced climbers, this path gave even them pause.

They each tied off their climbing ropes to a chimney, passing the rope around the chimney and through the loop of a figure eight knot at the end. Karl went first, using a descender clipped in to his climbing belt to rappel down to a window in the studio. It was locked.

Looking over at the other windows, he saw one at the far end of the building that was slightly open to the outside. He hoisted himself back up to the roof with a pair of ascenders from his pack of climbing gear.

"There's an open window down there," he whispered to Marco, pointing to the end of the roof. "We should be able to get in that way."

Unfastening the ropes from the chimney, they moved down to the other end of the palazzo. They had to walk gingerly, for the fragile, curved red brick tiles could crack at any moment, alerting someone inside to their presence. Or they could slip, since the tiled roof was steeply angled.

Refastening the ropes around the chimney at the other end, Karl again went down first, using descenders and a couple carabiners as a brake. Reaching the wall next to the open window, he peered in to see if anyone was inside that room. It was empty.

Looking over at Marco, he signaled with a thumbs up, then squeezed through the open window and into the room. A few moments later, Marco joined him.

Inside now, they both stood still, listening for any sounds beyond the room they were in. In the moonlit darkness they seemed to be in a storage space, with wooden boxes stacked here and there and shelves containing various jugs and smaller boxes. Marco took out a penlight from his pocket to better inspect the room.

His light focused on a familiar warning symbol on a box that made him gasp. *Explosives!* Crates of TNT, blocks of Semtex and C-4, and bottles of acetone, hydrogen peroxide, and other flammable materials. Enough incendiary components to take out a sizable chunk of the Most Serene city of Venice. And that would explain the open window, for venting.

Each man looked at the other, thinking the same two thoughts.

What was all this intended for?

And fire didn't seem like such a good idea now.

They needed a new plan.

FIFTY-TWO

"Our best option now would be to take Gallucci and force him to open the safe," Marco suggested in a whisper.

"I agree," Karl said. "Best to assume there are other guards here, somewhere, so we have to be quiet about it. I don't think the guy downstairs is likely to hear us, but what if he has CCTV monitors?"

"We'll just have to take that risk. Be prepared."

They both checked the pistols in their shoulder holsters, rounds loaded, safeties off. Removing their packs, they went to the door, listened for any activity, and gently opened it.

The hallway was empty and dark, the wooden floors lined with Oriental carpet runners. Gallucci's bedroom was one floor down and at the other end of the building.

Making their way toward the stairs—which were exposed to the open four-story atrium in the center of the palazzo—they had to be careful not to make any sounds that would alert the guard in the reception foyer. Sound would carry well in the atrium.

They made it down to the third floor. So far, so good. If the guard had CCTV monitoring, he either wasn't watching it, or it was turned off and used only for recording, the more likely scenario given it was well after business hours and besides the guard, only Gallucci was in the building.

Creeping down the long hall leading toward Gallucci's room, the two men walked against the wall rather than down the center, so as not to risk squeaky floorboards in the old mansion. Another two long minutes and they were standing just outside the *capintesta*'s bedroom. They took out their weapons, raising them at face level, ready for whatever lay beyond.

Taking a deep breath, Marco ever so quietly turned the door handle, opening the door just a crack. The lights were out in the room now. Gallucci must have gone to sleep.

Marco pushed the door open wider, just enough for them to get inside. After each of them slid through the opening, Karl gently closed the door behind them.

Suddenly, the room filled with blinding bright light. Angelo Gallucci stood there, a double-barreled shotgun aimed directly at both Karl and Marco. Instinctively, both men rapidly raised their pistols and aimed them at Gallucci.

"I've been expecting you gentlemen," he said with a tobacco-stained smile. "It took you long enough to get here. And it appears we have an awkward standoff. Lower your weapons. Now."

Marco was not so easily persuaded. "You lower yours first, *padrino*."

"At least you have the courtesy to address me formally," the Don said. "But you people have caused me no end of problems. What is it you want here, anyway?"

"Just the book," Marco said calmly. "The one you call the Coscia Journal."

"I'm sorry to disappoint you, but I do not know what you're talking about."

"Now who's being discourteous?" Karl asked. "We know it's in your safe. Giuseppe told us before you had him killed." Karl had only made an assumption of the fact, but imagined he was right based on logic alone. And Gallucci's reaction confirmed it.

The old man's eyes narrowed and his face hardened. "That sniveling *puttana*. Couldn't keep his mouth shut when he didn't get what he wanted. No matter. What's done is done. I've already called for the guard. Things will go easier if you give up now." Just then, the guard cautiously opened the door behind them, his own weapon drawn. "Drop your weapons," he growled.

Thinking fast, Marco had a risky idea, depending on whether or not the old Italian knew German. Addressing Gallucci as if he were cursing him in German, he said simply, *"Karl, nach rechts fallen lassen!"*

Understanding Marco's subtle command, Karl instantly dropped to his right on the floor, turning his SIG toward the guard. At the same time, Marco dropped to his left and pulled the trigger of his Glock expertly aimed at Gallucci's left shoulder, which caused Gallucci to fire as well, the reflexive blast from the shotgun spraying buckshot well above Marco and Karl, but directly into the guard's face. His body flew back into the hallway as the shotgun's recoil pushed the now bleeding Gallucci onto the bed behind him.

Karl leapt up and onto the old man, yanking the shotgun away from him. Marco turned around to look down the hallway, pistol raised, waiting for anyone else to appear. No one had come yet.

As Karl frisked Gallucci for other weapons, he inspected the wound. It would require medical attention soon, but he would still be capable of opening the safe.

"Get up," Marco demanded. "Is there anyone else in the house?"

Ignoring the question, the old man moaned in pain as his left hand instinctively reached for the wound. Withdrawing his hand, he found it was covered with blood.

"What have you done to me?!" he cried. "Get me to a doctor!"

"Only after you open your safe and give us that journal," Marco said, grabbing the man and standing him up. "Let's go."

"I can't do that!" he said, fear in his voice. "It's been in our hands for over three hundred years! It is our legacy."

"Well, it's under new management now," Marco quipped. "I'll ask you one more time. Is anyone else here?"

"No, just the one guard and myself. I haven't had time to replace those you've already killed off."

With Karl supporting Gallucci on one side and Marco on the other, they led him up the stairs to his office next to the studio, cautiously watching for others to show up in case the *capintesta* was lying.

Reaching the safe, Gallucci looked at Marco, a pleading look in his eyes. "Isn't there anything else I can give you instead of the Journal? Money? As much as you need, just take it and leave."

"No thanks, just the Journal."

Gallucci sighed, then spun the dial on the large Gardall safe back and forth, entering the combination as Marco mentally recorded the chosen numbers. A turn of the handle and the door cracked open. Gallucci's hand went in first, fumbling for the Glock, but Karl held firmly to the Don's arm, expecting a move like that. He retrieved the pistol, secured the safety and tucked it behind him inside his belt.

"Nice try," Karl said. "Here, sit down at the desk and rest. We'll get you a doctor soon." Gallucci fell into his chair. As he did, his hand went to the desk as if in support, but his thumb curled furtively under the edge as he pressed a hidden button.

While Karl kept an eye on Gallucci, Marco looked inside the safe. Sitting on a top shelf was a leather satchel, which he pulled out and laid on the desk. Opening it, he removed a thick leather-bound book, clearly well-aged. Lifting back the cover, the first page inside was labeled *"Il Giornale Coscia della Camorra Veneta"* —The Coscia Journal of the Veneto Camorra.

Quickly flipping through the pages, Marco was amazed at the vast number of famous paintings recorded over the centuries. But reviewing it further would have to wait. They had to find medical treatment for Gallucci and then be on their way.

"Freeze!" two voices shouted at the same time as a pair of guards ran into the room holding Uzi submachine guns. "Drop your weapons!"

Taken by surprise, Marco and Karl reluctantly set their pistols on the desk, then held their hands up. Two more armed guards were coming up the hall. They were outnumbered.

Gallucci looked at his prisoners, offering an explanation. "I didn't lie. They weren't in *this* house. They were in an adjacent apartment equipped with an emergency alarm I tripped." That black-stained smile again.

"Now grab that book and get me to a doctor, fast!" Gallucci shouted to his men. "Then take these two down to the basement and kill the bastards."

The last two guards to enter stuffed the Coscia Journal into its leather satchel, then supported Gallucci between them, helping their boss down the stairs and out the front door to a waiting boat. For an old and injured man he moved sprightly, motivated to save his own life despite the pain—but he was still losing blood.

Marco and Karl dragged their pace as much as they could as they descended the stairs, their minds racing for options as they heard Gallucci's boat take off outside. Their captors had yet to take the Don's Glock from Karl's backside, hidden as it was under his jacket.

Just then, two quick shots rang out from behind them. Both guards fell. Karl looked up to see Lukas standing at the top of the stairs behind them, his SIG Sauer ready for any more comers. Karl first checked to make sure the guards were dead or immobilized, then ran back up and hugged his partner.

"Your timing couldn't have been better!" he gushed with relief. "How did you know?"

"I saw four men rush over from an apartment next door and figured you might need some help," Lukas obliged.

Marco was already planning ahead, texting Hana to bring their boat up to Feudatario's dock—*fast*. Then he ran upstairs, passing Karl and Lukas, and returned to the explosives room to grab their backpacks. While there, he pulled out two sticks of dynamite from one case and tossed them in his pack. Then he went into Gallucci's office to retrieve his and Karl's pistols from the desk.

Racing back down the stairs, he glanced at the two Swiss Guards as he kept moving toward the entrance. "Alright, let's get out of here and get that book back! Hana's waiting for us."

CHAPTER
FIFTY-THREE

Having received Marco's text message, Hana revved the engines of the Aquariva from across the wide canal and sped toward the dock in front of Palazzo Feudatario. As she crossed the water, she noticed a red Invictus 280 speedboat with three men in it race away from the dock and take off to the south.

Approaching the landing, she spotted Marco, Karl and Lukas running out of the palazzo's entrance and heading toward her. She brought the boat up to the dock and all three men scrambled aboard, tossing their bags on the aft deck.

"Hang on!" Marco yelled, instantly taking the helm as Hana moved aside. He pushed the throttle forward as far as it would go. The nose of the Aquariva flew into the air, the powerful twin Lamborghini V-12 engines roaring to life as the team sped after Gallucci's craft.

"It's that red boat up ahead," Hana shouted, pointing with one hand while holding onto Marco tightly. "I saw three men get in carrying a bag."

"Yes, that's Gallucci and his two guards with the Coscia Journal. He's injured and needs medical attention, so they're likely heading to a private doctor, or maybe some safe house.

"Those guys are carrying Uzis," Marco warned her, "so I want you to stay down on the deck if any shooting starts. And put on a lifejacket." He looked at her caringly. "Please?"

Hesitant at first, Hana complied with his request, slipping her arms through one of the orange vests.

Both boats were mid-canal now, having just passed under the Rialto Bridge between the San Polo and San Marco sestieres, their wakes throwing up fierce waves of water. Hearing the loud engines, then seeing the boats heading toward them, the few gondoliers out this time of night braced their own craft for the oncoming turbulence, shouting obscenities with furious hand gestures to the offending drivers as each boat passed. One gondola capsized, throwing its driver and passengers into the chilly waters.

Marco's powerful Aquariva was gaining on the Invictus as both reached the lagoon at the mouth of the canal, passing the jetty end of the Dorsoduro. In less than a minute they would be out in open water.

Rounding the confluence of the Grand Canal at Piazza San Marco, two Carabinieri boats—blue lights flashing and two-toned sirens wailing—joined in on the chase. Marco saw Dominic and Dario Contini in the lead police boat, now just a hundred meters away.

Hearing the staccato bark of Uzi bullets, everyone aboard the three following boats took cover. A few of the bullets struck the hull of the Aquariva, others spitting the water surrounding it. Each boat began zigzag maneuvers that, while slowing them down a bit, at least provided more of a moving target.

"We have to stop that shooter!" Marco shouted to Karl and Lukas. "I'll try to get closer so you can take him out. Stay low."

Lukas took one side of the boat just behind the windshield while Karl took the opposite side, their SIGs steadied on the gunnels. With the police boats shining bright spotlights onto Gallucci's boat—bouncing as they were off the wake of the

Invictus ahead of them—both Swiss Guards took aim at the man with the Uzi perched on the aft seat.

Aiming was a challenge. Both Karl and Lukas got off shots, but missed their mark.

"Can't you get any closer?" Karl yelled. Marco punched the throttle again, aiming directly for the Invictus.

"Hana, get down on the deck and stay there!" he shouted as he himself ducked. She obeyed his command, holding fast to the back of Marco's chair as the boat repeatedly bounced high off the waves.

The two Carabinieri boats had separated, the one carrying Dominic and Contini now taking the far starboard side of the Invictus while the other boat held to the port side, with the Aquariva following directly behind. Gallucci was surrounded. Still, they sped on undeterred.

Lukas steadied himself again, standing now and leaning against the side of the boat, his pistol no longer held against the gunnel. Taking aim at the shooter, he fired off one, then another, then a third shot. Though the Invictus was riding through smooth water, their own boat was riding its wake, making it even more challenging to make a clean hit.

"Marco!" he shouted. "If you can get as close as possible, then slow down to prevent us from riding their wake, I think we can get a better shot." He looked over at Karl, who understood the strategy and prepared for it himself.

Marco thought for a moment, then saw the logic. Taking the risk of being hit, he sped up to within twenty meters of the Invictus, crouching low behind the windshield as Uzi shot peppered the air around them.

Then he shut down the throttle. The Aquariva instantly slowed, leveling out with just mild rocking. Karl and Lukas stood, steadied themselves against the side of the boat, and took shots at the shooter. At least one hit its mark. The man went down, the Uzi bouncing off the stern of the Invictus and splashing into the water.

That left the injured Gallucci and the driver, who, though occupied, also had an Uzi. Marco slammed the throttle forward again, the bow of the Aquariva lifting high as the powerful Lamborghinis thrust the boat forward.

The loudspeaker on one of the Carabinieri boats issued a stern statement: *"This is the police. Stop your boat immediately and prepare to be boarded. This is your only warning."*

The Invictus kept moving at top speed, its twin Volvo Penta engines matching the top 40-knot limit of the Aquariva.

Marco motioned for Karl to join him at the helm.

"You've got to take out the driver as well," he urged. "We can use the same tactic as before."

Karl gave him a thumbs up, then moved to tell Lukas of the plan.

Just then Marco saw something being thrown high into the air from the Invictus, something fiery and heading their way. It had the sparkle of a fuse.

Dynamite!

Turning the wheel hard to starboard, Marco shouted, *"Everyone down! Incoming!"*

The ocean on the port side of the boat exploded with such force that a huge corona of water rose fifty meters into the air. The blast just barely missed them, but everyone aboard was soaked.

"Motherfuckers!" Marco yelled. "Lukas, there are two sticks of dynamite in my pack. Take one out and be prepared to light and throw it on my call."

"But, what about the Coscia Journal?!" Hana pleaded. "What's more important, stopping them or destroying everything?"

Marco checked himself, realizing his reaction wasn't the best course, given the primary objective.

"No, you're right," he admitted. "Never mind that, Lukas. Just kill the driver."

As Karl and Lukas took up their positions for the next round, suddenly the Invictus starting slowing, then came to a complete stop, drifting in the water. Warily, Marco slowed their own boat, keeping a distance, ready to speed up if more dynamite were seen flying toward them.

The Carabinieri boats slowed as well, also cautious of the unexpected action.

A man, presumably the driver, was shouting across the water.

"I surrender!!" he said, his hands clearly held high in the air, the boat bobbing in the now calm water. "Don Gallucci is dead. There is no need to run anymore."

The police boat carrying Dominic and Contini slowly approached the Invictus, two Carabinieri officers aboard training their pistols on the driver. When it reached the boat on the starboard side, the two officers jumped on board, handcuffing the driver.

Marco sidled the Aquariva up to the port side of the Invictus. Karl fastened a line from their boat to a cleat on the other, holding the two boats together.

Dominic jumped off the police boat and onto the Invictus, seeking the satchel carrying the Coscia Journal. His eyes searched the dark floorboards around the crumpled body of the Camorra leader. Nothing. Saying a quick prayer, he gingerly turned Gallucci's body over and there it was: the secreted journal that could unravel 300 years of thievery. Retrieving it, he then joined his team on the Aquariva, fist bumping with Marco, Karl and Lukas and hugging Hana tightly. Adrenaline coursed through each person as the flashing blue lights cast pulsing illuminations on everyone in the four boats in the middle of the otherwise dark lagoon.

Marco jumped on board the Invictus to make sure Gallucci was indeed dead. He knew the man had a serious wound, and was surprised he'd stayed alive as long as he had. But the loss of blood, precipitated by the bouncing of the boat in its attempt to escape, had finally drained the life out of him.

The Camorra would need a new leader now.

CHAPTER
FIFTY-FOUR

Venice's Marco Polo airport was bustling with tourists as Renzo Farelli purchased his one-way first class ticket on British Airways to the island of Vanuatu in the South Pacific.

He had discreetly settled what business affairs he dared to in La Serenissima and packed what little he wished to take with him, telling no one of his plans, just that he was taking a brief vacation to the United States. To New York City, in fact, where he could take in some of the finest art museums in the world. Yes, yes, he told everyone, he would return shortly.

He had two hours to kill before the flight, so he passed through the golden doors of BA's private Executive Club Lounge to relax and enjoy a Bloody Mary to calm his nerves.

Farelli had heard about Don Gallucci's sudden death the night before and felt reasonably safe, given the probable turmoil of finding a new *capintesta* in the meantime.

It was the perfect moment to leave. He had eight million euros in his Swiss bank account—more than half of that thanks to Eldon Villard—and was more than ready to enjoy the fruits of his life's hard work.

The lounge was busy that morning, and most tables were

already taken. Farelli chose instead to sit on a wide tufted-leather bench set against a free-standing interior wall overlooking the tarmac, watching as the planes taxied back and forth, wondering where people might be heading off to. Such a wide world, with so many places to visit. Maybe one day he *would* go to New York, after things had settled down.

A burly gentleman with a newspaper ambled over to where Farelli was sitting and took a seat next to him. Not too close, a respectable distance, as he opened the newspaper wide and scanned the headlines. A few minutes later, another man settled on his opposite side, setting his coffee on the glass table in front of him.

While not especially anti-social, Farelli preferred his own personal space, and started to rise to find a new spot to sit.

Before he could get up, the man on his right held up a hand to his arm, pulling him back down.

"Excuse me, but aren't you Renzo Farelli?" the stranger asked.

The burly man reading the newspaper edged closer in, his large frame now pressing against the Venetian.

"Who wants to know?" Farelli asked indignantly. "Would you mind, signore? I'm trying to leave."

The man on the right pulled out a silenced Israeli Masada pistol and furtively shoved it into Farelli's right side. "Please, sit back down."

"How did you get a gun in here?!" Farelli asked in a panic.

"It's easy when you're a cop with a badge," the man whispered. "But you must remain quiet, Signor Farelli. Monsieur Villard wanted us to tell you 'Bon Voyage,' and that he sends his fondest regards."

The man on his left leaned over, pressing the open newspaper in front of Farelli, masking his entire face and upper body. The man on the right had reached into his pocket and withdrawn a small hypodermic needle filled with a precise combination of Pancuronium Bromide, Sodium Pentothal and

Potassium Chloride. Without Farelli even knowing what was happening, the needle was suddenly thrust into the right side of his neck.

His head slowly fell to one side, and he instantly stopped breathing.

Newspaper Man made sure Farelli's body was properly positioned to sit up on its own, as if he were sleeping, while Needle Cop simply picked up his coffee and took a last swallow. Both men then stood up and walked away in different directions.

As he sat in the Queen Anne chair in the library of his Parisian villa in Muette, Eldon Villard fumed at the fact that he'd been cheated out of €25 million. He'd tossed through the night reminding himself it was but a small fraction of his net worth, and yet a man of his means did not get to where he was by being taken advantage of—unless he deemed it a worthwhile strategy to his long-term investments. Even then it was controlled, by him. But that was not the case with Feudatario Restorations, and the terrible outcome he'd suffered at the hands of those fools, all of whom were now dead.

He couldn't very well come forward to the authorities, since he was treading on illegal ground himself and he had no inclination toward such exposure. No, that was not an option.

Still, the more he thought of being taken, the more worked up he got. *He* was the one who took advantage of people, not the other way around, dammit! He reached over to rub his left arm, one more thing that was bothering him.

He finished off the half glass of cognac he was drinking, staring into the fire, thinking of his secret stash of paintings in the freeport. Though it brought a brief smile to his face, he couldn't shake the psychological irritation of losing the Raphael *and* his money.

But now it was even physical irritation. *What is it with this arm?!* he thought, massaging it again. *Why is it numb?*

Suddenly, Villard's chest lurched up, his eyes bugged open, and he flopped back down onto the leather armchair. He sat there in terror, not knowing what was happening to him.

Another seizure, worse than the first, and this time when he landed in the chair, he couldn't breathe.

Confused, his mind was racing but his body wouldn't respond to any commands he gave it. He could only get one word out before death took him in the next instant.

"Luxembourg."

CHAPTER

FIFTY-FIVE

I n his fourth-floor office of the Secretary of State's palace, in the shadow of St. Peter's Dome, Cardinal Enrico Petrini had just finished perusing his copy of the Coscia Journal, as kindly provided by Father Dominic.

"This is quite the indictment here, Michael," Petrini said, his face grave with concern. "There is yet quite a lot to do, rounding up the works of art that belong to the Church—if they're even accessible at this point."

"I agree, Eminence," Dominic acknowledged. "It was a real eye-opener for many of us, especially Marcello Sabatini. It will be his job to take on this mission, of course, but I don't envy the time and resources he'll require to carry it out."

"Oh, I'll give him whatever he needs to bring back our priceless treasures. It may take a great deal of arm-twisting for many of these big-name museums who have no idea they 'own' works of art that actually belong to the Church. I can see us in court for years over this. But this evidence weighs heavily in our favor.

"How can I ever thank you, Michael?" he asked. "Our history owes you a great debt."

"Well, this was hardly my doing alone," Dominic protested.

"Marco Picard led the effort all the way. It's he who really deserves credit for this."

"Then perhaps His Holiness should honor him with a papal knighthood," Petrini suggested, then agreed with himself. "Yes, absolutely. I shall arrange for it immediately."

"I might also suggest some form of recognition for Sergeant Karl Dengler and Corporal Lukas Bischoff, Eminence. They went above and beyond in this gamble, risking their lives on too many occasions."

"Yes, we must do something for them as well, I agree. And I also intend to deal with Bishop Torricelli and Cardinal Abruzzo —though more harshly, of course—since their names feature prominently in this Journal. I'd assumed Abruzzo would be untouchable as Patriarch of Venice, but with this kind of proof of his corruption, the Pope would not hesitate removing him with valid justification."

"Not to mention that cache of explosives found in Abruzzo's building. Marco informed the Carabinieri about that, which will be added on to their prosecution charges."

Dominic looked thoughtful for a moment, then looked up.

"One question I've had for a while now, Eminence, is how has such an elaborate scheme been going on for so long in the Vatican without anyone ever mentioning it?"

"I've been worried about that as well," Petrini said, a sadness coming over him. "I expect men of good will are often turned by the thought of such vast personal gain, especially as made possible by the Camorra, not to mention the severe penalty for going up against them. So despite their good intentions, fear and greed came together at the right place and time over the centuries. I'm sure the Camorra actually groomed people to serve their bidding here and made sure their replacements were just as compliant. And on it went.

"And as you must know, once you're in, you can never leave the Mafia. Once Eve had a bite of the apple, she was doomed."

"I see your point," Dominic admitted.

"Speaking of old times," he continued, "we would never have gotten this far without the posthumous help of Antonio Vivaldi, who centuries ago pointed us in the right direction. We owe him our gratitude as well."

"Yes, of course. Perhaps the Holy Father can say a Mass in his honor," Petrini suggested. "He was a fellow priest, after all."

EPILOGUE

I t was a brilliant spring day as the *sampietrini* set up the ceremonial stand and guest chairs in the Vatican's Courtyard of Saint Damascus. Flags representing the Vatican, the Swiss Guard, Italy, Switzerland and France lined the backdrop as the Vatican florists laid out a dozen large arrangements embellishing the stage.

As two of their number, Karl Dengler and Lukas Bischoff, sat in seats of prominence on the stage, the remaining 133 Swiss Guards—dressed in their colorful striped Renaissance gala uniforms with red plumed helmets—marched out into the courtyard in formation, the pontifical military band playing official Swiss Guard and papal anthems.

Also sitting on the stage were Father Michael Dominic, Marco Picard, Hana Sinclair, and Agent Dario Contini, along with Cardinal Enrico Petrini and various other cardinals and bishops connected with the Vatican Museum and the Apostolic Archive. On the center of the stage was a white throne for His Holiness.

As the band played, various honored guests were ushered in, taking seats in the audience. Once everyone was present, the Swiss Guard Band began playing the Pontifical Hymn as the Pope was escorted into the courtyard. Everyone stood until the

Holy Father took his seat and gave his blessing to the crowd. Then the Master of Ceremonies approached the microphone.

"Your Holiness, honored guests, ladies and gentlemen…"

The MC went on to introduce those to be honored and the reasons for their courage and valor in restoring precious works of art to the Vatican Museum. The MC asked for each of the six honorees to stand and approach His Holiness.

With the Commander of the Swiss Guard standing next to him—holding a pillow on which were laid out various medals—the Pope was handed the prestigious Benemerenti Medals to present to Hana, Karl, Lukas, and Contini. As he looped the beribboned medals around their necks, he kissed each of them on both cheeks and gave them his blessing and personal thanks.

Marco then stood before His Holiness and was given the most esteemed medal of the Pontifical Equestrian Order of St. Gregory the Great, making him an official knight of the papacy in recognition of his personal service to the Holy See and to the Roman Catholic Church.

Michael Dominic was called up next. The Pope awarded him the Order of Pius IX, the highest papal order currently awarded, for his leadership in the operation.

On the bark of their commander's order, the entire Swiss Guard contingent came to attention, smartly snapped their heels and saluted all awardees for their bravery. As flags fluttered in the warm breeze, the Swiss Guard Band struck up another tune, and the audience burst into applause.

Hana looked admiringly at Marco. "Does this mean I now have to call you 'Sir Marco'?"

"I don't think it works that way unless you're British," he said, smiling. "But since I am French, you could call me 'My Lord'…"

"I think I'll just stick with 'Marco'," Hana said coyly.

Cardinal Petrini sidled up to Dominic as the audience continued to applaud. He took him by both shoulders and looked into his brown eyes.

"I couldn't be more proud of you than I am today… my son."
Petrini's eyes glistened on the verge of tears. Dominic, his own
emotions taking hold, embraced Petrini tightly, then turned
away lest he break down. He then hugged Hana and shook
hands with his friends as the Pope was escorted off the stage and
back into the Apostolic Palace.

～

"So, what's next for you two?" Dominic asked Hana and Marco
as they walked through the papal gardens.

Hana looked up at the beaming Marco. "We're going back to
Paris, of course, and I've got enough for a great story here, so I
expect I'll be busy at the computer for a while. And you?"

"I've got a lot of catching up to do in the Archives," Dominic
said, as he looked into Hana's eyes wistfully. "But I'm really
happy for both of you having found each other. You're an
excellent match." He reached up to rub his eyes as Hana
wrapped him in an endearing hug.

"Take good care, Michael," she said. "I'll be thinking of you."

"Same here," he said, wiping his eyes again. Then he turned
to Marco.

"Marco, I couldn't ask for a better man at my side throughout
this ordeal. In some ways I owe you my life. You take good care
of Hana, now. We'll see each other again, I'm sure."

"You are a damn fine man, Michael. I'll stand with you any
day. *Au revoir mon frère.*"

Dominic smiled, then turned and walked away, his head
bowed, his hand brushing lightly against the trimmed top of the
boxwood hedge bordering the Grotto of the Virgin Mary as he
returned to his life of devotion to the church through his
dedication to protecting—and unlocking—the treasures of the
Vatican Secret Archives.

～

AUTHOR'S NOTES

Author's Notes

Thank you for reading *The Vivaldi Cipher*. I hope you enjoyed it and, if you haven't already, suggest you pick up the story in the other books preceding this one—*The Magdalene Deception, The Magdalene Reliquary* and *The Magdalene Veil*.

When you have a moment, may I ask that you leave a review on Amazon and and possibly Goodreads? Reviews are crucial to a book's success, and I hope for this series to have a long and entertaining life.

You can easily leave your review by going to my Amazon book page for *The Vivaldi Cipher*.

If you would like to reach out for any reason, you can always email me at gary@garymcavoy.com. If you'd like to learn more about me and my other books, visit my website at www.garymcavoy.com, where you can also sign up for my private readers' mailing list for news, giveaways, and to be among the first to learn of forthcoming books.

With best wishes,

Gary McAvoy

Fact vs. Fiction

Many readers have asked me to distinguish fact from fiction in my books. Generally, I like to take factual events and historical figures and build on them in creative ways—but much of what I do write is historically accurate. In this section, I'll review some of the chapters where questions may arise, with hopes that it may help those wondering what's real and what isn't.

Prologue: Cardinal Pietro Ottoboni was an actual figure in the Church, as described, and a major benefactor of the arts. And yes, he did father between 60-70 children among his many mistresses; times were certainly different back then. He did fall ill and die during the papal conclave of 1740, but as far as I know he died of natural causes. I'm the one who poisoned him. I do not know if he knew Antonio Vivaldi, though it's highly probable he did.

The devious scoundrel Cardinal Niccolò Coscia was also a real life figure and was heavily penalized for misappropriation of Vatican treasury funds. And yes, there was mystery connected to the extreme reduction in his punishment.

Antonio Vivaldi was in fact a priest, which—having a longtime appreciation for Vivaldi's work—surprised even me when I discovered it in my research. He spent decades of his life teaching violin to young girls at an orphanage called the Pio Ospedale della Pietà (Devout Hospital of Mercy) in Venice, Italy.

Chapter 1: The proliferation of pigeons—and the serious destruction they cause to buildings in Piazza San Marco—have been described accurately. They have become a real menace, and tourists are discouraged from feeding them since their nesting in the buildings, as well as waiting for food, does incalculable damage to the ancient structures.

Venice's Biblioteca Marciana (the Library of Saint Mark) does have the oldest actual texts of Homer's *Iliad*, and the only autograph (meaning handwritten by the author) commentary of Homer's companion work, *Odyssey*, from the 12th century. All descriptions of these works are accurate.

Chapters 2 and 8: The images of the Vivaldi documents are not authentic and were digitally prepared for this book by me and my music collaborator Dr. David Loberg Code, Associate Director of the School of Music and Professor of Music Theory and Technology at Western Michigan University. However, as a manuscripts collector myself, I *have* come across such authentic material, and it does have a similar appearance. I prepared the images using antiquing software, though couldn't achieve a more handwritten effect like I'd hoped.

Chapter 3: I've spent a great deal of time in Venice and, like Michael Dominic, count it as my favorite city in the world. (If only the cruise ships would leave, it would be a much better place.) The magnificent palazzos on the Grand Canal feature prominently here, and my descriptions of them are as I recall and as I have photographed them.

The Camorra, as many readers may know, is an actual Mafia organization in various regions throughout Italy. It has a flatter organizational structure but the same criminal enterprises as other Mafia clans. I doubt they have much influence in La Serenissima—since Venice has its own Mala del Brenta organized crime group—but the Camorra's presence elsewhere and its long history did come in handy for the story. My descriptions of the Camorra clan here are largely fictional, though.

Chapter 6: I count myself fortunate to have come across Dr. David Loberg Code and his ingenious Solfa Cipher (see Acknowledgments), which served as the initial inspiration for this book. I've loved codes, ciphers, and cryptology in general since that was part of my job in the US Army decades ago, and bringing Vivaldi into the world of secret codes made perfect sense and a good foundation for this work.

Chapter 7: Palazzo Grimaldi and its story is completely fictitious. Other than the fact that the House of Grimaldi is over 800 years old and does have an illustrious history, I know nothing of the family's estate holdings throughout history, nor whether or not they ever had a palazzo in Venice.

Giulia Lama was a real and outstanding female painter in the all-male world of artists in 18th-century Venice, and she struggled to maintain her notability despite men taking credit for —no, actually stealing—her work.

Chapter 8: Count Giacomo Durazzo was, in fact, the owner of the Vivaldi manuscripts—some 300 concertos and 20 operas—in the late 1700s, purchased from a Venetian senator named Count Jacopo Soranzo, who acquired them from Vivaldi's brother Francesco after Antonio died in 1741. Two brothers from the Durazzo family inherited the manuscripts in the late 19th century, and eventually they were sold off to library museums.

Chapter 10: Harry's Bar is among the most beloved landmarks of Venice, having been the hangout for Ernest Hemingway and others mentioned in the book, along with so many more celebrities as well as folks like you and me. As longtime readers know, the foods I write about all come from actual menus from

AUTHOR'S NOTES

real restaurants mentioned, many of which I've actually dined at over the years. Ah, if only Venice were closer to Seattle....

Chapter 11: Yes, the Vatican does indeed have 70,000 works of priceless art in its inventory, 50,000 of which are tucked away in storage most of the time. Seems a shame, really, that so few people will ever get to see them.

The artworks I describe are all authentic pieces by the artists mentioned; none of that is fictional, apart from the forgeries I invented.

Chapter 12: Carnivale is Venice's annual, months-long gala celebration similar to New Orleans' Mardi Gras. Costumes are a big and very serious part of it, and the long history I described about them is spot on. Antonia Sauter's famed atelier is *the* place to buy couture costumes, as is Ca' Macana for the most exquisite genuine historical masks Venice has to offer. I'm almost one hundred percent sure the Swiss Guard would never be permitted to wear their official gala uniforms at a costume party; but hey, it's my book.

Chapter 18: The processes for establishing authenticity of a painting are all depicted accurately here. There are many more, of course, but in the interests of time and prevention of boredom, I omitted the others.

Chapter 20: The Vatican very probably has its own internal restorations team and would likely never send paintings out for such work. But using an old established firm in Venice was crucial to the plot; hence, the use of the fictional Palazzo Feudatario.

Chapter 27: Shockingly, it is true that, day and night, 12 cars are stolen every hour in Italy! And the Fiat Panda is the most popular for thieves. Having rented one on a particular trip from Milan to Lake Como, I can't imagine why.

The process described here for aging canvasses to antique them is accurate, and a favored method used by forgers ("old cigarette butts soaked in rainwater?!" Yep.)

Chapter 28: I am not a runner, but for those who are, this course through Venice is, I am told, one of the best for taking on the city's interior. If you ever get there and need some exercise, give it a try.

Chapter 31: Just a little sidebar here. In laying out Marco's scheme for getting the drop on the bad guys from a bridge, with Hana driving the boat below him, I actually used a detailed canal map of Burano island to do this. Imagine my surprise, then, to find that the specific yet random bridge I chose—the only one that would work for the scene—actually *did* cross a canal called the Rio Assassini—the River of Assassins! Coincidence?

Chapter 34: The processes described here are the actual methods used by forgers for creating their faux masterpieces. Today's fakebusters are scrupulous in analyzing pigments as described. Thomas Hoving, former director of New York's Metropolitan Museum of Art, once wrote that he believed nearly *half* of all art he had evaluated for museums in his long career was fake. So, *caveat emptor.*

Chapter 39: Italian trains have two classes of car: First Class and Second Class. The difference in cost is minor, only a few euros, but First Class seating is more spacious, with fewer seats per compartment, and usually quieter. There is more room for luggage and it will generally be less crowded, since most passengers typically travel in Second Class. Just FYI if you're ever considering between the two.

Like the Vatican, the Uffizi Gallery in Florence most likely does their own restorations in-house, not sending them to a fictional palazzo in Venice.

Chapter 41: Just so you know, €25 million for a Raphael is certainly within the range such paintings go for. There are only 184 known Raphaels extant today, but as one of the most prominent and distinguished artists of all time, his work is in great demand (by the few who can afford it).

Chapter 42: When I first introduced Apple's AirTag tracking discs in *The Magdalene Deception*—long before they would be officially released, and based only on tech rumors at the time—I was holding my breath that the company would not fail me, or worse, change the name. Thankfully, AirTags were released in mid-2021 (I wrote that book in late 2019), and they worked as well for saving Hana in this book, too.

Epilogue: The prestigious Vatican medals and awards described here are actually used by the Pope for valued services rendered to the Church.

General Notes: I've really come to enjoy Marco Picard and his involvement with Hana. Having introduced him in *The Magdalene Veil*, I didn't realize he would become so prominent in future stories, but I do like the way Dominic struggles with his feelings for Hana, and the challenges his calling has burdened him with. However, some early reader feedback tells me they feel bad for Michael and are upset with Marco having taken Hana. To which I say, stay tuned…

All firearms mentioned in the book are as described. Glocks are made of a highly durable plastic, favored for their lightness by police departments worldwide. The Swiss Guard uses SIG Sauers as their primary weapons of choice, though they have a wider assortment based on the demands of each operation.

ACKNOWLEDGMENTS

I have had the grateful assistance of many friends and colleagues in the writing of this book, without whose help it would have been a more challenging project.

Special thanks first to Dr. David Loberg Code, Associate Director of the School of Music, and Professor of Music Theory and Technology, at Western Michigan University, for his brilliant and creative assistance with Solfa Ciphers and musical cryptography, which served as the inspiration for this book. For more information on the Solfa Cipher, visit https://wmich.edu/mus-theo/solfa-cipher/secrets/

Thanks also to Greg McDonald, whose fine mind I am honored to say was at my beck and call, as we weaved through some of the more complex plotlines this book required from time to time. Greg's way of looking at things complements mine, and his help on every book has been invaluable.

Yale Lewis, my friend and attorney before he retired (not from our friendship, thankfully) brought a great eye for detail, and his constant rereading and "processing" of material helped me reshape it for the better.

My friend of forty-plus years, Kathleen Costello, was always there on a moment's notice, pushing me toward the light of better grammar, plotting, and scheming. And to my other lifelong friends Renee Bell and Karen Flannery for their trendy fashion advice (not for me; for the characters).

I owe thanks to my Launch Team, that hardy band of early readers who helped to reshape the final version into what it has become, and especially to Ron Moore, whose proficiencies across a wide range of expert areas clarified many salient points.

And to my esteemed editor, Sandra Haven, without whose seasoned wisdom and unvarnished feedback I would be at a loss for just the right words, and more.

Finally, I wish to thank all the readers of my work, whose incredibly positive reviews and ongoing encouragement make writing these historical adventures all the more worthwhile.